# The Ache Within Me

Rozia Bell

Banks & Bell Legacy

ISBN:
979-8-9989231-0-4 (paperback)
979-8-9989231-3-5 (Ebook)
979-8-9989231-4-2 (Audio)
Cover design by Samantha Sanderson-Marshall
Published by Banks & Bell Legacy, LLC
www.roziabell.com

First edition 2025

Printed in the United States of America

# Dedication

In the depth of my soul, there resides an admiration and affection for you, dear Karma. With boundless love and gratitude, I dedicate these words to the essence of who you are and what you represent in my life. It is through your gentle touch that I have come to understand the delicate dance of energy that shapes us. With each breath, each action, I feel your loving embrace guiding me towards growth and understanding. In moments of joy, you celebrate me. In moments of challenge, you offer me the gift of perspective. I cherish you, Karma, for you are not merely a concept, but a beloved partner in this journey of my life. With each step I take on this adventure, you walk beside me as a gentle yet unwavering companion. May my love for you shine brightly.

You are the biggest pain in my ass, but I offer my deepest respect and gratitude to you, Karma.

# Trigger Warning

This book contains themes of trauma, sexual assault, domestic violence, emotional abuse, infidelity, mental health struggles, incarceration, and complicated relationships with self and others. There's also a generous helping of questionable choices, overthinking, and people falling in love with people who should *absolutely* come with warning labels.

If you're in a tender place, please take care while reading.

And if you find yourself saying, "Girl…what are you doing?" Just know… you're not alone.

# Chapter 1

## In the After

*Dear Young Reya,*

*I don't really know where to start, or what to say, because this isn't the letter you were expecting. I know you probably thought that by now I would have it all figured out. That I'd be happy, strong, and full of light. But the truth is, I'm still here, still feeling so lost sometimes. Even though I'm surrounded by people who love me, I often feel like I'm alone. Like I'm still that little girl, sitting in the dark, waiting for someone to see me.*

*But here's what I need to tell you...what I wish someone had told me back then: It's okay to not be okay. It's okay to feel sad when your heart is aching. You don't have to push it down, hide it away, or pretend everything is fine. I'm telling you this because I need to hear it, too. Sometimes, I don't even know why I feel so heavy inside. Maybe it's just something we have to live through, something we have to feel, so we can understand what true happiness feels like when it finally comes.*

*I'm giving you permission to feel every tear that falls, every moment of hurt. Don't hold it in for anyone. Don't bottle it up* because you think it will make others more comfortable. That will only make the sadness linger longer. You are allowed to cry, little one. You are allowed to feel lost and confused because those feelings don't make you weak. They make you human.

But listen, I need to tell you something else, too. There will be moments, even small ones, when happiness will sneak through the cracks. There will be glimpses of joy, moments when your heart feels light. I know you won't know what to do with them because they won't last long. But please, please learn to hold on to those moments. Grab them, clutch them tight, and never let go. Even when the darkness comes back, those moments of light are real. Don't let the sadness steal them from you.

I don't have any answers, little one. I wish I could promise that everything will be okay and easy and perfect, but I can't. What I can promise is this: you are strong enough to face whatever comes your way. Every hard thing you go through will shape you, but it Will. Not. Break. You. You have an incredible strength inside of you. Every challenge, every struggle, every heartache will shape you into something more resilient, more capable. And though it may seem overwhelming at times, none of it will defeat you. Though happiness may seem distant now, it's worth chasing. And I promise I won't stop until we find complete joy in our souls.

I love you. I'm here, and I will always be here. Even when it feels like no one else is.

With all my heart,
Your Older Self

I set the pencil down and stare at the uneven lines of my handwriting bleeding across the page. The ink blurs under the weight of my tears, each droplet splashing down onto the fragile, metaphorical younger version of me captured in these words. The paper feels damp beneath my fingertips, cool and soft, as if it, too, is succumbing to my sorrow. A lump rises in my throat, and I swallow hard, trying to keep the flood at bay. I am about to leave for therapy, but I needed to purge some of this weight first. I needed to give my younger self the words I wish she'd had back then, an assurance she wasn't alone. That she *isn't* forgotten. That I still feel her trembling spirit deep within me and that, somehow, I'm trying not to give up on her.

Sitting at my wooden desk, the surface nicked and worn, and familiar under my arms, I let my emotions take over. The color, a muted green, was supposed to feel calming. But today it feels heavy, like moss overtaking the edges of a neglected stone. The pink walls surrounding me offer little solace, their cheerful hue almost mocking my melancholy. They were meant to be a symbol. A declaration that I finally had a favorite color. Instead, they feel suffocating, a bubblegum cage closing in around me. The faint smell of soil and damp leaves wafts from the plants on my shelves, a reminder that life can still exist, even in the shadowy corners of despair. The books lining the walls sit steadfast, their vibrant spines full of lessons I tell myself I'm not too old or too fractured to learn.

In front of me, pinned to the wall above my computer, are crayon-scribbled pictures my daughter made years ago, their colors bright but chaotic. My chest tightens when I look at them. They tug the corners of my mouth into the faintest of smiles, but the smile comes with a sting, a needle laced with guilt. I've talked about this in therapy too many times to count. The guilt for leaving her, guilt for not being the mother she deserved. Dr. Jenson always says I have to live "in the after" but the before looms over me like a shadow. I can still see her tiny hands clutching the crayons, her voice bubbling with excitement as she explained her drawings.

One picture in particular catches my eye. There are green clouds drifting lazily above red grass. Two stick figures stand in the center, one tall and one small, both in matching dresses. The smaller one looks up at the taller with a smile that only a child can draw: lopsided and pure, and radiating adoration. The scene feels like a storybook land, detached from reality. It's a world we could've built together if only happiness had been enough to bind us. A world where green clouds hang in a sky that never rains, and nothing is broken.

My gaze falls back to the journal in front of me. My newest letter to my younger self sits there, the ink scrawled desperately, as though I could somehow reach through time and shake her, tell her to hold on. I wish I hadn't been dealt such pitiful cards. I wish I could have been her hero.

A shuddering breath escapes me as I swipe at my eyes with trembling hands. My cheeks are sticky, my throat raw. Therapy is calling, and I know I can't be late. My movements feel mechanical as I rip the page from the journal, the paper crinkling in protest. I ball it up, pressing it into a tight, angry sphere before tossing it into the wastebasket by the door. The sound it makes as it lands, a hollow thud, reverberates in my chest.

Throwing the paper away feels like more than just discarding a journal entry. It's a quiet refusal. A refusal to carry the weight of a truth I'm not ready to live with. That letter held a version of me I'm still ashamed of, still grieving, still trying to love. By crumpling it, I'm trying to silence the ache within me. To deny the guilt that clung to every word. Maybe it was too honest. Maybe it touched something too raw.

I hesitate, one hand resting on the back of my chair. My heart feels heavy, like a weight I can't set down. For just a moment, I allow myself to wish, fiercely, desperately wish, that I could love myself. That I could be someone worth loving.

# Chapter 2

## In the After

Tick.

"I want you to close your eyes," Dr. Jenson says, his voice gentle, soothing, like he's trying to lull me into safety. His blue eyes fix on me, unwavering but kind. I take a shaky breath, my fingers fidgeting with the shredded edge of a tissue. My hands don't know where to land, so I fidget.

Tick.

The clock looms behind me, its steady rhythm oddly comforting, like a distant heartbeat in an empty room. I hate the clichés of therapy, "close your eyes, picture the beach, find your happy place." It always felt like a joke. Sand? Sand gets everywhere. In your hair, between your toes, clinging to your skin long after the beach is gone.

Tick.

But he doesn't rush me. He lets the silence stretch. Lets me breathe. Lets me wrestle with the fear of being seen. For a moment, I understand why people fall for their therapists. Every time I come here, I feel like I matter.

I feel heard.

I feel important.

Dr. Jenson's patience feels like a rare gift. It would almost be easy to believe he cares, if I didn't know better. If I didn't remind myself that he's paid to listen to me unravel.

I twirl the tissue I've been holding in my hand between my fingers. I notice the white tissue against my almond complexion. The contrast is sharp, and I stare at it. I'm glad I am finally done crying about how overwhelmed life had become. Depression came fast and hard.

Tick.

Dr. Jenson is quiet. Still, I close my eyes. I let the air settle in my lungs. What's my happy place? Not the beach. No, it's something quieter, softer. A forest, maybe. A place where the ground is gentle, where the scent of wildflowers chokes out every ugly thought in my head. I can feel the grass beneath my feet, the wind in my hair. The trees whisper to me, drowning the noise I carry inside.

For a moment, my lips tilt into a faint smile. A brief, fleeting smile.

Then, tick.

That little glimpse of happiness is evidence enough that I am in my happy place. I'm no longer in the small office surrounded by bottles of water and tissue for all the crying crazies of the world. I'm no longer staring at the many accolades Dr. Jenson has hanging on the wall. I'm no longer sitting on a brown, leather couch fidgeting with my hands, I am in my happy place.

Tick.

"I want you to think about…" He says and pauses. The weight of his words settles between us, heavy and inevitable. Little does he know, I am already in my happy place. Overthinking every situation has put me ahead in this assignment. I focus on the gentle trees I'm imagining in my head. I even wiggle my toes that are tucked safely away in my black sneakers and visualize them in a field of grass so vast, you can't see where it ends or begins.

One point for Reya. Zero points for this situation.

"I want you to think about…the girl in the dugout."

No ticks.

No heartbeat.

No breathing.

The question hits me like a thunderclap, sharp and sudden, shattering the fragile world I thought I understood. The sound of it reverberates in my mind, freezing time itself. Everything about what is normal, familiar, and happy disintegrates, crumbling to dust inside of me. The air grows thick, heavy, and motionless. The tears trembling in my eyes is the only movement left in a world that has gone utterly still. There are no more warm memories, no more gentle sunlight filtering through trees. Even the earth beneath my feet feels unsteady, as if it, too, has been swallowed by this moment. My chest tightens, the weight of the question pressing down like a force I cannot escape, leaving nothing but the slow, inevitable rise of tears spilling over.

Breathe, Reya. You have to breathe.

Tick.

Time slams back into motion like a freight train, and the sudden rush of oxygen burns my lungs. The impact is crushing, a force so unexpected it knocks the air from me all over again. The swelling pressure in my chest shatters, exploding in a torrent of raw, unstoppable emotion.

Tears spill over my eyelids in a relentless flood, and a

strangled sob of agony escapes my throat before I can stop it. It's not just crying—it's breaking. My mind reels, spinning out of control as the weight of everything crashes over me, drowning out reason, leaving nothing but the overwhelming tide of pain. My mind begins to race. How does he remember that story? He must have dozens of clients. Clients that are more fucked up in the head than I am.

Yet, he remembered.

His voice breaks through the fog. "What made that girl stay in the dug out?" I can feel him looking at me. But I am determined more than ever to keep my eyes closed. "The fear of disappointing Josh? The fear that you wouldn't be liked if you left? The need to feel accepted? I want you to really think about why that girl stayed."

Stop. Stop. STOP!

I inhale trying to stop the rush in my head. The swelling in my eyes and the lump in my throat has become too uncomfortable to bear. I open my mouth to speak, then close it again. The room is getting smaller.

Smaller, smaller.

My breath is shallow, and my hands are trembling as I pick up the entire box of tissue, I am going to need them.

I am getting frustrated with how patient he is being with me. He sits there and lets me process. He doesn't try to rush my thoughts.

"I…" I stop. I look at Dr. Jenson and furrow my eyebrows. I…what? I don't remember? I don't want to talk about it? I don't want to relive that again?

Zero points Reya, one point for this situation.

# Chapter 3

**Before**
**14 years old.**

The sun was blinding, the kind of relentless heat that stuck to your skin like guilt. Josh and I sat on the bleachers, the silver metal warming uncomfortably beneath us. He leaned back, legs sprawled out like he owned the field, a crooked grin stretched across his face.

"Why aren't koalas considered bears?" He asked suddenly, his voice playful.

I frowned. "Because... they're marsupials?"

"Nope. Because they don't have the right koala-fications," he said, laughing like it was the funniest thing he'd ever heard.

I laughed, too, though I wasn't sure why. His laughter was contagious, his attention intoxicating. Nobody had ever liked me like this. Laughed with me like this, *talked* to me like this. Despite his buck teeth and the fact that he was shorter than me, Josh made me feel like he cared. For the first time in weeks, I didn't feel like I was fading into the background.

"I like you," he said, as if it were the most natural thing in the world.

The words lodged in my chest, unfamiliar and warm. No one

had ever said that to me before. Not my parents, not my friends (not that I'd had any friends).

"Thanks," I mumbled, my face heating under his gaze.

"You know," he began, leaning in conspiratorially, "we've been talking for two weeks now. Don't you think it's time we… you know… took it to the next level?"

The next level.

I knew what he meant. I wasn't stupid. But I didn't want it.

"What do you mean?" I asked anyway, stalling for time, hoping my hesitation would make him change his mind.

He leaned in and whispered something in my ear. It caught me by surprise. I knew I did not want to have sex, but I definitely did not want to do what he was asking me for. I looked down at the bleachers we were sitting on. Although the bleachers were silver in color, it was covered in orange sand that distorted the look of the metal. My hands felt gritty to the touch, and my hair was sticking to my forehead. It was hot outside, and the Las Vegas air felt heavy. I watched as other students walked by; some looked at us, but most could care less that we existed.

Story of my life.

Josh grinned and leaned closer, his voice dropping to a whisper. When he said it, I froze. My stomach churned, a mix of confusion and dread.

"Josh, I don't think…"

"Come on," he interrupted, his tone light, like he was teasing me. "It's not a big deal. Don't you want me to like you?"

His words hit me like a slap. Of course I wanted him to like me. More than anything.

He repeated himself, louder this time, "Can you do that thing to my duck?"

I pretended I didn't know what that meant. I thought if I could pretend long enough, he would give up. "I don't know what that means."

He looked at me with a smile, "I made it up."

"Do the thing with your duck?" I took a deep breath in and contorted my face as if I were really thinking. "Hmm," I mumbled it a few times under my breath.

"You don't get it?" His eyebrows furrowed and he sat there with his mouth slightly ajar. He looked at me as if this were a pop-quiz and there was only one correct answer, and I was failing.

He had just called me smart not even 4 minutes ago, I didn't know why I was acting so stupid in that moment. I didn't know why I couldn't just tell him how I really felt.

He smiled at me with those bucked teeth of his and said, "If you still don't understand, I can show you better than I can tell you. I know somewhere we can go," and in one swift motion, we were off the bleachers and walking on the path toward the baseball field. I followed him, my feet dragging against the gritty dirt. The baseball field stretched out before us, wide and empty, and fenced in, with the dugout looming in the distance.

We didn't walk hand-in-hand, we didn't talk as our strides became coordinated. We were just there, two people walking to the baseball field. I wasn't nervous, I wasn't happy either. I didn't know what to say or how to feel.

We walked by a student who was wearing a long white t-shirt and black jeans. His hair was cut low, and he looked like he had no business standing next to the fence. As we were walking past, Josh walked over and talked to him. I waited patiently where Josh had left me. My body began to tense up, my heart began to race. I became nervous in that moment, but I couldn't explain why. I liked Josh. Or, I liked what Josh could be. If I were being honest, I hardly knew him at all.

The gate to the baseball field had a lock on it so he said we had to "hop the fence". We could go in the dugout, and no one would be able to see us. He told me Gerald was going to keep lookout in case somebody did come. Everything he was saying felt wrong. Everything we were doing felt wrong. But he threw his backpack over the fence and started climbing. Looking toward the dugout, it felt like a trap; dark and enclosed. But Josh didn't hesitate. He hopped the fence, laughing when he landed on the other side. "Come on," he called, holding out a hand.

I hesitated, the sharp metal of the fence digging into my palms. Everything about this felt off. But when he looked at me like that, with expectation and something like affection, I couldn't say no.

So, I climbed.

The dugout smelled of sweat and stale air. The orange dirt clung to my shoes, the concrete floor coarse beneath my feet. Josh dropped his bag on the bench, his movements casual, rehearsed.

And then he smiled.

"Let's do the thing to my duck," he said.

"Josh, I don't think…"

"You'll be fine," he said, already undoing his belt. "It's easy. I'll show you."

I should've turned around then. I should've listened to my gut.

Instead, I laughed nervously and smiled. I walked over to him, I got on my knees, and I put my face down to his belly button. I smelled it, and it smelled sweaty and gross. It felt wiggly and squishy in my hand, but when I looked up at him, he had the biggest smile on his face. I had the ability to make him happy, and I remember feeling like I was somebody. Like I finally met someone who liked my brain, who liked my humor, who liked me sweaty and all.

I was only down there for a minute or two before I was too grossed out to keep going, but it felt like a lifetime. "Was it OK?" I had asked him as I got up. Self-conscious about what I had just done and looking for reassurance, I dusted myself off and looked at him.

"It was OK, but you need practice." He stood up, zipped his pants, and buttoned them. "You stay here while I make sure the coast is clear. When I give you the signal, come out."

"What's the signal?"

"I'll say 'coo'." He held his hand to his mouth and cupped his fingers like he was doing a bird call.

I did what I was told. I stayed put and wiped my mouth. I hawked up a loogie and spit it out. I walked back-and-forth. Then I stopped to listen. I could hear him climbing the gate. I could hear when his feet touched the ground. And then I started pacing again as I waited for the call. I didn't hear what came next because when I turned around, Gerald was behind me. He was unbuttoning his pants and sat on the shirt Josh left behind. "What are you doing?" I had asked him.

"Josh said that you needed practice. So here I am." He said with his arms in the air and a smile on his face.

"But I don't like you, I like Josh." I exclaimed, but he told me if I really did like Josh that I would do this. That this would be the only way for Josh to like me back. So, I got on my knees once more. This time not as long. But this time when I looked up, he didn't look happy. He stood up, pulled his pants up and told me to wait while he checked for the coast to be clear.

I waited.

Another guy came into the dugout.

Then another.

By the fifth guy, I realized that there was no way for me to get out of there. By the seventh guy, I stopped trying to explain that I only wanted Josh because they all said the same thing: "This is what Josh wants you to do." I stopped trying to remember their names, they were just a blur in the wind.

By the tenth guy, I began to cry. I didn't want to be down there anymore, but I didn't know how to get out. No one was going to save me. When the next boy came into the dugout, I cried and got back on my knees. He pulled his pants down and sat on the bench like all the ones before him, but this guy looked at me.

"Are you okay?" He had asked me with concern.

I cried even harder, "No, I'm not. I don't want to be here anymore. I only wanted Josh to like me. Now I just want to go home, but this is the only way." I said between sobs and tears. I put my face by his bellybutton, but he put his palm to my forehead then stood up.

"You should go." He said while he put his pants back on.

"I can't." I cried.

"Reya, there is a line of guys out there waiting for you to top

15

them off. And they don't care about you. If you don't go now, you will be down here all night."

*A line of boys?* I thought to myself. I don't know why I didn't think it would be so many, I guess after every boy that came down, I thought it would be the last. I didn't think there would be a line. I began to wonder if Josh had this planned all along. Was that the reason Gerald was waiting by the fence? I couldn't allow my mind to travel too far. I needed to focus on how I could get out of this situation. There was only two ways out of the dugout, but once I was out, I would still have to climb the fence and walk past that line of people.

I had two options: I could stay in the dugout. Or I could leave the dugout. But to me, both options were equally terrible.

The walk of shame was the lesser of two evils.

I walked up the three steps and tried to put my head around the structure to see if there was a way out without being seen. There wasn't. I was embarrassed. I climbed to the top of the fence, I jumped down, I grabbed my backpack, and I had to walk by every boy in that line. They all looked at me. Some laughed. Some looked disappointed. None spoke to me.

Josh never talked to me again.

# Chapter 4

## In The After

The clock ticks, steady and unyielding.

"I don't know," I finally gain the courage to respond. My face is damp with tears, and my nose is raw. My hands clutch the tissue so tightly, it feels like the only thing grounding me to this room. I am very aware of how pathetic I must look, like a wounded animal still fighting for some dignity. "I'm not sure what kept me in the dugout." I close my eyes and try to forget that day, along with so many others. My eyes sting as I steal a glance of Dr. Jenson, his calm presence like a stone in the storm. His notebook sits in his lap, pen at the ready, but he doesn't rush me.

"Do me a favor," Dr. Jenson interjects. He leans forward slightly, his tone gentle but probing. "I want you to concentrate on how you were feeling when Josh left the dugout."

I close my eyes as the memories claw their way to the surface. The sting of rejection, the desperate need to belong. "I felt like I made a friend." I admit. Rapid tears start falling from my eyes with that statement and my voice crack on the words.

*I felt like I made a friend.*

The weight of that truth crushes me.

Dr. Jenson jots something down. "And when the next guy came, what did you feel then?"

"If I'm being honest," I take a deep inhale. I open my eyes and look at Dr. Jenson, hoping he doesn't judge me for my next comment. He is writing something in his notepad and doesn't see the subtle turn of my head, so I close my eyes once more. "If I'm being honest, as each person came down, I felt more and more helpless. I felt more and more alone." I pause, the words sticking in my throat like thorns. "But at the same time, with each person that came into the dug out, I felt like I gained another friend."

My eyebrows crease as I think about how broken I must have been. How stupid I was. I shake my head from side to side and stare at the tissue I'm holding in my hand. What was once a perfect square, soft, white, and almost transparent is now bawled up into a million wrinkles and grey from the moisture. Not the same size as it once was, it is now heavy and soaked in pain, and it'll never go back to that pure white color, it'll never go back to that perfect square. It has too many tears absorbed into it now. It's holding too much sorrow and the weight of my failures. I throw the crumpled tissue in the bin and grab four more.

Dr. Jenson is as patient as ever. He lets me process. Allows my mind to race and wander. He doesn't try to fill the silence, he doesn't try to comfort me, he just waits until it feels right.

"You know that isn't friendship, right?" He says softly, his voice steady but firm.

I nod, but the truth doesn't settle in. I won't allow it to. My head knows it wasn't friendship, but my heart clings to the lie because it's easier than facing the emptiness.

Dr. Jenson waits. He still doesn't rush me or fill the silence, and the weight of his patience feels unbearable. I crumble under it.

"I don't understand why I stayed," I whisper. "I could have left. There was no one holding me there. No barriers."

"Exactly," he says, and his words cut deep. "That's why I brought it up today. You came in feeling overwhelmed, didn't you?"

I nod, wiping my face with another tissue.

"And why are you overwhelmed?"

"Because everyone needs me!" My voice rises with frustration, the dam inside me breaking. "I was being stretched so thin I felt I was going to rip."

Dr. Jenson's pen pauses mid-air. "Why didn't you just say no?"

I stare at him, stunned by the simplicity of his question. "Because... because they might think I'm unreliable."

"And so, you let yourself drown under the weight of their demands," he says gently, his voice cutting through me like a blade. "Just like the girl in the dugout. She didn't say no either, did she? Because she was afraid of disappointing someone. Because she thought that if she spoke up, she would be thrown away. But Reya..." His voice softens, but the gentleness only makes it worse. "They threw you away, anyway, didn't they?"

His words hit me like a punch to the gut, the air rushing from my lungs as if I had been physically struck. For a moment, it feels like the walls are closing in again. I want to deny it, to argue, but his words settle too deeply into the raw, aching truth I've tried to ignore.

*They threw me away anyway.*

The truth echoes, bitter and sharp. I gave everything, every part of myself, to be good enough, to be wanted. *To be loved.* But no matter how much of myself I poured into their bottomless void of expectations, it was never enough. *I* was never enough.

Why is it so easy for people to discard me? The question twists like a knife in my chest. I try so hard, sacrifice so much. I sacrifice bits and pieces of myself until I'm not sure what is left. I smile when it hurts, say yes when I want to say no, I give love when all I want is to feel it in return. But it is always the same. People take and take, and when I'm empty, they leave.

Why am I so easy to leave behind? My mind races, clawing for answers, but all I feel is the crushing weight of loneliness. The kind of loneliness that comes from giving everything I have and still being left alone, discarded like an afterthought.

His words echo again, louder this time. *They threw you away anyway.* The truth of it is unbearable, yet impossible to escape.

"This isn't the same," I protest weakly, but even I don't believe it.

"I think it is." He says, his tone solid. "I think you feel like if you were to say 'no' to your boss, he would have no use for you and he would throw you away. I think you want so badly to be liked, that you will go through great lengths to ensure that, even at the expense of your health, your happiness, and your dignity."

He looks at me and I bow my head. My defenses crumble. There is something about his deep, blue eyes that penetrate my soul. This man has torn down all my defenses. Taken down all my walls. I want to hate this man, but instead, I admire him.

"Why did you choose me to be your therapist, Reya? I'm an old white man from Kentucky, why did you choose me?" He puts down his pen and notepad and looks directly at me.

I blink, startled by the sudden shift in conversation. "Because…because you specialize in sex addictions," I answer while blowing my nose. I look at Dr. Jenson from the top of his bald, shiny head to the loafers he is wearing. The plaid button up shirt and blue jeans are plain and simple. His soft blue eyes are obstructed by the glasses sitting on his nose. The wrinkles and discoloration on his face shows he has spent time in the sun in his lifetime. But overall, he is an average looking middle-aged white man.

"I don't think you have a sex addiction, though," he says. He looks up at the clock, only 10 minutes left in the session. He wheels his office chair over to a brown filing cabinet that has three drawers. He hesitates as he decides which drawer to open before pulling out a paper. "I want you to do this for homework. It's a worksheet that I created to help people understand what they are feeling. It says, 'Why do I have sex?' and there is a list of reasons. For example, there are statements such as: I have sex because it feels good. I have sex because I like to feel in control. I have sex because it makes me feel more attractive. And so on. I want you to just circle the ones that apply to you."

He wheels his chair over to me and hands me the paper. He pauses and lets his fingers linger on mine for a moment while looking in my red puffy eyes. "I think you use sex as a way to feel wanted. To feel like you matter. But it's not the sex you're addicted to, it's the validation. And that's what we need to work on. The only way we are going to improve, is if we keep showing up." He takes his hand back like he realizes the gesture is a mistake. "I'm not judging you at all. I have patients who have done worse things than you could possibly imagine, but it's my job to ask the tough questions, and you're doing great."

With that, he stands up and offers me a hand to help me off the couch. As I take his hand and stand, he reaches both arms in front of him to welcome a hug. Although I am towering over him now that we are both standing, I let myself melt into his arms. It's warmth I didn't know I needed.

He pulls away from me and opens the door to his office. "See you Friday, Reya." He says as he ushers me out.

"I'm looking forward to it." I say with a hint of sarcasm. *I am not looking forward to it.*

After navigating through the hallways, the bright afternoon sun catches me off guard. I have to shield my eyes from the harshness of it. As I make my way to my car, my hands begin to tremble. My heart begins to race. My legs seem to respond before my mind can understand what is happening because I am heading toward a bush. I crouch down and begin heaving into the dirt. It is a visual representation of the disgust I feel inside.

# Chapter 5

## In the After

As I pull into my driveway, I have no idea how I made it home. My mind was not on the road. It was in every direction but the correct one. I thought about Josh, I thought about that girl all alone with no one to talk to. I cried the entire drive home thinking about Dr. Jenson and how he has created a space for me to feel what I have suppressed for so long.

The driveway feels like a sanctuary as I cut the engine. My hands rest on the steering wheel, trembling slightly. My eyes are red and swollen from the therapy session, but I can't let Tim see that.

I take a deep breath, willing myself to pull it together. I glance in the rearview mirror and practice a smile. It's not convincing, but it will have to do. I grab my purse and my keys, plastering on the grin as I walk into the house.

Immediately, I'm hit with the aroma of fried chicken and roasted potatoes. Tim has been cooking, anticipating my arrival. The smell consumes my nostrils and takes over my senses. The pretend smile I put on in the car is a sincere one when I enter the kitchen. My stomach begins to growl, reminding me I hadn't eaten all day.

"Hi, babe," I call out to him as I walk in.

"Hey lady, I'm in the zone." He responds. Tim is standing at the stove, focused, flipping chicken in a cast-iron skillet with one hand and stirring gravy with the other. Smoke rises around him threatening to set the alarm off, so I move to open the window.

Then I open the sliding glass door. In this moment, I am so happy that I met Tim. To come home to a cooked meal takes the stress off me, and I realize that this is my happy place. I turn around and walk to the bar stool by the sink and lift myself onto the chair.

"Thank you so much for cooking, I had a rough one today." I say to him trying to sound as in control of my emotions as possible. It's comical watching him avoid the popping of the grease.

"Aww, it's my pleasure." He keeps stirring the gravy with one hand as he turns to look at me. His tall muscular frame looks great in his tank top and his shorts hug him perfectly. His complexion is the deepest shade of brown, and it makes his teeth look extra white against his skin. "How was therapy?" His presence is steady and reliable. It's a stark contrast to the chaos swirling inside of me.

I hesitate a beat too long. "It was fine," I say. He hates talking about my past. He hates when I tell him about the person I was before my life changed so drastically, so I avoid those conversations at all costs.

"What did you guys talk about?" He asks me with a genuine look on his face before he turns and tends to the food. His tone is casual with a hint of curiosity beneath it.

I don't want to talk about that.

As I try to find the words to say to him, I look around the kitchen. There is not a single surface uncovered. Not only is there flour in the air, but there is also flour on every surface. Raw chicken sitting on the counter next to vegetables. Oil on the floor and on his face. Knives and forks and spatulas in an unorganized mess scattered on the countertops. Dishes piled in the sink sitting in cold, dirty dish water.

"Nothing in particular," I finally say hoping the response is good enough for him but arming myself for battle if it isn't.

"Really, Reya?" He puts down the metal spoon he was using to stir the gravy and turns to me. "You've been gone for hours, and you didn't talk about anything?"

I can tell he's getting agitated by my answers, but I double down. I would rather fight than confront my demons. Not today.

"I ask you all the time not to use a metal spoon with my nonstick pans. It scratches them. That's why I bought plastic cookware." My chest tightens at what I'm about to do, but I have to.

He stares at me, clearly unimpressed with my attempt to change the subject. "Don't deflect, were you really in therapy?"

He questions me like I'm hiding something. I'm already on edge and now he's questioning if I was really in therapy? Tim doesn't need to know everything, he doesn't need to know about the memories I dredged up, or the things I'm still trying to make sense of.

And he *definitely* doesn't need to know about the secrets I've been carrying.

Fight accepted.

"Yes, I was in therapy, you can call the man and ask him yourself. Yes, I have been gone for hours, and when I left, this house was spotless." I purposefully look around the kitchen. I intentionally wipe a finger across the counter and look at the exposed marble countertop where my finger had been. It's surrounded by the fine particles of flour. I look at the dirty towels bawled up on the counter in front of me.

"I'm in the middle of cooking," he says in an exasperated huff. "Cooking dinner so you could have a hot meal when you got home."

"I guess your mom never taught you to clean while you cook?" I roll my eyes at him and take note at the dig I just took. This fight has nothing to do with her, or with Tim, really. But I really don't want to talk right now. I stand up and the sound of the chair scraping the floor fills the air. I grab the bottle of water and head toward the stairs.

"Dinner is almost ready, Reya." Tim puts both hands on the counter in front of him and tries to control his temper. He hangs his head toward his chest as he clenches his teeth.

*I'm starving.* "I'm not hungry," I lie as I make my way up the stairs. Part of me hates the fact that I wasn't brave enough to tell him what I'm feeling. I'm feeling insecure, self-conscious, and inadequate. But most of all, in this moment as I walk to my room and shut the door, I feel alone, and I know it's my fault.

In the bedroom, I collapse onto the bed, burying my face in the pillow as the day's events replay in my mind. Dr. Jenson's questions and the memories I've spent years trying to bury are front and center. And now the weight of Tim's unspoken accusations are clawing their way into my consciousness.

I know he sees through me.

But the truth?

The truth is something I'm not ready to face, let alone share.

# Chapter 6

**Before**
**10 years old**

We were walking.

The world felt too big, and I felt too small.

My mom was walking ahead of us, gripping the leash like it was the only thing tethering her to sanity. Her steps were hurried, but deliberate. Milo, our German Shepherd, stayed close at her side, his ears perked and his body tense.

I clutched my sister Ava's hand as tightly as she clutched mine. I wasn't sure if it was her fear or mine that made her grip so firm, but I didn't dare let go.

We were walking.

The sound of our footsteps on the cracked pavement echoed in the quiet street. The air was sharp and cold, biting at my exposed skin. My pajamas were too small, the fabric pulled tight across my arms, and I shivered with every step. Ava had given me her jacket, leaving her in a thin pink T-shirt that did little to protect her from the chill.

Ahead of us, my dad loomed like a shadow, his figure cutting through the faint streetlights. He stalked after my mom with a kind of intentional menace, his long strides eating up the distance between them.

"Call 911, Reya," my mom said, her voice trembling but strong. She didn't slow down, didn't look back.

The phone was heavy in my hand, the numbers already punched into the keypad, but I couldn't press the call button. My chest hurt with guilt and fear. If I called, I'd be betraying my dad. But if I didn't...

"Call them now!" She shouted, glancing over her shoulder.

Milo's growl rumbled low and threatening. My dad's movements slowed, his steps measured as he eyed the dog warily.

I swallowed hard, my fingers trembling over the phone. I couldn't do it. I couldn't choose. I loved them both.

How was I supposed to choose?

Ava tugged my hand, pulling me closer to her. "Reya, we have to," she whispered, her voice breaking.

"I can't," I whispered back, my throat tight with unshed tears.

Ahead of us, my dad stopped abruptly. His hand twitched at his side like he was considering his next move. Without warning, he lunged toward my mom, and everything erupted into chaos.

Milo leapt, his teeth bared and a snarl tearing from his throat. He met my dad head-on, snapping and growling, forcing him back. My dad stumbled, glaring at the dog like Milo was the problem, not him.

"Call them!" My mom screamed again, her voice cracking under the weight of her desperation.

I couldn't move. My fingers were frozen, clutching the phone like it was a lifeline, but I couldn't bring myself to press the button.

We had nothing but a cellphone and a leash. We had no destination. No goal. No end. We were just walking. It felt like we had been walking endlessly, but I could still see our home behind me. It looked so familiar with the overgrown weeds in the yard. There was no garage. There was no "Welcome" sign. There was nothing inviting in front of our house. Just dirt. Just weeds. But it was ours.

If we were to keep walking in our current direction, we would hit the main road. I turned my attention toward the cars that were zooming past. Red ones, black ones, white ones, and I wished one of them would save us. I wished one of them would turn down our street. I wished that this would all just be over.

Suddenly, as if Dad heard me, he granted my wish. He turned on his heels and started walking toward our house. He smiled at me as he passed, but it wasn't a happy smile.

Mom ran toward me and grabbed the phone from my hand. Milo was no longer in attack mode, and he was happy to see me. He was always happy to see me. I loved the way his brown and black fur tickled my skin and how his nose was always wet and cold. I even loved his teeth and smelly breath. Other than my sister, Milo had been my closest friend. We got him 8 years ago when I was just a baby, and we grew up together. There wasn't a time when Milo wasn't by my side. I ran my hands in the fur on his head as he smelled my face. His tail wagged and I felt safe.

I heard my mom on the phone. Her voice was panicked and cracked, "Hello, my husband is trying to kill me, I am on Belcrest Street walking toward Peachtree. Please send help!"

She hung up.

Tears were swelling in her eyes, but she didn't cry, she just looked toward the house. Despite the crisp winter air, she smelled of sweat and the fear was radiating off her skin. Her hands were trembling when she hugged us, but her hug was reassuring all the same.

My mom turned to face us, "I need you girls to be brave, okay? When the police come, tell them I'm wearing a black shirt and walking toward Peachtree. Tell them I have the dog with me. But you have to stay here and wait for them."

*Stay here?* Without her?

"No," Ava said, her voice trembling but firm. "We can't stay here."

"You have to," Mom insisted, her eyes darting between us. She put both hands on Ava's shoulders. "I'll come back for you. I promise. Just stay here."

She turned and ran, Milo by her side, his growl rumbling in the cool air.

I wanted to scream. I wanted to run after her, to grab her hand and beg her to take us with her. But Ava pulled me back, her arms wrapping around me tightly.

"Stay here," she whispered, her voice shaking. "We have to stay here."

Dad walked past us with steady intent, his face twisted in anger. His stride was fast and determined. Focused. His gaze was set. I felt my sister go rigid and she tightened her grip on my hand, so I turned to look at her. As terror consumed her entire body and tears threatened to spill from her eyes, she grabbed my head and held it tight in her chest. Her heart was pounding so hard I could feel it against my cheek. Or maybe it was my heart. The two beats blended together, fast and frantic, as if they were fighting to keep us alive.

BANG.

I jerked away from Ava, my eyes wide and uncomprehending. The sound echoed in my ears, deafening and all-encompassing. My mom screamed, a sound so raw and agonizing it sliced through me like a blade.

I turned toward the noise, my body trembled violently.

Ava tried to pull me back, her hands gripping my arms, but I couldn't look away. I couldn't move.

I dropped the phone. It hit the pavement with a dull thud, but I didn't hear it over the sound of my mom's sobs.

The terror I'd felt before was nothing compared to the crushing weight of this moment. I was frozen, a little girl in too-small pajamas, staring at the lifeless body of the only creature who had made me feel safe.

I didn't cry. I couldn't. The fear hollowed me out, leaving no room for tears.

In the faint glow of a streetlight, I saw him.

Milo.

The world narrowed to that one awful sight. Milo, who had always been there, always protected us, was gone.

Just… gone.

He was lying in the dirt, his body still and wrong in a way I couldn't understand. Blood pooled around him, dark and glossy, spreading like a shadow.

"No," I whispered, the word barely audible.

The only sound I could hear was Ava's whispered mantra as she held me close: "Be brave, be brave, be brave."

# Chapter 7

## In the After

The blare of my alarm jolts me awake, cutting through the haze of restless sleep. I slap it off, the sound lingering in my ears like a cruel reminder of everything I want to forget. My chest feels heavy, my body sluggish, as if the weight of yesterday has sunk into my bones.

I reach out instinctively, my hand brushing cold sheets on Tim's side of the bed. He's already gone. A pang of guilt flickers in my chest, but I shove it down before it can take root.

*I guess your mom never taught you to clean while you cook.*

I think about the words I said to him last night before I stormed out of the kitchen and a sense of disappointment sweeps over me.

My mind shifts to the dream I just had; I imagine therapy opened some old wounds I was trying to keep suppressed. I try to bury those memories deep within me, so I never have to think about how dark my life was then. I used to have this same dream often as a kid and I remember trying to fill in the details that conflicted. But every time I woke up, I would have more questions than answers. Milo was my best friend. He was the closest thing I had, and he was killed by my father. I haven't had another dog since Milo. I can't handle the pain of losing something so innocent again, but mostly, I don't want to think about what happened after Luther killed Milo.

I tap on my nightstand to find my glasses. I feel an empty water bottle on my fingertips, the bag of chips I finished off for dinner last night. I feel a cord and follow the length of it all the way to my phone and unplug it from the charger. When I finally find my glasses within the cluttered nightstand, I head downstairs for a cup of coffee.

Three unread messages and two missed calls.

One missed call from my mom.

One from Tim.

I listen to the voicemail from my mom first before going to my text messages. I'm not ready to deal with accountability from last nights argument. I press play on the voicemail, her voice filling the quiet room.

"Hey, Reya. Just calling to check on you. I heard you quit your job, and you've been feeling…overwhelmed. I just… I want you to know it's okay to take a break. Lord knows I could use one myself with everything I'm dealing with. But whatever's going on, remember what I always say, when life gives you lemons, you make lemonade."

I roll my eyes, her words as grating as ever.

Lemonade.

She's been spewing that cliché since I was eight years old, but what does it even mean? When life gives you shit, you're supposed to sugarcoat it and pretend it doesn't stink?

Still, her voice sticks with me, a ghost of the past I can't shake. I picture her lying in that hospital bed, her body bruised and broken, and a familiar knot forms in my stomach. It's the same knot I feel every time I see her, every time she tries to act like everything's fine.

My mind wanders back to my dream. *Be brave*, my mom had told us before my life shattered for the first time. I need to visit her more, but I can't stand the sight of her. Every time I look at her, I see the woman who couldn't protect herself, let alone me. I love her, but I hate that loving her still feels like mourning someone who never got the chance to be whole.

I open the messages from Tim:

> I'm going to my dad's house, I'll be home soon. Dinner is in the microwave if you still want it.
> -8:13 PM

> I'm sorry, babe. I shouldn't have asked about therapy. I trust you, and I know you wouldn't lie to me. I called because I wanted to hear ur voice.
> -10:27 PM

> I've been drinking too much with my dad, I know you wouldn't want me to drink and drive, so I'm going to just stay the night here. I love you and I'm sorry.
> -12:12 AM

I sigh at how patient that man is with me and how awful I have been with him. I think about how good the food smelled when I walked in the house yesterday. And if I am being honest with myself, under different circumstances, I would have loved the opportunity to connect with Tim on a deeper level. To talk to him about why my heart is so sad, but I don't trust him with those intimacies, not anymore. I reply:

Good morning love. I'm assuming you expected to spend
the night there because you went to work this morning.
So, you must have brought a change of clothes. That's
weird. Lol Enjoy your day…
-Reya

The sarcasm makes my lips curl as I take a sip of my coffee and let the heat of it burn the inside of my mouth a little before I swallow it. I grab my purse, pull out the homework from Dr. Jenson and throw it on the table. "I will deal with you after I clean this mess of a kitchen," I say aloud for no reason in particular.

I don't want to fight with Tim, he has been my rock through all the chaos. He has been someone constant in my ever-changing corner. He knows how to handle me when I'm being unreasonable, and if I'm being honest, times like last night is a prime example. I need to tell him the real reason I have been so overwhelmed. The real reason I have been depressed and shut down. I hate keeping secrets from him, but it feels easier to bottle it up snugly inside my heart and never let it out.

I grab a broom from the closet and begin sweeping. Typically, I like to start from the top and work my way to the floors because wiping the counters can be messy. But today, there is so much flour and flakes on the floor, I clean out of order, which makes me mad about last night all over again. Tim is a great man, but completely useless around the house.

I put on some music and sway to the beat. Cleaning is therapeutic for me. I can turn off my brain and let my body do the work. I can listen to feel good music and actually allow myself to feel good.

# Chapter 8

## Tim

The crack of dominoes on wood is the only thing keeping the silence from getting awkward. I line up my last tile and slam it down like I'm summoning thunder. "Domino, muthafucka."

Dad doesn't even flinch. "Man, if I had a dollar for every time you got cocky just before losing, I'd have enough to finally pay your mom back for the 46 years she has put up with my ass."

I laugh and lean back in the rickety chair, sipping from the red cup beside me. Bourbon. Cheap, harsh, perfect. It burns just enough to remind me I'm still in here somewhere. "You're already in the hole, old man. Just admit you raised a champion."

"I raised a smartass with too much bourbon and not enough common sense," he mutters, squinting at his tiles. "You still chasin' that girl?"

My smile tightens.

"I'm not chasing her," I say. "She's my fiancée." I laugh at my old man sitting across from me. The lines on his face make him look older than he is. The lines of a man that has lived

He grunts. "You are living with a woman who is looking past you…not with one that sees you."

I exhale, scratch my chin. "I know."

Silence hangs for a moment. Not awkward, just honest.

Then he burps, shifts in his chair, and says, "But hell, she fine. I'd be blind too. I'd put up with a lot for her."

I smirk. "Thank you, Dad. That's exactly the emotional support I was looking for." Being with my dad is easy. He doesn't expect anything from me. He doesn't want anything from me but a game of Dominoes. Maybe a beer or two. We can laugh, or we can be silent. But we are comfortable. The hardest conversations we have are always about Reya. I know she doesn't love me.

I know, she doesn't. But I hold out hoping that one day she will. The time I had with Nola was a mistake. I just felt so unappreciated. So invisible, that when Nola showed interest, my head couldn't say no. I didn't like Nola, I just wanted to feel like a man again.

"Support? Nah, we're talkin' facts. That woman has the kind of pain in her eyes that can make men stupid. Like gospel music in high heels. Do you think she loves you?"

I take a long sip. "No."

"You okay with that?"

"No."

"Are you going to leave?"

"…No."

Dad chuckles and slaps the table. "Now that's my boy. Goddamn idiot. But my idiot."

I grin, not because it's funny, but because if I don't, I'll fall apart. The bourbon helps silence the ache inside of me. So does being here. With him.

Reya doesn't understand how I feel. How she makes *me* feel. And I can't tell her. She is already so hard to connect with. This is her world, I'm just living in it and hoping one day she will love me back.

My dad reaches for a jelly doughnut from the paper bag on the counter, bites in without looking.

"You ever think maybe she's broken because you're too whole?"

"I'm not whole," I mutter. "I'm just quieter about being fucked up."

He shrugs. "Same difference. The world doesn't know what to do with a man who bleeds soft."

I pull my phone out, thumb hovering for a second. Then I type: I've been drinking too much with my dad. I'm just going to stay the night here.

And I hit send.

Another domino clacks on the table.

"Shit," I mutter. "You win again?"

Dad leans back smug, powdered sugar on his lip. "Domino, son."

# Chapter 9

## In the After

When Tim walks through the door, his presence fills the room like a warm light. He smiles at me, that easy, forgiving smile, and I feel the tension in my shoulders tighten.

"Hey, Reya," he says, setting his bag down. "How was your day?"

"It was fine," I reply, my tone clipped.

He pauses, studying me. "You sure? You've been quiet lately."

I shrug, not meeting his eyes. "I don't know. Maybe I'm just tired of you asking the same boring questions every day." The words come out sharper than I intended, but I don't apologize.

Tim blinks, his smile faltering for a second before he recovers. "Ooookaaay," he says slowly, walking over to the fridge. "Anything you want to talk about?" He pulls out a beer and pops it open.

"No," I say quickly, grabbing a bottle of water and twisting the cap off. "And before you ask, no, I didn't do anything productive today. Is that a problem?"

"Reya," he says softly, turning to face me. "Why are you doing this?"

"Doing what?" I snap, my voice rising. "Existing? Taking up space in your perfect little world?"

His brow furrows, concern etched across his face. "You know that's not what I mean."

I scoff, crossing my arms. "You're just mad I'm not some Stepford wife who worships the ground you walk on."

He takes a step closer, his voice steady. "I don't want a Stepford wife, Reya. I just want you to let me in. I want you to be vulnerable with me for one damn second. Whatever's going on with you, we can figure it out together."

His words hit too close to home, striking at the heart of everything I've been trying to avoid. I look away.

"There's nothing to figure out," I say coldly. "Stop trying to fix me. I'm not some charity case for you to save."

He takes a deep breath, his jaw tightening. "I'm not trying to fix you, Reya. I just love you." Those three words are too much. They're always too much.

I laugh bitterly, the sound hollow. "Yeah, well, maybe you shouldn't."

The silence that follows is deafening. I can feel his eyes on me, searching for something, but I refuse to meet his gaze.

"Okay," he says finally, his voice barely above a whisper. "I'll stop asking for now."

He walks away, his footsteps soft against the floor, and the guilt crashes over me like a tidal wave. I hear him moving around upstairs, the faint creak of the floorboards as he changes into more comfortable clothes.

I collapse into the chair, the weight of everything pressing me down as if gravity itself has turned against me. My hands tremble as I bury my face in them, trying to muffle the storm raging inside. Tim deserves better. Better than this mess I've become…better than me. I can't let him in. Not when I'm barely holding the fractured pieces of myself together. Not when the secret I'm hiding feels like a jagged, rotting thing that could cut through us both and leave nothing but devastation in its wake.

The thought of letting him see me makes my stomach churn. If I let him in, he's going to see the cracks. He's going to see the twisted, ugly parts of me I've spent years hiding. My heart isn't just wounded; it's blackened, and hardened with rot. And my soul… my soul feels like it's been drowning in sorrow for so long it's forgotten how to float.

I can already imagine the look on his face when the truth hits him; the dawning realization that I'm not someone to be loved. I'm someone to be feared, pitied, avoided. I'm someone you leave behind.

So I'll continue to push him away before he gets the chance. It's better that way. If he leaves because I'm cruel, because I'm cold, because I make him hate me, I can live with that. I'll tell myself it was my choice. I can carry the weight of being the villain in his story—it's a role I know how to play. But if he sees me, the real me, and leaves because he can't love what he finds… I don't think I could survive that.

I'd rather be hated for being heartless than pitied for being unlovable. Because deep down, I already hate myself enough for the both of us. It's easier to live with the monster I've made of myself than to face the truth that I was never worthy of love to begin with.

\*\*\*

The next morning, I stand in front of the mirror, freshly out of the shower, with beads of water still clinging to my skin. The bathroom is filled with steam, the air thick and suffocating, but the worst part is the reflection staring back at me.

I lean in closer, my face coming into sharp focus. The first thing I notice is the blemishes. Small, red marks scattered across my skin like a map of everything I've done wrong. My fingers twitch as I run them over a new pimple forming on my chin, the skin angry and swollen.

I squeeze, hard. The white pus erupts onto my fingertip, and for a moment, there's satisfaction. A small, fleeting victory. But the relief fades as I catch sight of the scar beneath it, another reminder of my relentless picking.

My nose, wide and flat, takes center stage on my face. It's shaped like a bell pepper, a cruel detail that's always drawn attention I didn't want.

I glance at my wild hair that coils in defiance and never falls the way I want it. My edges frizz out like static, stubborn and unruly, a quiet rebellion against every attempt I make to keep my life neat or controlled.

Then there are my breasts.

I look at them with the same mix of shame and anger I've felt since I was a teenager. They're not just small; they're misshapen, flat, sagging as if gravity had given up on me early. The skin is loose, and the nipples are large, dark, and textured.

"They're not that bad," Tim had said the first time I'd shown him. Those words echo in my mind, a cruel reminder that even the person who loves me can only manage lukewarm acceptance. He doesn't touch them. Doesn't look at them. And I don't blame him. After several years of Tim pretending like they weren't there while they dangled in his face, and him flinching anytime they went near him, I finally built up the momentum to ask him to play with them. Tease them. Touch them. But he refused.

"You're just so insecure about them, I don't want to do or say the wrong thing to make you mad at me." He had told me.

"But I'm asking you to touch them." I proclaimed.

"And now I'm telling you I'm not comfortable with them, I'm sorry." And he did look genuinely sorry.

God doesn't make mistakes. That's what people say, right? But looking at myself, I can't help but feel like an exception to the rule.

I grab a towel, wrapping it tightly around me, like armor against the thoughts threatening to drown me. The mirror is still there, still watching, still judging.

I turn away.

Downstairs, I pour myself a cup of coffee, trying to shake the heaviness that clings to me like the steam from the bathroom. I scroll through my phone, avoiding texts from Tim. He's probably still upset after last night, and honestly, I don't have the energy to reassure him right now.

Instead, I reread an old message, one I shouldn't have saved but can't seem to delete.

> I think about you all the time. I can't help it. You're
> intoxicating.

The words feel like a whisper against my skin, warm and dangerous. My thumb hovers over the screen. Delete. Save. Delete. Save. I don't know what I'm holding on to, validation, maybe. Or something darker.

My phone buzzes with another message.

> Don't forget our session today. Same time.

The familiar knot forms in my stomach. Therapy. I know I should feel relief (this is supposed to be helping me, after all) but the sessions are starting to unearth things I'm not ready to face.

As I stand in the parking lot of the *BeBetter Therapy Center,* I close the door to my car and take one last glance over of my outfit. I chose to look casual today. I put on a green spaghetti strap dress that goes to my knees, paired with black tennis shoes. I put in my favorite gold earrings and wore my best gold necklace. I wanted to wear something that would make me feel attractive, even if all I'm going to do is talk about why I have so many dysfunctional thoughts in my head.

"Hello, I'm here to see Dr. Jenson," I say to the receptionist at the desk. She is average looking with blonde hair and red lipstick. I can tell she is trying to combat the visual signs of aging by caking on foundation. I bet she uses anti-aging cream at night to feel better about herself.

"He will be with you in a moment, you can have a seat." She gestures to the chairs that are placed in a half circle around her desk. I take my pick in the corner in case the lobby begins to get full before the Doctor comes to get me. Where I'm positioned, I will only have to sit next to one person instead of a person on either side of me. Social anxiety is rearing its ugly little head already even though I am the only one in the office besides Anti-Aging Allison sitting at her desk.

I look at the magazines scattered on the table in front of me, but ultimately, I pull out my phone. Tim text:

> I love you cutie-bootie. I hope you allow yourself to be
> happy today because you deserve it. Ur awesome.
> -Tim

I thank him for the message, and I add a few kissing emojis to seal the deal.

"Hey, Reya. Come on back," Dr. Jory Jenson calls from the entrance of the hallway, his voice warm, familiar. His demeanor is always composed, collegiate, and confident. But there's a flicker of something else today.

Something softer.

I rise and follow him, my hips swaying just slightly, just enough for him to notice.

I want him to notice.

No, I don't.

The receptionist watches me like a hawk.I flash her a slow, deliberate smirk.

"How's your day been?" Dr. Jenson asks as we navigate the maze of narrow, beige hallways. He smells like cedar-wood and ink, the kind of scent that clings to books and brilliant minds.

"You know what, not terrible," I say, offering him a coy smile. "I don't have a job anymore, so I've just been on the couch catching up on some reading."

He gives a low chuckle. "Well, that doesn't sound terrible at all." He opens the door to his office, gesturing toward the couch like a gentleman. "After you."

His office is dimly lit; the walls lined with degrees and shelves of dense academic texts. It smells like roasted coffee beans and ambition. The leather couch beneath me sighs when I sit. It's aged and familiar and worn in the best places. Like him.

He takes his usual seat then rolls his chair closer to the filing cabinet, pulling out another worksheet. "So, did you have time to take a look at your paper?" He asks crossing one leg over the other with a professor's grace.

My heart jumps. I dig through my purse looking for the paper and find it, relieved. "I did. But I couldn't find anything that really jumped out to me," I admit. "I looked at it all day yesterday, but nothing felt right."

"No problem," he says, his reading glasses perched low on his nose as he scans the worksheet. "Let's take a look together."

He reads aloud, "The top five reasons people engage in sex: pleasure, love, curiosity, opportunity, and orgasm. None of these appeal to you?"

I glance down at the list, pretending to consider it. "Not really."

"What about Tim? Would you say that you love him?" He asks, placing the paper in his lap and locking eyes with me. His voice is calm, but I see the flicker of interest, his pupils dilate slightly but he doesn't blink.

I exhale, pretending to be vulnerable, but watching him closely. "I just feel like I'm stuck. Like I'm going through the motions with Tim, but nothing really matters." I pause, carefully choosing my next line. "Even the people in my life…" I look away, biting my lip.

Calculated.

"What about them?" He prompts, gently.

"I don't think I've ever really loved anyone," I say, my voice thick with practiced grief. His eyes soften. I never really knew love until…

"That's a big statement, Reya. Why do you think that?" His voice cuts through my thoughts.

I shrug. "Maybe I don't know what love is supposed to feel

like. Maybe I've never seen a good example of it…" I trail off. Let him imagine the rest.

"Do you feel loved by anyone now?"

"Tim loves me," I admit, quiet and a little ashamed. He shows me every day. I know he loves me. I just don't know how to accept it.

"And do you love him?"

I pause too long. "I care about him."

"There's a difference between caring and loving," he says. "Do you think you're afraid to love Tim?"

"No," I say quickly. "I just… I don't think I'm capable of it. Not the way he deserves." And I mean it.

He studies me, the corner of his mouth twitching into something like sympathy. "What about yourself? Do you feel capable of loving yourself?"

I laugh a sharp, bitter sound. "Have you met me?"

But he doesn't smile. "Reya, if you can't love yourself, it's going to be hard to let anyone else in. Including Tim."

I shift on the couch, the leather creaking beneath me. I cross and uncross my legs slowly. "It's not that simple." I don't *want* to let Tim in. Tim deserves someone other than me, *better* than me.

"No," he says. "But it's worth exploring because you deserve love, Reya."

The words sting. Not because they're harsh, but because I want so badly to believe them.

But I don't.

Not really.

I look at him, his sleeves rolled up, a single ink pen tucked behind his ear. He is clean, cut, poised, the type of man who grades essays with red ink and gives firm, fair lectures. The type of man who should not be looking at me the way he is right now.

And yet, I find myself wondering...*is he interested in me?*

I glance away, hoping he can't read the storm behind my eyes.

My mind wanders instead. Why does the idea of being loved feel like a threat?

I want the attention, the affection, the validation. I want it so badly it hurts.

It's like I'm stuck in a loop.

I chase love with a hunger that can never be satisfied...and when it shows up, offering me everything I ever claimed to want...I push it away.

Because deep down, I'm not afraid of being hurt...

But of being seen.

"Reya," Dr. Jenson says, snapping me back into the room, his pen frozen in his hand, "What do you want from therapy? What's your end goal?"

I blink at him, caught off guard. "I...I want to feel proud of myself," I whisper. I inhale at the thought.

"You should feel proud of yourself," he says firmly, his eyes lock onto mine. "You've been hurt, yes. But not beyond repair."

His voice is too kind. It wraps around me and makes my stomach flutter. The way he looks at me makes my breath catch. It's too intense, too knowing, like he can see everything I've worked so hard to hide.

I look away before he can see what's behind my eyes. "I don't know if I believe that."

He leans back, a sigh leaving his chest, and he doesn't say anything for a moment.

I wonder if he thinks about me after I leave. If I've found my way into his perfect little world of books and boundaries.

And if I have…

How long until he lets me stay in his world?

"That's okay," he says. "We'll work on it."

He shifts in his chair. "It might help if you walked me through some of your other sexual experiences. Sometimes the way we've been touched explains why we keep pushing love away. Maybe I can better understand why accepting love feels so unsafe for you."

# Chapter 10

**Before**
**14 years old**

The walk to the bus stop felt endless. My backpack was too heavy, my shoes too small, and the science project in my hands was awkward and unwieldy. But I didn't care about any of that. Kenny was walking ahead of me, his head held high, and I was three steps behind, exactly where he told me to be.

Where he told me to *stay.*

I didn't know much about Kenny. He was a junior, older, and cooler in ways I didn't understand but desperately wanted to. When he first spoke to me at school, it felt like a spotlight had landed on me for the first time in my life.

"You're different," he had said, his voice low and confident. "I like that."

It wasn't a compliment, not really, but I latched onto it like a lifeline.

*Different.*

Maybe that could mean special.

Now, as we walked, I tried not to trip over my too-tight jeans or scuff the shoes I had borrowed from Ava. I'd wanted so badly to look good for him, but the shoes pinched with every step, and my legs ached from the weight of my bag.

When we reached the bus stop, Kenny sat down on the bench without a word. I tried to sit next to him, but he shot me a glare so sharp it made my stomach drop.

"Don't," he said, nodding toward the ground. "Just stand over there."

I swallowed the lump in my throat and obeyed, stepping away like I was something to be hidden.

When the bus finally pulled up, I climbed on with a nervous flutter in my chest, still hopeful to be near Kenny.

But once we were inside, the distance between us only grew. Kenny disappeared to the back, laughing with his friends like I wasn't even there.

I stayed near the front, gripping the metal pole and swaying with the rhythm of the bus, trying not to take up too much space.

I told myself it didn't matter. He had invited me over. That meant something, didn't it?

When we finally got off the bus, I followed him down streets I didn't recognize, past crumbling apartment buildings and graffiti-covered walls. The neighborhood felt foreign and a little dangerous, but I didn't say anything.

"This is it," Kenny said, gesturing toward a dingy building with peeling paint and broken windows.

I nodded, trying to hide my unease as we climbed the creaking stairs to his apartment. Inside, the air was stale, the faint smell of smoke lingered in the walls. The living room was bare except for a few folding chairs and a TV sitting on the floor.

He led me to his room, and my heart pounded in my chest. The mattress on the floor was covered in a rumpled sheet, and clothes were strewn everywhere. There was no decoration, no personality. Just the stark reality of someone barely making do. There were no signs of family, or traditions, or the usual findings in a home that was occupied.

"Take off your clothes," Kenny said, his voice casual, as if he were asking me to hand him a pencil.

I froze, my heart skipping a beat. "What?"

"You heard me," he said, pulling off his shirt.

My stomach twisted. I didn't want this. I didn't want to be here anymore. But I thought of the way he'd smiled at me in the hallway, the way he'd made me feel seen when no one else had.

"I thought we were going to talk," I said weakly, my voice barely audible.

Kenny laughed, shaking his head. "You think I brought you here to talk?"

I could feel the tears welling in my eyes, but I blinked them back. "I… I don't think I'm ready," I stammered.

His expression hardened, the easy grin fading. "Then why are you wasting my time?"

His words landed hard, like a punch I hadn't braced for. I'd come all this way, hoping for something I couldn't even name, and now I was ruining it.

"Okay," I whispered, my hands trembling. "But I don't want to take off my shirt, is that okay?"

"I don't care," he gestured for me to take off my pants.

The room was quiet except for the sound of his breathing and the occasional creak of the mattress. My body felt foreign, like it didn't belong to me anymore. I closed my eyes and let my mind drift, trying to escape the painful moment.

"No stop, I think something's wrong. I think you're in the wrong hole." I began to cry.

"There are only two holes down here, it's either this one or your ass. You choose." He said, but he didn't relieve any pressure.

The pain was more than I could bare. It was a pain unlike I had ever felt before. "Can you stop for a second?" I pleaded.

"No," he said, and he pushed further inside of me.

I cried out in pain.

"Yes, do that. I like that." He said between breaths.

My pain...turned him on? Tears filled my eyes as my face contorted to the unpleasant pressure I was feeling. He continued to move over me with a force that felt more like punishment than pleasure. He grinded against me, rough and relentless, and the opposite of gentle.

"I'm almost done." He grunted.

I was throbbing in places I didn't even know existed. I couldn't understand what had just happened or why I felt this way, or why it hurt so bad, but I just wanted to leave.

When it was over, Kenny rolled off me, his movements abrupt. "That was boring," he said, pulling on his pants. "You need to loosen up or something."

I didn't respond. I couldn't. My thighs ached, and my chest felt hollow.

My phone buzzed, and I scrambled to grab it, desperate for an excuse to leave.

"I will be there in ten minutes," my mom's voice said. "Be ready."

Kenny stood up. "Great, you got blood all over my bed." He said, I could tell he was angry.

"I'm sorry." But where had the blood come from? I put my hand between my legs and the pain I was feeling became a visual when my hand came back stained red. My body began to tremble when I saw it, and I couldn't stop shaking.

He threw a dry, crusty towel on the bed near where I was sitting, and I wiped my hands. I could hardly move, but I made myself stand. My legs were weak, my pelvis hurt.

He walked into the bathroom.

My phone rang, "Hello."

"I'm on my way." Click.

I called back. "Mom, I'm not ready."

"I don't care, Reya. Get ready, I have to go to work and I'm already running late. I am on my way." Click.

I didn't want to walk. I *couldn't* walk. But I had to. My legs were wobbly and burning. I heard water running from the sink when I knocked on the bathroom door where Kenny was.

"Hey Kenny, I have to go."

"Okay."

I hadn't had time to process what had just happened. My shirt had blood on it, but it could easily be hidden. I put on my pants that were too tight, shoes that were too small, my backpack that was too heavy and grabbed my science project that wasn't good enough, and I headed to the door. Kenny followed behind me but passed me when we made it downstairs. He led us in a direction that we hadn't come from, but toward another busy street.

He took us to a bus stop and sat down. I was allowed to sit next to him now since no one was around, and he lit a cigarette. The bus stop already smelled like urine and must, and now the smell of the cigarette was making me sick.

"How long do you think it will take for the bus?" I asked him.

He looked up and down the street. We seen the bus going in the opposite direction on Lamb Boulevard and he pointed. "You see that bus coming? That means the bus we're waiting on will be here in 30 minutes."

*30 minutes?* "I don't have 30 minutes. I have fifteen. At most." I said, I begged for a solution with my soul and crying with my eyes.

"Then you're going to have to run, because the bus won't be here for 30 more minutes. This is Cheyenne. Next you have Carey, Lake Mead, Owens, then Washington."

"Can you at least run halfway with me, my bag is heavy."

"No." And with that, he got up and walked toward his apartment building.

I had no choice; I took off running. My science fair project was a tri-fold cardboard that answered the question: *Does the way a paper is folded influence how fast it will burn?* It had glitter, and examples, and right now it was aerodynamic and made it hard to run.

My phone rang.

I couldn't answer, I was on a busy street with cars that were looming by me when I was supposed to be in a quiet library studying. I would say my phone was on silent.

I ran.

The phone rang.

I ran.

The phone rang.

I threw the science project in the rocks next to a brick wall, I didn't need it. I already got a grade for it, and it was slowing me down. I made it to Carey Ave and looked at my phone. It had been 6 minutes and 9 phone calls. If it were to take me six minutes for each block, that would be twenty-four minutes just to make it to Washington, then I would still have to run a block up toward the school.

Today would be the day I die.

The phone rang.

I couldn't answer. Not yet.

I ran.

I couldn't breathe but I couldn't stop. Tears were filling my eyes. My legs hurt, my feet hurt, and it felt like I was running in a body that didn't belong to me. My hips were different. My legs were different. *I was different.*

I ran.

Lake Mead.

I looked at my phone, I had to answer. 34 missed calls. She was furious.

"WHAT THE HELL, REYA. I already told you I was going to be late for work. You got me walking around this damn school looking for you. I don't have time for this."

Click.

She was so quick to hang up all the time. If she would have stayed on the phone a little longer, she would have heard me say I still wasn't ready. I still had to get to Owens then Washington.

Zoom.

Zoom.

The cars were passing me by without a care in the world. I hoped they were all getting a good look at me because this would be the last time anyone was going to see me alive. I took off my shoes. No shoes were better than shoes that were too small. I wish I could abandon my backpack, but I needed it. I put my shoes over each hand and took off running again as I gasped for air.

When this was all over, me and Kenny were going to laugh. I was going to break through those barriers of his. Those barriers that made him not want to talk to me. Or be seen with me.

Zoom.

Zoom.

The phone rang.

I ran.

The cars zoomed by.

I ran.

Owen's. It had been twenty minutes since I started this run, and I had about twenty minutes more. I wished I could just call my mom and tell her that I went to a friend's house. I wished I could cry to her and tell her how much pain I was in.

Instead, I ran. I ran from the pain. I ran from the pressure. I ran toward what was waiting for me when I reached her car. As I ran, I hoped my mom wouldn't lash out at me. I hoped she would see that something wasn't right and show me some compassion, because what I really needed was a mom. A friend.

I ran.

I gasped for air while my backpack rose and fell with the momentum of my legs which caused my shoulders to ache.

I was at the crosswalk of Lamb and Washington. I was so close. I just need to run up the street, and I would be on campus at least. Something big and loud was approaching me from behind and I turned to see the city bus zooming toward me.

Kenny said it would take thirty minutes for it to come. That meant I had been running for thirty minutes. That meant my mom had been calling me for thirty minutes, without hearing so much as a word from me. I had to answer.

102 missed calls. She was pissed.

Breathe.

"Hello, mom I came out and I didn't see you, so I went to the back the school. Where are you?"

"Reya, I'm in the spot I'm always in when I pick you up. Hurry. The. Fuck. Up."

Click.

*She seemed calm*, I thought to myself sarcastically. I took off running. Faster than I ever ran before. Up Washington, I was now running against the traffic and with all the cars that came toward me, I began to panic. I still had to stop and put my shoes on, but it felt as though there was no time. I didn't want this; I didn't want any of this.

***

After not talking the entire drive home, we pulled into the driveway. The entire drive, all my mom could do was breathe heavily and grip the steering wheel as she tried to control her anger.

"Where were you, Reya?" She had asked me between gritted teeth. We were parked now and sat in the car while she waited for answers.

"I was…" I stopped to think. I wanted to tell her where I was. I wanted to talk to her because I *needed* to talk to her. But I could tell by the death grip on the steering wheel, and the look she had in her eyes that she wouldn't understand. "I was in the library."

*Whack.* Right across the cheek.

"Don't lie to me, where were you?" She asked again as her breaths became more intense than ever.

I grabbed my cheek with my hand. I couldn't tell her. Not now. Not with her looking like that. I had to double down.

"My phone was on silent so I didn't hear it ring."

"Your phone was on silent?" Tears were starting to form in her eyes. And I was confused. Why was she about to cry? "Your phone was on silent?" She asked again.

*No.* "Yes." I held my cheek. My feet, my legs, my lungs, my nose, my insides, and now my cheek, were all in pain. I looked at the floor. I wanted to take off those stupid shoes. And those stupid pants.

Without another word, she got out the car, closed the door and walked into the house. I couldn't move. Now that the adrenaline wore off, I felt the aches all over even more. I could hardly pick up my backpack, I couldn't get my legs to move but I forced it.

I walked into my room, put down my backpack, grabbed some pajamas and headed for the shower. The warm water against my skin felt so good. I cried as I seen all the dried-up blood running down the drain.

No one today asked me how I felt.

Sad.

Or what I wanted.

A friend.

Or if I was okay.

No.

I had just had sex with someone I hardly even knew. I never

put too much thought into what my first time would be like, but I think I would have envisioned candles, or music, or kissing, or *compliance.*

At that time in my life, it felt like I cried every day. Every single day there was something new to cry about, and every single day the tears stung my eyes and rolled down my cheeks. And that day had been no exception.

I turned the water off and took a long slow breath. I looked in the mirror and said, "Tomorrow will be better." I gave myself a weak smile before I walked out of the bathroom.

I walked across the hall to my room and started to shut the door when I saw my dad, Luther, walking toward me.

"Where were you?" He asked me, calmly.

*At my boyfriend's house.* "In the library," I responded. He didn't look mad, but I never knew with him.

"I know that's the lie you told your mama, but I'm asking you now. Where were you?"

*I don't trust you.* "At the library" I doubled down. I stood there trying to hide the shaking in my hands. He looked at me like he could hear my heart racing, but he didn't say anything. "I was in the library, so I put my phone on silent. I didn't hear her calling."

"Okay, if that's the lie you want to stick with, I can't help you." He said as he walked toward the kitchen and away from me. I watched him walk away. My mom was mean, but Luther was meaner. I would rather feel the wrath from my mom than deal with anything Luther could cook up.

I knocked on Ava's door.

"Come in." She invited from her bed.

"Thank you for letting me wear your shoes." I told her.

"I didn't think they would fit you." She laughed as she said it.

"They didn't, my feet are barking like a dog." We both laughed and I sat on her bed.

"You know you're not allowed to sit on my bed." The laughing had stopped, and she looked at me.

"I'm sorry," I stood up. "I just wanted to ask, how was your first time?"

She stopped combing her hair and looked me in my eyes. "Why would I tell you that? So you can run and tell our mom?"

There it was. That space between us. It hadn't always been there. But over time, Ava got tired. Tired of shielding me. Tired of being the strong one while I crumbled and came crawling back for comfort. I always needed her to tell me it would all be okay…until one day, she didn't. The distance didn't show up all at once. It stretched in moments like this.

"No, I just…"

"You listen to me on the phone and repeat everything you hear. You're a tattle-tell, I would never tell you my business." She was cold. She was harsh. She was matter of fact.

*Please believe me that I wasn't going to tattle. I just wanted to know if it was supposed to hurt. Or if it was supposed to be an enjoyable experience. And if you wanted to have sex, or did you feel pressured. And I'm confused and I could use someone to talk to. And you're my only friend.* "Never mind." I said as I fought back the tears. I put my head down like a dog with its tail tucked, "Thank you for letting me wear your shoes," I said again.

She didn't acknowledge the second thank you, I guess the first one was enough. And she didn't acknowledge my exit. I pulled her door shut behind me, careful not to let it click too loud, as if noise might make the moment more real.

I stood in the hallway, frozen between two closed doors. My parents' room was dark, silent, shut tight. Behind me, Ava's door was just as closed. There was no light spilling from either side. No voices. No footsteps. Just me in the middle, staring at the tile, trying to keep it together, trying not to feel like a ghost in my own house.

Kenny never talked to me again.

# Chapter 11

**Before**
**14 years old**

Two months later, I had met Andrew. And Andrew was the complete opposite of Kenny. He was so full of emotions. He was happy all the time and his smile could light up a room.

His skin was the color of lightly toasted bread, and he was one of the tallest people in school. He was on the Volleyball team and was walking through the gym when he saw me for the first time.

I don't remember how our relationship escalated so fast, but I was happy when it did. So, when he asked if I wanted to hang out with him after school, I was ecstatic. "But I don't want to have sex." I had told him.

"Okay, we don't have to," he said to me with a smile on his face.

I smiled back as we walked to his place.

We walked next to each other down Washington and we talked about Volleyball. We were ditching practice so we could be together, and it felt like a fairytale. We talked about what his favorite sport was (baseball) and what he wanted to do after high school (play baseball).

"My family is home, I hope that's okay," he had said.

"It's okay," I responded. It was better than okay. I was going to meet his family. And we were going to have dinner together and this was what high school was supposed to be about. Meeting new people and building relationships. I daydreamed the entire walk to his house. I was one of the tallest girls in the school, he was one of the tallest boys, and we were together. I was so happy to be walking with him, I let my feet guide me and I lived in my fantasy.

When we crossed Lamb, we came to apartment buildings that looked modest and worn. As I walked into his home, there were stairs as soon as you walked through the door. On the right side of the stairs, there was the dining room then the kitchen. On the left side of the stairs was the living room, and that was where he took me to meet his mom and sister.

His sister was sitting between her mom's legs getting her hair done. His mom was on the couch braiding. She was surrounded by hair products, combs, and brushes.

"Hello," I said to the pair of them as I walked in.

"Hey mom, this is Reya." Andrew said as he walked over and kissed his mom on the head. "We're going upstairs."

"Okay," she said without ever taking her eyes off the braid she was working on.

I followed Andrew upstairs, we went into his room, and he shut the door. He took off his backpack and his gym bag.

I looked around his room, he had trophies and certificates every where in an unorganized array on his walls. He had jerseys hanging up and a football on the floor. It was the sportiest room I had ever seen. It was the kind of room I envisioned every teenage boy to have.

He began to walk toward me, and he put his hands on my waist. He whispered in my ear, "Lay down."

My eyebrows furrowed at the command. He knew I didn't want this. And as his hands went to the button on my pants, I stopped him.

"Your mom is downstairs, what are you doing?"

"So." He had said as he proceeded to take my pants off.

"Andrew, stop. I told you I didn't want to…"

He pushed me on the bed and pulled my pants and panties to my ankles. "What do you think I invited you over here for? To talk? No." He pulled his basketball shorts off and got on top of me. It hurt just as much as the first time. And I didn't want it. But I learned from the first time that fighting and protesting wasn't going to stop anything, so I complied.

When he finished, he got up and put his clothes on.

I pushed down every feeling I had, got up and put my clothes on too.

I wasn't sure what to do next so I thought I would talk to him. "So do you think you guys will win conference this year?" I asked as I put my shoes back on my feet.

"What are you doing? Get out." He said as he opened the door to his room.

I looked at him and cocked my head to the side. I didn't understand what was happening. I stood up and walked closer to him. "What do you mean?" I asked.

Once I got closer to him, he led me into the hallway. I looked up at him and said, "I thought we were going to talk or something."

He looked down at me. My back was to the stairs as I looked at him in confusion. "You still think I invited you over here to talk?"

He laughed a little then raised his foot off the ground.

He kicked me in my stomach.

Not being prepared for the kick caused me to lose my balance and I rolled all the way down the stairs. I didn't feel any pain when I made it to the bottom. I couldn't comprehend what had just happened. But when I looked up and saw Andrew laughing at the top, I realized he kicked me down on purpose. He walked out of sight and came back with my backpack, tossed it at me then disappeared behind the hallway again. I heard his door close.

Perplexed as to what had just happened, I looked over toward his mom and sister. His mom looked at me and shook her head then hit her daughter on the shoulder with a comb.

"See, this is what I be telling you about. You need to be careful who you give yourself to. These boys will embarrass you out here." She turned her attention to me. "Maybe your parents will teach you not to go home with just anybody." She let her gaze linger on me for a moment, then went back to braiding hair.

# Chapter 12

## In the After

Dr. Jenson is looking at me with such sympathy. "I'm so sorry that happened to you." He says. And I can tell he means it. The leather couch beneath me creaks as I shift nervously in my seat, my fingers tugging at the loose thread on my dress.

I laugh (nervous habit) and say, "It's okay. But Andrew talked to me a few times after that." I avoid Dr. Jenson's gaze, staring instead at the notepad resting on his knee. The scribbles on the page look like a foreign language from this distance, and I wonder what they say about me.

He jots a few notes on his paper. Surprisingly, I didn't cry when I tell him about Kenny or Andrew. I shake my head and roll my eyes at the memory of it. "After the situation with Andrew, I remember a girl named Jasmine. I was sitting outside in the quad area alone, and she walked over to my table. And I remember thinking to myself, *Yes! Someone is finally going to sit with me.*" I rapidly grab a few tissues from the box at this memory.

"She had a few boys following behind her. She came and stood on the table I was sitting at and she turned to the crowd. She yelled to them, 'Her? Her right here?' As she pointed at me, she said, 'This girl right here is a hoe?' The crowd yelled back:

'YEAH!' And all I could do was look at her. I *stared* at her. Then she jumped off the table and everyone laughed at me. After that, I would eat my lunch in the girls' bathroom, or pretend I needed extra help in my Psychology class." I wipe my eyes dry at that memory. This memory hurts worse than the rest.

I adjust myself on the couch. It is getting hot in his office, so my skin is starting to stick to the leather couch. Dr. Jenson lets me adjust. He lets me fidget. He lets me think. We sit in silence for a few moments more.

"After that, I decided I was going to be the one in charge of me. I wasn't going to let men take advan…"

"Boys." He interrupts me. His voice cuts in low and firm.

"Huh?" I look up at him.

"Boys, Reya. They weren't men. They were boys. And you were a *child*. That should have never happened to you." His tone is unlike anything I've heard from him before: shaken, almost raw. He takes off his reading glasses and presses his thumb into his eyes like he's trying to push the memory out of his skull. Like what he heard was more than he was prepared for.

"Nothing happened to me. Everyone was having sex in high school." I interject.

He looks at me, really looks at me. "No…they weren't."

He reaches out his hands and grabs mine. He holds them. "No, they weren't. What happened to you wasn't normal. It *isn't* normal, Reya. No one should have to go through that, and I'm sorry you had to go through that alone." His grip is warm, grounding. His thumb brushes across my knuckle, and it sends an odd tingle up my arm.

"I never talk about what it was like for me in high school

because it's embarrassing. Most people just called me a hoe without knowing anything about me. But I don't think I *went through* anything."

His hands tighten just slightly around mine before he pulls back, clearing his throat as he returns to the safety of his chair.

"Where were your parents through all of this?" He pulls his hands away from mine and sits up straight. The sympathy in his voice is gone. He is back to Dr. Jenson.

"They were there. Physically." I say as I look down at my tissue.

"But not emotionally?"

The air feels heavy and I struggle to breathe. "They had their own stuff to deal with," I say, defensively.

He nods, his expression calm but focused. Understanding. "So you learned early on to take care of yourself. To keep quiet. To not ask for what you need. Let's tackle one thing at a time here." He shifts in his seat, picks up the worksheet from his desk, but I can tell he hasn't emotionally stepped back yet. I can still feel him in the room, fully present.

He takes a deep breath. "I think you use sex as a way to make friends." He says while looking at the paper in front of him. "I think you're so used to feeling invisible, and being taken advantage of, that you use your body as currency."

I shrug my shoulders trying to keep it casual, even though I feel the sting of his words. "Sometimes I feel like people won't like me unless I'm on my back. Sometimes I feel like once they have sex with me, maybe they will realize that I am funny. And that I'm actually smart, and they will want to get to know me." A single tear falls down my cheek.

"Does it work?" He asks me.

"Sometimes." I say as I fidget with the paper.

"I don't think it does." He says as he pulls one leg over the other so his legs are crossed. His blue jeans are worn, and his shoes look freshly cleaned. The contrast feels like him: put together on the surface and softened in the places that matter.

"Kenny, Andrew, Josh. They never talked to you again, Reya. You won't make friends that way. You'll just make lifelong people that want to use you."

I shake my head at his assumptions. I have plenty of friends. The method works.

"I know you think they are your friends, but they are not, Reya. Tim, Tim is your friend. Ava is your friend. These men, they are not your friend." He tries to convince me, but I continue to shake my head. "Do me a favor, pull out your phone."

I know where he's going with this, but I comply anyway. I reach in my purse and pull out my phone. I instinctively unlock it, go to my messages, and scroll through. Mike. Dallas. Leven. Bobby. Victor. Quan. Vance. Kevin. All messages from people that I am *friends* with.

One point for Reya, zero points for this situation.

"I want you to call someone right now and tell them your car broke down and you need a ride. Anyone."

I take a deep breath; I wasn't prepared for a fake scenario. I go back to the top of my messages.

Mike. No.

Dallas. No.

Leven maybe, but I don't want to bother him for a fake scenario.

Bobby is married so no.

Victor. No.

"I can guarantee that Tim is the only person you would feel comfortable calling because you actually have a friendship with Tim."

I'm still not convinced with Dr. Jenson's theory. But I put my phone down and patiently wait for the session to be over.

"I'm going to give you homework. These past few sessions have been hard and heavy and thank you for sharing some of your most vulnerable moments with me. I appreciate your honesty. But you've spent so much of your life trying to be what others needed you to be...Do you even know who you are outside of that?" I look at him and wonder if I can even answer that question. *How* to answer that question.

He stands up and gestures for me to do the same. As I stand, he continues, "I want you to go home, and enjoy your fiancé. I want you to leave all the stress of therapy here, in this room and I want you to actually enjoy what you have at home."

I nod, unsure if I am able to do what he's asking.

The session ends with a familiar ache in my chest, a mix of vulnerability and exhaustion. I walk toward the door and think about what he's asking me to do.

But as I walked to the door, I pause. I look back at him.

And for a moment, I see it in his eyes. He's becoming invested in me in a way that's caught him off guard.

He goes back to shuffling papers and adjusting his glasses.

I take one more look at him and say, "Thank you," before leaving, his words linger in my mind, twisting and turning in ways I don't understand.

His eyes lift to meet mine.

He sees me, and I don't know if that makes me feel safe…or dangerous.

In the car, I sit for a long moment, staring at my reflection in the review mirror. The way Dr. Jenson looked at me flashes in my mind, his eyes steady and sharp and caring, like he could see right through me.

I shake that thought away and pull my phone out to dial Leven's number.

"Hello," he answers.

"Hey, my car just broke down, and I'm about 5 minutes away from your house, can you help me?"

There is silence on the other end of his phone.

"Don't you got a man?" He says it with no emotion in his voice, but I know what he's implying. "Where is he at?"

"He's at work," I lie. I know Leven will come. He has to come.

"Ummm, the game is on right now. Can you call an Uber and just get dropped off at my house until Tim gets off?"

"I *could* call an Uber, but I'm calling you." I say, with a hint of irritation in my voice.

"Never-mind, you can stay there with that attitude."

Click.

And with that, he hangs up on me and my fake scenario.

# Chapter 13

## In the After

I take Dr. Jenson's advice and live in the moment with Tim. When I open the door into our home, I smell a freshly cooked meal in the air, and today more than ever I decide I will handle the situation differently. When I walk into the kitchen, it's clean except for a few dishes in the sink and some spaghetti sauce on the counter. I kiss Tim on the forehead, "Hey, babe." I say to him.

"Hey, babe. I wasn't expecting you so soon. I'm sorry, I'm about to wash the dishes now." He says to me nervously. I hate that I have that effect on him, but I secretly love it at the same time.

"No, you keep doing what you're doing, I can help with the dishes. It smells great in here." I let my fingers graze across his back as I walk toward the sink and turn on the water. I look at him and we smile at each other.

"I take it you had a good session today?" He says as he stirs the sauce. "I'm sorry, I'm not going to ask about therapy, how was your day, Princess?" He changes the subject, and I appreciate him for it.

"My day was lazy; I think I'm ready to go back to work." I say to him. These two months have been great; I have been able to clear my head but I'm ready for the distraction now. I don't have the courage to explain to him why I really quit my job. I have only told Dr. Jenson, and when I told him, he looked at me with such sympathy and disappointment, I can't bare to have Tim look at me the same.

Me and Tim dance around the kitchen together and we sing to the oldies on the radio. *This* is my happy place. He walks up behind me wraps his arms around my waist, he kisses my neck and says, "It's about time you went back to work. You're a horrible stay at home fiancé." We both laugh at his joke, and I flick sauce at his face.

He makes me a plate of spaghetti, fried chicken, and garlic bread and we sit on the couch, our feet on the coffee table as we eat.

"I've been so selfish lately, how was work?" I ask between bites of bread. Tim is a terrible cook. The bread is burnt because when his timer went off, he was tending to the chicken and forgot to take the bread out. The fire was too high on the stove while he was deep frying the chicken, so the inside is raw. And he didn't cook the noodles long enough, so they are still crunchy, but I eat because he tries so hard to make me happy. I can risk ingesting salmonella to keep him happy.

"Work was cool," he says as he takes a bite of his chicken. "Mmm, I think this is some of my best chicken yet." He looks at me with a smile on his face.

I think before I respond, I could tell him how I really feel and ruin this beautiful, happy moment, or I can lie, and we can have a great night. I choose the latter. I've already been lying to him for years, what's one more?

"I think you're right." I smile and take another bite of chicken. Nope, still gross. I take a few bites then stand up. "Are you thirsty, babe?" I get the words out even though my mouth is filled with raw meat.

"Yea, a beer please." He says over his shoulder.

I shield my mouth with a paper towel and spit out the raw chicken before he notices.

"When was the last time you drank water? Would you like water instead?" I try to muster up my most innocent voice.

"Here you go." He says as he turns away from the movie to look at me. "I like to have a beer with my dinner. Is that a problem?" He asks me from the couch. The minor irritation is rearing its ugly head on his face.

It's not a problem for other people maybe, but Tim doesn't know when to stop. He can't just have one. He will drink until he is drunk. Or until he passes out. Or until he becomes someone I don't even recognize, and I hate those nights.

"No, one isn't a problem, but seven or eight is the problem." I say as I walk over to him with an open beer in one hand, and my bottle of water and napkin in the other. I sit the beer on the table. Tim picks it up and chugs the bottle until it is halfway gone, then wipes his mouth.

"When we first got together, you didn't have a problem with my drinking." He says as he scoots closer to me on the couch. Already I can smell the beer on his breath. I see the fizz still on his mustache and my stomach turns a little. "You never used to complain about my drinking." He takes another bite of spaghetti.

"I get that, but Tim, that was nine years ago. People's preferences change. Things are different now that we are living together, and your drinking is an issue." I try to say this as nice as possible. I shouldn't have mentioned this. I should have just brought him the beer.

"A few beers never killed nobody." He grabs my wrist and caresses it with his thumb.

"Okay, how about two beers tonight and we just enjoy each other. Fair?" I compromise with him.

"Fair." He agrees. "But what about after you go to sleep, can I drink more after you sleep? You won't even be up to notice."

I roll my eyes. This is really a sickness for him, and he can't even see it. "That's fine," I say, reluctantly. Taking a sip of my water. I take another bite of the chicken and spit it into the napkin when he isn't looking. I must admit, the outside is full of flavor and crispy and almost delicious. But the inside is soft, almost gooey in my mouth. Something isn't right with the texture, and I can't keep pretending that it's okay. "I want to go visit my mom tomorrow, can you come with me?"

"Of course," he smiles wide as he looks at me and I smile back. "I love moms." He puts a hand in the air while chewing a mouth full of spaghetti and I don't hesitate to meet his hand with my own. When our high fives meet, the sound brings happiness to my heart.

I don't deserve a man like Tim. He is patient. He is caring. He loves my family and my daughter, and I don't do anything but lie and keep secrets from him.

He laughs at the TV and my heart melts. I know eventually I can love him. I know one day I'm going to wake up and Tim will be the man of my dreams but today is not that day. A lot of the guilt has subsided after talking to Dr. Jenson. He understood that I don't think I love anyone. He told me it was normal for me to feel that way.

"Do you want to grab some flowers for her on the way?"

"Flowers for who?" Tim interrupts my thoughts and I'm thankful.

"For moms. I think she would appreciate some flowers." He says it so casually, he doesn't realize how nice that gesture actually is, and I wish I could love him.

"I would love that." I say as I put my napkin over my food because I cannot take another bite. I scoot in closer to him and cuddle up next to him on the couch. "Love you."

"Aww, I love you too." He takes another sip of his beer. "Now hurry up and go to sleep so I can get my drink on." He says jokingly as he kisses my forehead. I don't respond. I just laugh and nudge him with my shoulder.

I retreat to the bedroom, closing the door behind me and leaning against it. My chest aches, a gnawing guilt that I can't seem to shake.

Tim is a good man. Too good. And that's the problem.

I sit on the edge of the bed, staring at the framed photo on the nightstand. It's from our trip to the mountains last year. Tim's arm is slung around my shoulders, his face alight with laughter, while I'm smiling stiffly at the camera. I remember the moment clearly—the way he'd tried to make me laugh, the way I'd forced the smile for his sake.

I wanted to love him. I wanted to feel the same warmth and certainty that he seemed to feel every time he looked at me. But no matter how hard I tried, it wasn't there.

Being with Tim feels like wearing Ava's shoes: awkward, uncomfortable, never quite fitting right.

The first time he told me he loved me, I'd frozen. We'd been sitting on his couch, watching a movie, and he'd just... said it.

"I love you, Reya." The words hung in the air, heavy and suffocating. I'd smiled, nodded, and kissed him, but I hadn't said it back.

Not then. Not for months.

When I finally did, it had been out of obligation, not emotion. The look on his face when I said it had been worth it at the time: relief, joy, adoration. But now, I wonder if he could sense the emptiness behind the words.

I lie back on the bed, staring at the ceiling. My thoughts drift to therapy, to Dr. Jenson's words from earlier: *You've spent so much of your life trying to be what others needed you to be*, he'd said. *Do you even know who you are outside of that?* The question had stung, mostly because I didn't have an answer. I've spent my entire life molding myself to fit the people around me.

When Tim looks at me, he sees someone I don't recognize. He sees strength, kindness, beauty. But I don't see any of that. He just wants me to let him in, but every time I try, it feels like I'm walking into a trap.

I think about the nights when I lie awake, staring at the ceiling while Tim sleeps soundly beside me. He reaches for me sometimes in his sleep, his hand resting on my arm or his body curling around mine. I let him, but I never reach back.

It's not that I don't want to. It's that I don't know how.

The door creaks open, and Tim pokes his head in. "Hey," he says softly. "I made some tea. Thought you might want some."

He's holding a mug, steam curling up into the air, and his expression is so earnest it makes my chest ache.

I force a smile. "Thanks," I say, taking the mug from him.

He lingers in the doorway, his eyes searching mine. "I'm here if you need me," he says.

I nod, my throat too tight to speak.

When he finally leaves, I set the mug down on the nightstand and bury my face in my hands.

I want to be the person he thinks I am. I want to love him the way he deserves. But every time I try, I feel like I'm drowning.

# Chapter 14

## In the After

I wake up on the bed with Tim at my back. I usually don't like to cuddle because I run hot, but this morning I embrace how close he is to me. I embrace his chest on my back and his legs wrapped around mine. I scoot closer to him and instinctively he pulls me in closer.

"Good morning, cutie." His dry, raspy breath is warm on my ear as he nuzzles his face in my neck.

"Good morning, handsome." I say. It's rare for me to wake up next to him. Tim leaves two hours early for work in the morning, so he is gone by the time I normally wake up. And often times he spends the weekend at his family's house because he is too drunk to drive, or it was a late-night playing dominoes with friends. So, days where Tim is in bed when I open my eyes are always happy ones. "Do you want coffee?"

I lift my leg a nudge so he can release his hold he has on me, but he pulls me in tighter. "No," he breathes. "Stay here a little longer."

"No, I'm hot." I say as I force myself out of the entanglement and place my feet on the floor. "And besides, if I stay any longer, you'll want to do more than cuddle." I look at him and his manhood and I laugh. Our sex life was once prominent and frequent. But since seeing Dr. Jenson, I haven't been in the mood. Maybe it's the topics we talk about, or the feeling I get when I walk into his office, but sex with Tim has been the last thing on my mind.

"Is that a bad thing?" He asks as he turns from my side of the bed and readjusts the pillow he's laying on so he is propped up and watching me put on socks.

"No, it's not," I say, looking for the words to say. *Tell him the truth*. "I just really need some coffee." I lie. I hold his leg for a moment before I stand up and head toward the bathroom to brush my teeth. "I'll bring you some."

"I don't want any." He covers his head with the blue sheets that he is laying under.

"Good morning, Mom." I say as I sip my coffee.

"Good morning, Reya. What time do you think you will be here this morning?" Her voice makes me smile.

"I'm up and drinking coffee as we speak. I'll be there soon."

"Girl, we have coffee at the house," She laughs. "Well, I'm making breakfast, I'll make enough for you too."

She hangs up the phone without a goodbye. Without a departing word, but that is what I have come to expect from my mom. She is the nicest woman you will ever meet, but she is terrible with goodbyes.

I need to see her more often; she has been a rock through all the chaos of life's challenges. But seeing her makes me sad, and there is always a ball in the pit of my stomach when I look at her.

# Chapter 15

**Before**
**16 years old**

My body woke me up in the middle of the night. All I could hear was the steady buzz from my old alarm clock that sat on my nightstand.

Silence was a good thing.

I laid in my bed praying for the silence. It became my only solace in a life so confusing. I stared into the darkness as though I could make sense of the shapes in the shadows, and I listened. Something in my body woke me up every night around the same time. But that night, I couldn't seem to relax, my entire body was tense, and my breaths were slow.

I looked to my left at the small alarm clock: 1:00 AM. If there was anything but silence, there wouldn't be much I could do, but I felt like I owed it to my mom to listen. So, I listened.

My bladder was full, but I wouldn't dare go to the bathroom at this time. Not when there was silence. I closed my eyes and tried to steady my mind. I focused on the smell of my sheets. They smelled musty and a little stale, but it was a smell that was familiar and comforting.

I had to go to the bathroom. Maybe if I don't flush the toilet, we could still have a good night. It had been six nights of good nights, and I wanted it to last forever. I brought my hand to the top of my head to feel my hair. My scarf fell off in the middle of the night again. Great. Another obstacle to tackle when my alarm goes off. I sat on the edge of my bed and took a deep breath. My feet touched the ground, and I tried to focus my eyes on the darkness.

Keeping my room clean was impossible. There were socks and dirty clothes on my floor. Clothes were bulging out of my nightstand, and I instinctively moved my hand across the top of the dresser to find my glasses. I was careful not to knock anything off and disrupt the silence.

I couldn't keep sitting there taking deep breaths or my bladder would explode. I stood up as quietly as I could and began taking steps toward the door, careful not to step on anything that would make noise. I couldn't see any light shining through under my door. Luckily for me, the bathroom was right across the hallway. I only had to take 2 steps once I left my bedroom.

While holding my breath, I opened the door to my room as slowly as possible. The hallway wasn't all the way dark; some light was illuminating the living room which was causing my eyes to adjust better to the new scenery. Directly across the hallway from my room was my sister Ava's room. Her door was closed, and I didn't hear any movement on the other side of it. To my right I could see the door to my parents' room. The light was off, perfect. I didn't really think that my going to the restroom would cause a problem, but I never knew what would start the next string of chaos, so I tried to stay out of the way. Don't be seen. Don't be heard.

The first step off my warm and soft carpet and onto the cold, hard tile was jarring. I didn't even put my heel completely on the floor. I wouldn't dare.

Another step.

I had to remember to breathe.

Last step before I entered the bathroom, I held the door firmly and slowly opened it. Once I entered the bathroom, I pushed the door so that it was slightly opened so the faintness of the light will still shine through, but I could still have some privacy. I wouldn't dare turn on the light. I used my memory and the very faint illumination to guide me to my destination. There's no sound except the steady stream.

Safe. For now. I didn't flush. I didn't wash my hands. I was careful. I used the same stealth as before to exit the bathroom. Tip toeing and hardly breathing, I reached for the door, and I inhaled a quiet gasp. Mom is standing in the hallway reaching for the handle that was just pulled out of reach by me. But how? Why? *I was so careful.*

"Don't use the bathroom with the door open anymore." She whispered to me.

"I...okay." I whispered back. I was still too confused to process what she was saying, or why she was standing in front of me right now. She seen I was frozen in my tracks, so she held out her hand as if to usher me back into my room. She followed behind me and waited until I was comfortable in my bed.

"Good night," she whispered before she lingered a little longer in my doorway.

No. No. No. This wasn't right. She shouldn't be up. It was a quiet night. What did I do wrong? I was careful.

I seen light from under my door, which meant my mom was in the kitchen. I sat on my bed, but I didn't lay back down. Instead, I closed my eyes and listened for the noises. I heard the steady stream of water from the faucet. She was washing dishes? I heard faint clinks of glass from plates and drink-ware. *Be quiet, mom. Or you'll wake him. Wash the dishes in the morning.* I took deep breaths. In and out.

In and out.

In and…footsteps. No.

"What are you doing?" He spoke. He sounded tired, sleepy. Maybe that was a good thing.

No response.

"Did you not hear me? I said what are you doing?"

I couldn't see anything beyond my door, but with my eyes closed, I imagined the look in my moms' eyes. I imagined her feeling the same way I felt when I seen her at the bathroom door moments earlier. I imagined her being frozen in her tracks, her heart in her throat and unable to form words. But she must answer him. She must try. *Please, mom, answer him.*

I took a breath.

"I was just trying to wash the dishes so the kitchen would be clean when you woke up."

"Why weren't the dishes washed?"

"I ummm, I fell asleep. I didn't mean to I just…"

"Well, why don't you just come in the room and go back to sleep then?" He said to her.

With my eyes closed, I pictured my mom conflicted. She knew the kitchen must be cleaned before she went to bed. But she also knew not to go against his wishes. So, what does she do?

Either answer was wrong, and we both knew it.

The steady stream of water stopped. I heard more clanks of glasses, then I could no longer see the light under my door. I followed the footsteps across the hall with my ears. One soft and slow, the other hard and unforgiving. I heard their door close, and I waited. I laid back in my bed and waited for the inevitable. These nights came so often now, but I still cried. Why didn't she just do the dishes before she laid down? She knew. She should have learned her lesson. She should have learned from being with Luther for 17 years that there would be consequences.

There were always consequences.

"Luther, I'm sorry. I didn't mean to go to sleep. I was just so tired from…"

"Shut up. You think I want to hear…" He slapped her. "How tired you are…" He slapped her again. I knew the sound. It was distinct. It sounds more like a sting than a punch does. I knew the sounds of punches well. The sound of fist pounding flesh is unrecognizable. The sound my mom lets out is even more heartbreaking though. It was uncontrollable on her part. It was like a shriek of pain. It always caught her off guard even though she knew it was coming. But what could I say? It always caught me off guard too, even though I knew it was coming.

This is how my nights were, I was either woken up by the scuffle, or I jerked awake in nightmares from the last scuffle. Or sometimes, like nights like tonight, I woke up because my body hated me, and I had to use the restroom. Which caused me to hear scuffle from start to finish. Nights like those were the worse of nights. I laid there helpless. I listened. I judged my mom for not washing the dishes. I shook my head at her costly mistake. I listened to her suffer the consequences. Sometimes I cried. Sometimes I got angry, but never at Luther. Always at her. Why wouldn't she just leave? Why did she choose a man that beat on her? But mainly, why didn't she just do the dishes?

A punch landed on my mom. I wasn't sure where. Judging by the sound she made; I think in the gut. "Luther, stop." She said as she tried to catch her breath.

Definitely the gut.

I could hear what sounded like wrestling and I couldn't help but wonder how traumatized I had to be. I was sitting there laying in my bed, trying to envision how my mom was getting beat up. It had become such a common routine, I was trying to guess where the punches were landing.

*In the gut, 2 points for Luther.*

*She's still up and fighting 1 point for mom.*

*She hasn't backed down, she still has hope that he will have some sympathy, minus 3 points.*

*He knows no such thing.*

"Luther, STOP!" She yelled. I could tell she was fighting him back. Brave. It won't help, but brave.

"You want to sleep right? That's why you couldn't do the dishes?"

I heard more rustling. The buzz from the alarm clock had been overtaken by the noise from behind their door.

Then silence.

Wait, not silence, just quieter struggle? I imagined myself as the part of the ear that oversees listening. (The cochlea, I think.) In my mind I saw myself traveling down the hall, through the door of my parents' room and I followed the rustling. I wanted to know what was happening in there. I wanted to know my mom was safe…or as safe as she could be having not washed the dishes.

"Reya…" I heard that word clear as day. I held my breath. It sounded as though my mom called my name. She never called me. The protocol was for me and Ava to pretend like we were sleeping no matter what we heard. And when we woke up, we were to pretend like nothing happened. Why was she breaking the protocol? Why did she say my name? "Reya…he…lp…me."

The words were spaced out like she was gasping for air. But they were clear. She wanted my help. But what could I do? I was 16 years old, Five foot, five inches and barely 100 pounds. I was small, and I had never thrown a punch. Why was she calling me? I could stay in bed and pretend like this never happened. Pretend that I didn't just hear the craziest request from someone that I loved. I may not have respected, but I loved. Or I could stand up, right here, right now, walk up to the door, open it, and help my mom.

All of a sudden, I felt 10 years old again. My mom begging me to call the police, but I couldn't because I wasn't sure which parent to disappoint. Now that I was older, I knew it wasn't about who I would disappoint and who I wouldn't have. It was about who's life could I have saved. Maybe if I would have called the police the first time she asked, Milo would still be alive. Maybe if I would have called the police the second time she asked, she wouldn't have ended up in the hospital. Maybe we wouldn't be living here with this monster. *Be brave.* She had said to both my sister and me. But wait, my sister was older than me. Why didn't she call for Ava? Ava would have been more help to her than myself…

She saw me in the bathroom. She knew I was awake. *My stupid bladder.*

A shudder passes through my body. I didn't want to go in there. But maybe I was supposed to save a life that day. I stood up and walked into the hallway. It was supposed to be a quiet night. I sighed and put my hand on the doorknob of their bedroom, and I stood there, frozen.

"Reya...pl...ease. He's... go...ing ...to...kill...me." The words were shout out between breaths and scuffles. I twisted the doorknob and opened the door scanning the room for the abnormalities of what's to be expected from a fight. To the right their tan dresser looked to be untouched. The loose change is sitting in the corner as it always was. Unopened mail next to that. The bed looked as though it had been slept in and recently disturbed, but the top of Luther's head caught my eye. His black, short afro was bobbing up and down, barely visible. He was kneeling and I heard my mom gasping for air. I seen her hand reach up and grab his face. I heard him grunting, not even realizing I was in the room.

My body sprung into action without my minds consent. I rushed over to Luther and grabbed him by the hair. I tightened my fists around every curl and coil, and I pulled as hard as I could. He didn't even flinch. I had never hit anyone before, and I started crying at how uncomfortable it was. I didn't want to hurt him, but I didn't want my mom to die either.

Her small frame looked so helpless on the floor underneath the weight of him. I hit him in the head. *Take that!* I hit him again. One fist still in his hair, the other hitting the top of his head. He probably didn't feel the punches, but he knew I was there. Only a monster would kill a child's mom in front of said child. Was I dealing with a monster? Or a man who still had a heart?

"Get off her! You're going to kill her, are you crazy?" I said without releasing my grip on his hair. The lady on the floor was bleeding from her mouth and her nose but there was a fire in her eyes. A fire that said: *are you really going to beat me in front of my kid?*

Luther let go of her neck.

Reluctantly.

I released my grip on him as well…

Reluctantly.

I stood up, tears burning my eyes, but I refused to look away from him. He was unpredictable. He looked at me. Stared at me. I heard my mom gasping for breath now that her airway was open, but she didn't dare move. I held my ground as well.

He stood up. "Go get me a Slurpee," he said to no one in particular then he walked in the bathroom and closed the door. I wrinkled my eyebrows because what a weird request. A Slurpee?

My mom didn't miss a beat though; she got off the floor with grace and composure. "Go put some shoes on." She said to no one in particular and walked out of the room. I followed her, she made a right into the guest bathroom, and I made a left into my room to put on my shoes.

After what I just seen, we should have been packing our bags and getting the hell out of dodge. It's one thing to imagine what was going on behind closed doors, it was in a whole other league to be on the violent side of that door. And there was no returning from it.

Sitting in the car outside of 7-11, I didn't say anything the entire ride there, but now, I feel the need to ask. "Are you o…?"

"Don't." She held her hand up in the middle of my sentence. "Just go get the Slurpee…please."

I walked into the store and got the Slurpee.

# Chapter 16

## In the After

That memory doesn't just haunt my dreams; it seeps into every crack of my waking reality. Too often, Tim shakes me awake, his voice muffled by the haze of my screaming, or the violent shutter of my body trapped in another nightmare. I wake drenched in a cold sweat, heart racing, as if I had been running from something I could not outrun.

Memories are thieves of peace, leaving me, restless, and hollow. I think about my mom; how broken she seemed, how fragile she looked back then. I hated seeing her that way, consumed by a man who had turned love into something oppressive. I remember swearing that I would never be like her. I even imagined taking revenge on her behalf, freeing her from the grip of a man who didn't deserve her. This is why seeing her even now is so hard.

None the less, she is my mom. She is the one person in the world that I adore beyond any measure of love. So reluctantly, I sit my coffee cup down on the marble coffee table. I allow my fingers to linger on the cup while my mind races on the punches. The kicks. The bloody noses and the black eyes. As I walk upstairs and into the room, the sound of Tim's voice jolts me from my thoughts.

"Do you even love me anymore?" His voice carries a strange mix of vulnerability and accusation. I glance at him, lying under our thick, blue comforter, his face shadowed with something I can't quite place. He is operating under the impression that I even loved him from the start.

"What do you mean by that?" I respond. Deflection, good. Easy.

"Lately, I haven't been able to do anything right. If I cook," he rolls over to face me and I cross my arms waiting for the inevitable fight that is coming. "The food isn't cooked the way you like it. If I clean, it's not clean enough for your standards. What am I supposed to do?"

I laugh a sharp, bitter laugh that I can't suppress. "You want me to praise you for putting dishes in the dishwasher after three months of nagging? That's the bare minimum, Tim. I don't celebrate mediocrity, and you know that." I have no idea where this is coming from. I embraced him this morning and I thought we would have a good day. Apparently, we won't. And I'm okay with that.

"Let me finish." He says as he moves toward the edge of the bed. The only thing he is wearing are boxers, and he looks handsome. Cute. I can tell by the look in his eyes that he's hurt but is it wrong of me that this is when I am attracted to him the most. When he is hurting, vulnerable, and at his wits end? This is when I look at him and want to rip his close off.

"You won't touch me. You hardly even look at me. Is there someone else?" His eyes search mine, wide and pleading, and for a moment, I feel sorry for him.

But his accusations hit a nerve. I turn back, laughing hollowly. "Someone else? Someone else?" I laugh again, then clasp my fingers together and put my hands on the top of my head. "You really think there is someone else? There are so many flaws in that theory, I'm not even going to entertain that."

I walk away and into the bathroom. But I come back fueled with frustration, fueled with pent up anger. "You're the one that's gone all hours of the night. You're the one that's at your 'dad's' house," I put my fingers by my head to emphasize "dad's". "Because you are 'too drunk to drive'. Sometimes I don't see you for days, and *you* question *me* about cheating? That's rich." My voice rises as the truth spills out like venom, shaking the air around us. I laugh again; the crazy hysterical side is coming out.

I throw on the first clothes I see. I'm not just mad, my hands are shaking. My arms are shaking. My head is shaking. I can't stop this nervous neurotic laugh that has started, and I have a million thoughts going through my head.

"I guess I can't even express myself with you. I came to you with real concern, and you turn it into a me thing. Now, I'm the problem." There he goes, being all vulnerable and cute again. I have two options.

One: I can take a deep breath. Step away for a moment and come back levelheaded and just listen to the man that has loved me for nine years.

Two: I can make things worse, so I don't have to face my demons.

I have never been one to back down from a fight and I'm not sure if I should start now. I think about going to my mom's house. Being around her already makes me uneasy and I don't want to be riled up when I get there. But I also can't handle this conversation right now, either. I storm out of the room and into my office, slam the door and lock it. My hands tremble as I pull out my journal and turn a few pages.

Inhaling and trying to concentrate on calming my shaking body, I close my eyes and try to steady my breathing and my thoughts. I flip through the pages of my journal, and a familiar entry catches my attention.

*November 18th, 2022*

*I know I'm not perfect, and I don't pretend to be. I am actually…afraid. Afraid to be vulnerable. Afraid to get hurt. So, it's hard to believe that all I do is cry. I work so hard to build these walls around my heart to protect myself, but I am still crying.*

*Finding out about Nola and Tim broke something in me that I didn't know could break. I see her everywhere: in my nightmares, in my reflection, and every minute I feel inadequate. Tim says it wasn't physical, just attention seeking. But my tears don't know the difference between emotional and physical betrayal.*

*I remember seeing my mom cry. Hearing her cry…every night. And I never understood why she would stay with someone who brought her so much pain. And I will never forget what she told me. "I don't feel like I deserve any better." That response was so raw and so real and so…crazy to me. My mom. The nicest, most beautiful woman in the entire world didn't deserve to be happy?*

I should've known about Nola from the beginning. Not because of anything obvious. Just… the way she lingered. The way he lit up around her. The way my gut tightened the first time I saw them together at that company picnic.

I remember standing there, watching him laugh a little too long at something she said. He brushed me off like I was in the way. Like I was interrupting.

Later, when I brought her up (softly, carefully) he shut it down quick. Called her ugly. Said she was shaped weird. "Built like a troll," he said.

And I believed him. Or at least, I wanted to.

He was so convincing in his disgust for her that I almost felt bad for doubting him. I even caught myself defending her in my head. Telling myself she didn't deserve to be talked about like that.

That's the part that haunts me the most. That I was busy trying to protect a stranger's dignity while my own partner was betraying me.

I didn't find out in some dramatic way. No big reveal, no caught-in-the-act moment. Just slow, painful confirmation. A slip here. A lie there. And eventually, the truth showing up, ugly and undeniable.

It was *her*. The same woman he told me not to worry about. The same one he insisted he'd never touch.

And when I confronted him, he didn't even deny it. Just apologized. Just stood there looking small.

I remember messaging her, trying to stay calm. I told her that she was beautiful, and she had a nice body. But she needed to find her own man and leave mine alone.

She only responded to the compliment.

Of course she did.

That's what cuts the deepest. Not just that he cheated. Not just that he lied.

But that even in the middle of it all, I was still trying to be kind. Still trying to uplift the woman he used to help destroy me.

What a fucking joke.

\*\*\*

And now, sitting in my office, I think about all the bullshit Tim and I have been through in the past nine years. I take out a pen and just write. About nothing in particular. I wasn't the one mad this morning. But there has been a lot on my mind lately, so I write:

*February 3rd, 2024*

*I actually expect the worst from Tim these days. I know it sounds terrible, but that is 100% how I feel. He disappoints me more often than not. Before I go any further, let me explain so when I come back to reread this in a couple of months, I will have a better understanding.*

*A couple months ago, I let him in. Really in. I told him things few people knew. That I hated my breasts. That when I was little, I used to wrap rubber bands around my nipples, praying they'd fall off. That I hated my smile because people teased me about my gums.*

*He rubbed my leg. Told me I was beautiful. Took my hand away from my mouth and said he loved everything about me. Held me all night like he meant it.*

*That softness didn't last.*

*We argued about cleaning one day. I told him I wasn't*

*his maid. That I worked full-time, paid half the bills, did the shopping, the cooking, the everything and still had to clean up his beer bottles.*

*"You insecure ass bitch," he spat. "You don't even know how to love yourself. How could you love me?" Then he laughed in my face.*

*He weaponized everything I told him in confidence. And now he wonders why I don't talk to him. Why I don't trust him.*

*There he is, sitting in the next room, begging me to love him. But the truth is…I don't.*

*How could I?*

*My heart belongs to…*

My phone rings. It's my mom's number. I'm sure she is wondering where I am and when I'll be there. I silence the call because avoidance is winning today. I take a deep breath. I am a lot calmer now that my head is clear.

Do I want to go into the room, apologize, and hear Tim out? Or walk out the door and let this fester? If the roles were reversed, and I was in the room sad and confused, I would want him to come talk to me. So, I take a deep breath, and I walk in the room.

Tim pauses the TV and sits up; he looks at me with eyes full of apologies and compassion and I melt.

"Can we talk?" I say as I sit at the foot of the bed. I grab a handful of our blanket in my hand while I think of the words to say.

"That's all I wanted to do in the…"

I put my hand up to stop him. He is getting worked up

already and the conversation hasn't even begun. "I'm sorry." I pause and take a deep breath. Apologizing has never been easy for me, and right now it's the last thing I want to do. "I know I have been distant lately, and I'm sorry. You don't deserve it." *You do.* "And I should have expressed what is going on with me." *What's going on is I don't trust you. I don't trust you with my insecurities or my vulnerabilities and I damn sure don't trust you to be a man.* "I have just been emotional because of my therapy appointments; they have brought up a lot of things." I lie.

Well, it's a half lie.

"And I want to be there for you, but you won't let…"

I put my hand up again. "See, it's situations like this. I came to you, so I could express why I have been so distant, and you won't even let me do that without interrupting me." I stand up like I'm mad, I'm not. And earlier today, all he wanted to do was express and feel heard, and I wouldn't even let him do that. Now I am demanding something from him that I didn't offer moments before. Why am I like this?

"I'm sorry, continue." He sits back and puts his hand to his lips as if to say his lips are sealed.

"I'm done." I say as I roll my eyes and fight the tears that are forming. No matter how desperately I want to form a connection with him, I can't quite seem to. I feel like I am fighting myself, fighting Tim, fighting to just exist.

"I'm sorry, Reya. I am." He gets off the bed and walks over to me. He stops just inches from my body, and I tense up. Not because I think he will hit me. He's not Luther, but I flinch because he has entered my personal space, and I have never been comfortable with people getting close to me, physically or emotionally.

"I just love you so much. You are the most important woman in my life, and I hate that we've been fighting so much." Tim reaches his arms in front of him and puts his hands on my shoulders.

I relax a little.

Then I full on sink into his body. I let my entire body lose control of itself. He stumbles backward to keep himself and me from toppling to the floor.

I need a release.

A release from the frustration, from the tension. From the nights I have spent crying alone. From the wicked thoughts that are trapped in my head.

I pull my face away from him and I look at him.

He really is the most handsome when he is vulnerable.

# Chapter 17

## In the After

I decide to visit my mom. Not because she needs it. Not even because I need it. But to piss off Luther. That's it. That's the whole reason. A petty pilgrimage. A daughter's revenge.

Looking into Luther's eyes and letting him see exactly how much I hate him. How much I'm clinging to my mother just to remind him he no longer gets to hurt her. And to be honest, it is the closest thing I've had to joy in weeks.

So when I knock and *he* answers the door, I channel every ounce of emotional detachment I have and deliver the flattest, driest "Hello, Luther" the world has ever known.

"Hey, Rey," he says, trailing behind me like a bad decision. "How are you?"

"I'm fine. Is my mom here?" My voice is tight. Civil. Disinterested.

"She's coming." He sits at the kitchen table like he belongs there. I pivot and make a show of planting myself in the living room instead. That's the thing about passive-aggression, it only works if there is an audience. And right now, I'm performing for myself.

Then I hear footsteps in the hallway. The uneven shuffle. I already know it's her.

And when she appears, wrapped in a grey robe and fuzzy socks with one elbow sticking out a hole in her sleeve trying to get ready for company, I grin without meaning to.

"What's up girl?" She beams, eyes lighting up like she forgot I was a disappointment. "Why are you still growing? I swear you get taller every time I see you."

I laugh because I've been the same height since I was fifteen. But compared to her five feet of fire and dramatics, I'll always look like I belong in the WNBA.

She pulls me into a tight, one arm hug, patting my back like I'm still a little girl and not a grown ass woman just trying to keep it together.

"You want coffee?" She asks, already walking toward the kitchen.

"Sure," I say, following a few steps behind her, though my eyes flick to Luther, still camped out at the table like he's waiting for Jesus.

Clara glances over her shoulder at him, then raises her eyebrows at me in that *you-see-this-bullshit* kind of way and rolls her eyes so hard I think she's about to sprain something.

I press my lips together trying not to laugh.

She leans in slightly, voice low like we're conspiring. "Is he just going to sit there the whole time? Listening to our conversation like a background character with no lines?"

I can't help it, and I burst out laughing. "At least background actors get paid. He's doing it for free."

She stifles her own laugh, shaking her head. "A volunteer nosey person. That's a new low."

We settle on the couch with mismatched mugs, hers chipped

and mine from that one trip we took to Disneyland. Luther stays in the kitchen, pretending not to listen while also not doing a damn thing else.

"So," she says, curling one leg under herself. "Are you still allergic to peace? Or are you finally ready to settle down with Tim?"

I nearly choke on my coffee. "Damn, mom. Can we ease into it? Geesh." I roll my eyes and laugh.

She laughs as she takes another sip. "Just checking. You know I have to get one in." There is a warmth that fills the space between her words. Like she is trying to say *I love you* without making it too heavy.

"Me and Tim are fine," I say into my mug. I don't really want coffee, but it is comforting all the same.

"Just fine?" She raises an eyebrow at me. "People say they are 'just fine' when they don't want to admit they are running from something. Or towards something."

"Mom, we are good." I say with my most convincing voice.

"I've been married to Luther long enough to know that peace and orgasms are supposed to come in the same package."

I nearly spit out my coffee, "Mom!"

"What? I'm grown. You're grown. We can talk grown. And let me tell you something right now, if a man can't make your life easier and your knees weaker, you're wasting your time, and your moisturizer."

I start laughing so hard my stomach hurts. My mom has the best way of giving advice.

She keeps going, like she's been saving this wisdom just for today. "I have been through too much, Reya. I've worked two jobs, raised two kids, and managed to get cussed out only once a week. That's my resume. So I know what I'm talking about. You keep trying to find love that feels like a rescue mission, when you should be looking for somebody who feels like the house you finally get to go home to."

I blink at her, caught somewhere between laughing and crying. "Damn, that's actually kinda beautiful."

Clara shrugs. "I have my moments."

She takes a sip from her chipped mug like she didn't just drop a truth bomb in the middle of the living room.

We fall into an easy silence, the kind you only get with someone who's seen you cry, seen you fail, seen you leave and still kept your seat warm.

In the kitchen, Luther coughs loudly. On purpose.

Clara glances toward the sound and mutters, "Ain't nobody talking to you." She says low enough that only we can hear.

She leans in closer, dropping her voice. "I give him three more months before I start hiding his keys and claiming he is losing his mind when he complains."

I fall back into the couch laughing, eyes wet from the joy of it, from the absurdity of it, from the love of it. And for a second, I let myself believe I'm safe here. That time has undone the damage. The love, even in piece feels like it's enough.

But the walls in this house remember.

I do too.

Clara was never allowed to fall apart. Never given the space to be soft. She was always performing strength just to survive the day. And now here she is, giving me joy like it costs her nothing, when I know damn well it costs her everything.

From the kitchen, Luther's voice breaks the moment. "Clara, are you going to clean up or what?"

Just like that, her shoulders drop. Barely. But enough. The light in her eye's dims, and she sets her mug down gently, like anything louder might shatter the illusion we've built.

"I guess our time is up," she says softly.

Her smile doesn't reach her eyes this time.

I want to scream. Or throw the mug. Or tell her to leave him for good. But I don't say anything. Because I know she won't leave. Not yet.

Clara stands, smoothing the front of her robe, already slipping back into her role.

I sit there, coffee cold in my hands, watching the woman who raised me walk away like she always does: quiet, resilient, and half swallowed by a man who never deserved her.

# Chapter 18

## In the After

I sit in Dr. Jenson's office feeling lighter today, almost taller. The leather couch feels more like a comforting embrace instead of the suffocating, judgmental surface it used to be.

"How are you doing today, Reya?" He asks, crossing one leg over the other, his usual polished and deliberate demeanor intact. His bald head catches the light just enough to make it oddly reassuring, a beacon of familiarity in the storm that is my life. I can't quite explain why, but it is starting to feel like home here on his couch.

"I'm not terrible, thank you," I say softly, shifting slightly. "How are you? How was your vacation?"

His mouth curves into a small, knowing smile. "My vacation was much needed. Thank you for asking." His tone is casual, but his words hang in the air longer than they should, and I find myself savoring the exchange more than I'd like to admit. I forget sometimes how much I enjoy talking to him. It's too easy, too... comforting.

His wife must be lucky, I think to myself. She gets to bask in this logical, empathetic, steady presence all the time. A man who listens. A man who offers clarity without judgment. A man who can make you feel like you're the only person in the room. I can't help but compare him to my fiancé (my messy, reactive, impatient fiancé). I tell myself I'm here to learn, to grow, to bring some of this balance into my own relationship.

"Reya, I have to say," he interrupts my spiraling thoughts, his smile widening. "You've made tremendous progress."

"Really?" I blink, caught off guard. "I don't feel that way. I feel like all I've done is cry and tell you how broken I am. Over and over. And over."

"That's the point," he says, beaming. "Healing isn't always about finding a resolution. Sometimes it's just about talking. Sometimes it's about saying the things you never thought you'd share. Growth is letting yourself be vulnerable, and for you, Reya, I think growth has been allowing yourself to be happy. Finally understanding that your past doesn't define your worth."

I look at him, and this time, I let the silence stretch. No tears. No knee-jerk deflections. Just the heavy weight of his words settling over me.

"Reya," he continues, his voice softer now, "When you first walked through that door, I could see how much you were carrying. The heartache. The regret. But today, you seem…lighter." His eyes linger on me, scanning, searching. It feels like he's peeling back layers I didn't even know I had, his gaze uncomfortably close to the insecurities I try to hide. "You've done the hard part: unloading."

He wheels his chair to his desk, retrieving a notepad. I watch him, my hands twitching in my lap. Months ago, I fidgeted because I was drowning in shame and grief. Today, I fidget because I can't reconcile the praise he's giving me with the truth he knows. The secret that feels like a poison I've been feeding myself, drop by drop, while hiding it from Tim. How can he be proud of me, knowing the darkness I've confessed here?

"I think we're ready to add another homework assignment to your session," Dr. Jenson says, breaking into my thoughts. "Now that we've faced the choices that broke you, let's work on building you back up."

I nod, biting the inside of my cheek to keep my expression neutral. The idea of moving forward terrifies me. Moving forward means letting go of the comfort that has been my companion, my tormentor. It means letting go of the strange solace I feel in this room, *with him.*

"Let's start with making friends," he says, his voice cutting through the haze in my mind.

"I have friends," I say quickly, forcing a smile. It's a lie. We both know it.

"As we discussed, those men aren't your friends, Reya," he replies sharply, his tone dropping an octave. "They're just waiting for the opportunity to use you. I want you to experience real friendship. The kind that's not… transactional."

His voice sounds almost husky like there's more he wants to say and for a moment, I wonder if I've imagined it. Then again, imagining things has become a habit lately.

"I want you to take a class," Dr. Jenson says, his tone lighter now, but his words carefully chosen. "I know you like cooking. Maybe try a cooking class. Or join a hiking group, you've mentioned how much you enjoy being outdoors."

He listens.

That's what makes him dangerous. I mentioned the outdoors once, buried in a rant about Tim, and somehow, he remembered. He *always* remembers.

"Thinking about joining a group gives me anxiety," I admit, already dreading the idea. He knows this about me. He knows everything about me.

"I'm aware of your social anxiety, Reya," he says, leaning forward slightly, his voice gentle but firm. "That's why I'm suggesting these activities with strangers. Things you enjoy doing. Your anxiety doesn't come from being around people; it comes from your past."

The words hit too close to home, but I let them sit in the air.

"What I'm suggesting," he continues. "Is meeting people who know nothing about you. They don't know your past or your mistakes. You get to choose who they see. And I encourage you to just… be yourself. Because yourself is pretty amazing."

His smile is radiant, genuine, but it makes my stomach tighten. Does he believe that? Really? Or is this just his job?

I find myself smiling back anyway, laughing softly. "Okay, I'll do it… for you."

"I appreciate that," he replies with an easy smile. "But ultimately, you're doing it for yourself. And I think you'll find there's nothing to fear."

He picks up his notepad, scribbling in that annoyingly unreadable way of his. My eyes follow the motion of his hand until he suddenly pauses, the air in the room shifting as he leans back. His posture becomes rigid, his expression tightening into something more serious.

"There's one more thing I need from you, Reya," he says, his voice quieter, heavier. "I need you to walk away from Leven. Let him go. Let his friendship go. Free yourself from the hold he has over you."

My lips part in shock, a cold chill spreading through my chest. "What does Leven have to do with anything? He's just a friend." I haven't thought about Leven since I called him and lied about my car breaking down (thank you Dr. Jenson).

Dr. Jenson's jaw tightens, his gaze sharp. "No, he's not."

The words come out clipped, almost biting. There's something unfamiliar in his tone, something I don't know how to place. Is it jealousy? Disgust? Concern? Is he being a protective therapist? A concerned friend? Or something else entirely?

"Reya," he continues, his voice softening now, almost pleading. "I can't make you do anything. And I won't force your hand. That's not my role here. But I'm urging you to step back from that situation. Just enough to see how destructive it is to your progress."

His eyes lock on mine, searching. The intensity makes me look away. I know he's right (at least, I think he's right) but his insistence feels too personal, too pointed.

"Leven... needs me," I say, my voice barely above a whisper. "I don't think I can just—"

"Then do it for me," Dr. Jenson interrupts, his voice dropping to a low, almost intimate register. "Do this one thing... *for me.*"

I freeze. He's not looking at me anymore. Dr. Jenson, the man who prides himself on maintaining eye contact no matter how uncomfortable the conversation, won't look at me now. It's a stark contrast, and it leaves me reeling. Is he ashamed of what he's asking? Does he know how selfish this sounds?

"Okay," I say finally, "for you."

His shoulders drop in relief, and his smile returns soft, hopeful, and radiant.

But deep down, I can't shake the feeling that I've crossed a line I don't fully understand.

I drive home feeling distant, as if therapy has scraped off just enough weight for me to breathe easier. But the relief is fleeting. It dissolves the moment I hear Dr. Jenson's voice replay in my head. *Healing isn't always about resolution.*

I shake my head, gripping the wheel a little tighter. No resolution? Then what the hell am I doing? If there's no finish line, no milestone to track my progress, then how do I know if I'm actually healing? It feels... unfinished. Like I'll always be reaching, always waiting for something to click into place that never will.

The thought unsettles me.

The streetlights blur as I drive, my mind slipping into the chaos of the last few months. The lies. The secrets. The guilt. The way I sometimes wake up in the middle of the night and feel like I'm suffocating under the weight of it all. And then there's him, Dr. Jenson. His voice, his presence, the way he looks at me when I say something honest. It makes me feel... wanted.

I exhale sharply, trying to shake my thoughts away. *He doesn't want you, Reya. He's your therapist.* And yet, every time he speaks, I feel like he understands me better than anyone else ever has. Including my fiancé.

That should terrify me. But it doesn't.

I used to believe I'd live a slow, meaningful life. Taking my time, appreciating the ride instead of rushing through it. But all I do is run. Run from the truth, from my choices, from the parts of me I don't want to face. Maybe that's why I keep seeking something outside of myself. Why I keep ending up in places I shouldn't be, in beds I shouldn't be in. Because if I stop, if I slow down long enough to sit with the mess I've made, it might swallow me whole.

*Healing isn't always about resolution.*

Maybe Dr. Jenson is right. Maybe healing isn't about fixing everything. Maybe it's just about not falling apart.

# Chapter 19

## In the After

As I approach the group a few days later, I have to focus on not falling, a dull pressure settling just beneath my ribs. My breathing feels too shallow, my steps too hesitant, as if the earth beneath my feet might shift at any moment and swallow me whole. The crisp morning air carries the scent of damp earth and pine, a reminder that I am far from the places where I usually feel in control.

I scan the faces around me. Normally, this would be the moment where I pick my mark—the man whose eyes would linger just a second too long, the one who would find my laughter intoxicating, the one who would make me feel powerful with the simplest look. But not today.

Dr. Jenson's voice echoes in my mind.

Meet people.

Connect.

No sex.

It shouldn't feel like an impossible task, but it does.

"Hi," I say, the word small and unsteady as I step into the loose circle of hikers. I avoid making direct eye contact, afraid that even a flicker of familiarity could send me slipping into old habits. I'm out of my element, but at least the hike itself is familiar. My body knows the rhythm of it: the steady incline, the burn in my calves, the way the air thins as the elevation climbs. But this? This standing among strangers, this attempt at honesty? It is foreign terrain.

A few people murmur polite greetings in return. I exhale, grateful for the pleasantries. They are safe, easy.

"Alright, it looks like Reya is the last to arrive," the leader announces with a smile. "Let's start with some introductions."

I freeze.

Shit.

Of course they want introductions. Why didn't I prepare something? My mind scrambles for words, but all I can think about is Dr. Jenson. His piercing blue eyes and the way he tilts his head when I say something revealing. His voice, steady and sure, whispering, "*You can do this.*"

I swallow hard and force myself to believe it.

"Good morning," I start, but my voice feels like it belongs to someone else. "My name is Reya. I'm 32 years old."

Why did I say my age? No one cares about my age. My fingers twitch as I force myself to keep them at my sides. I want to fidget, to shrink. I wish the leader had gone first and given me some kind of framework. The silence stretches for half a second too long, pressing against my chest. Say something else.

*Anything.*

"I've done this hike before, but never with a group." I swallow against the dryness in my throat. "I, uh, wanted to meet people with similar interests." That sounds fake. *Do I even have interests?* "And I hope we have a great time."

It's the most generic thing I could have said, but the group still offers warm smiles and a collective, "Hey Reya."

Relief crashes into me like a wave, and I let myself breathe.

The woman next to me, dressed entirely in black, offers a small smile. "Reya is definitely more of a people person than I am."

If only she knew.

"I'm Shay," she continues. "I signed up for this hike to push myself out of my comfort zone. I don't normally do well in groups, so… I'm a little nervous."

Her honesty is disarming. I nod at her, my throat too tight to say anything meaningful. I envy the way she admits her fears so easily, while mine coils inside me, twisting themselves into something uglier.

The introductions continue. There's Brandon, tall and lanky with dark skin glowing under the rising sun. His locs spill from beneath his cap, and I immediately know I need to stay away from him. He seems like the type I could pull into my orbit, the type who might let me use him as a distraction.

Then there's a heavyset woman, Wendy. She is younger with a kind face and soft edges. I glance at the trail ahead, wondering if she'll struggle with some of the steeper inclines. And then there's Mike, broad shoulders, strong arms, the kind of man who won't let her struggle alone. I recognize the way he looks at her before the hike even begins. He's already decided to be her hero.

And here I am, still trying to decide who the hell I even am.

There are twelve of us in total, five women, seven men. Too many temptations. Too many ways to slip into old patterns.

This will be one of the hardest things I have ever done.

Every man here is beautiful in his own way; from sharp

jawlines to soft smiles, from dreadlocks to buzz cuts, from lean builds to sturdy, protective frames. Normally, I would spend this time figuring out my next move. Who I could toy with. Who would make me feel something, even if only for a moment.

But I came here for something different.

Dr. Jenson's words echo again.

*Meet people.*

*Connect.*

*No sex.*

My stomach twists. More than anything, I am afraid. Afraid that I have nothing to offer beyond my body. Afraid that without seduction, I am nothing at all.

My hands begin to tremble. Sweat pools at my lower back despite the cool morning air. What do I say to these people? What can I possibly contribute if I'm not selling some version of myself?

My fingers curl into my palms.

*A hoe.*

*A liar.*

*A cheater.*

These are the words that have defined me for so long. They cling to my skin, stain my bones, whisper in my ear every time I try to imagine being anything else.

But here, now, I have a choice.

Who can I be in this moment?

I don't know.

But for the first time, I think I might want to find out.

\*\*\*

The first few steps of the hike are always the hardest—the moment when my body realizes it has to work, my muscles screaming before they've even been put to the test. The morning air is crisp but dry, filling my lungs with a sharpness that reminds me I am alive. The dirt beneath my boots is loose, kicking up fine dust that clings to my leggings. The desert landscape stretches around me; the kind of emptiness that makes a person feel small. But here, among the towering red boulders and twisted Joshua trees, I find a strange kind of beauty.

Still, my mind is restless.

Who decided this path was worth walking? Who saw this landscape and thought, "Yes, let's carve a trail through it!"

And who am I if I'm not carving my own path the way I used to: through flirtation, seduction, and lies?

A voice interrupts my spiraling thoughts. "Good morning," Wendy greets me, her voice soft but warm. She falls into step beside me, her movements careful as we navigate the first decline. "Did you say you've done this hike before?"

I glance over at her. Her breath is already labored, and I see the uncertainty in her eyes. She's nervous. I know that feeling well.

"Yeah," I say, masking the fact that I'm already feeling the strain in my legs. "It's, umm… It's a little challenging." I laugh, as if that will make it sound less intimidating.

She exhales sharply, smiling but hesitant. "That's what I'm afraid of. Do you think I can do it? I don't want to embarrass myself."

The way she says it, lighthearted but careful, tugs at something in me. That old familiar feeling of not being good enough.

I look at her, our strides syncing up. "Hiking is all about mind over matter. I think you can make it, but *you* have to believe you can." I pause, considering my next words. "And if you ever start to feel like you can't make it, you can lean on one of us."

I mean it.

At least, I think I do.

She glances up at me, her face half-hidden by the shadow of her cap. The way she tilts forward with each step tells me she's already feeling the effort. I don't judge her for it, but I do wonder why she picked this hike, of all hikes. It's not an easy one. It's not the kind of thing you do on a whim.

"Do you hike often?" I ask, trying to ignore the sudden pang of jealousy I feel toward her. Why? Maybe because she had the courage to put herself out there, to do something difficult, without the safety net of seduction. I wish I could be like that: brave in a way that doesn't rely on being desired.

"Nope," she laughs breathlessly. "This is my first time ever!"

I blink at her. *Ever?*

"How long is it?" She asks, still grinning but with an edge of fear beneath her voice.

"It'll take two to three hours to reach the hot springs." I try to focus on that, the reward waiting at the end of this struggle. The crisp, clear water against my aching muscles. The way the steam will curl into the sky.

Her face falls. "So, this is an all-day thing?"

I can't help but laugh. "Yeah, pretty much."

She groans, but it's lighthearted. And for the first time, I think I could really like her. She's easy to be around, unpolished in a way that feels... safe.

"So, what made you sign up for this?" I ask, genuinely curious.

Her answer hits me like a gut punch.

"My daughter just committed suicide."

The air shifts, the weight of those words heavy between us. The wind whistles through the canyon, carrying the scent of sunbaked earth and sage, but all I can focus on is the way her voice trembles.

"Oh my God," I whisper. "I'm so sorry."

Tears sting my eyes, surprising me. I don't even know this woman, and yet, I feel her pain like it's my own.

"Thank you." She tilts her head toward the sky, blinking rapidly. "Yeah… about a week ago."

A week? My mouth goes dry. I can't imagine that kind of grief; raw, fresh, like an open wound.

And suddenly, I think of Delilah. I haven't talked to her in weeks, and sometimes I pretend that it's okay. But it's not.

Right now, I miss my daughter.

"My job told me to take some time off," she continues, her voice thick with emotion. "And being at home just makes me feel… sad."

That last word is so simple, yet so full of devastation.

I stop walking. Before I can second-guess myself, I reach for her, wrapping my arms around her heavy frame.

She stiffens for half a second before melting into me.

And then she starts to cry.

We stand there, the sounds of the desert muffled by the quiet ache of shared sorrow. I cry too and concentrate on transferring some of her pain into me, so she doesn't have to carry it alone. I imagine it radiating off her and running through my veins like it were my burden to carry all along.

"Thank you," she whispers.

"You're welcome," I murmur, meaning it more than I thought I would.

When we start walking again, the silence between us is different. Not awkward, not heavy. Just there.

"Can I ask you something?" I say after a while.

"Sure."

"Is this something you want to talk about, or are you here to escape it?"

She exhales, considering. "I don't know. No one has asked me that yet."

Something about that stings. How many people have tried to comfort her without actually seeing her?

I let my instincts guide me. "How old was she?"

"Twenty-five."

I nod; my steps deliberate. "What's your favorite memory of her?"

She takes a moment to think, then turns to me, eyes softening. "We went to a concert together once. A Wu-Tang show. For some reason, she thought I was cool then. It was the first time I felt like she saw me, not just as her mom, but as a woman trying to figure life out."

I let that memory linger for a bit longer.

"So who was the better dancer out of the two of you?" I ask with a smile on my face.

"Oh, me. Hands down. And don't let the electric slide come on out here in this desert." She gives me a look of knowing then snaps her fingers and laughs. She is a beautiful woman with a smile that could light up the world.

"I'm proud of you," I say, surprising myself. "It takes courage to open up like this."

She blinks back more tears, and we walk in silence. A comfortable, much-needed silence.

We catch up with the group, falling back into place just as Mike turns to us.

"How are you ladies doing?" He asks, flashing an easy grin.

"I'm well," I reply, and I let my gaze linger on him just a second too long.

Old habits.

I think of Dr. Jenson. *Why is it always him?* His face is the one I see when I need comfort. When I need clarity. My heart clenches at the realization that Tim, my partner of nine years, doesn't do that for me.

I swallow the thought.

Mike steps closer, his voice low. "Where are you from, Reya?"

"Vegas," I answer. Then I smirk. "Let me guess… you're from California?"

He laughs. "Yeah, how'd you know?"

*Because they always are.*

And yet, even as I flirt, even as I play the part that comes so naturally to me, my mind drifts elsewhere…to a pair of blue eyes, to a steady voice that sees through me.

To the one man I can never have.

And God help me… I want him anyway.

# Chapter 20

## In the After

The sun hangs heavy in the sky by the time we reach the hot springs, our bodies slick with sweat and exhaustion. The once cool morning air has been swallowed by the desert heat, thick and suffocating, pressing against my skin like an unwanted embrace. The scent of sun-warmed rock and mineral-rich water lingers in the air, mingling with the faint musk of bodies that have worked too hard to get here.

For a moment, I let myself revel in the feeling of accomplishment. I did this. I survived this. And yet, even now, I am restless.

I strip down to my bathing suit first, unbothered by the others still standing around in their hiking clothes. My tan two-piece is strategic. High-waisted to hide what needs to be hidden, cut just right to accentuate what needs to be seen. A compromise between my insecurities and my need to be wanted.

Dr. Jenson said no sex.

He never said I couldn't be desirable.

As I spray sunscreen over my body, the mist cooling my overheated skin, I catch a glimpse of my reflection in the water. My tattoos stand out against the deep gold of my complexion; inked stories etched permanently into my flesh. I wonder if anyone sees them the way I do, not just as artwork, but as armor.

"Hey, can I get some of that?"

Brandon's voice pulls me back to the present.

I turn, and there he is, standing too close, the sun catching the deep brown of his skin, highlighting the sharp lines of his jaw. His dreadlocks are tied up neatly, his smile easy, inviting.

Fuck.

This was the one man I told myself to avoid. The one who looked too easy to pull into my orbit. And yet, here he is, holding out his hand for my sunscreen.

I pass it to him, keeping my expression neutral. "Of course. I tell people all the time that skin cancer does not discriminate." I laugh, casual, friendly. Innocent.

He chuckles, shaking the bottle before spraying it over his legs. "I'm Brandon, by the way. I don't know if you remember from the introductions. And you are…?" He gestures toward me with the bottle.

"Reya," I say, smoothing my braids into a bun atop my head. The distinct scent of sunscreen lingers in the air, mingling with the sharp freshness of the river below.

"Nice ink," he nods toward my arm, squinting. "Wait… is that…" his eyes widen with amusement "…Yoo, do you have Harry Potter tattooed on your arm?"

Heat rushes to my face, and for a split second, I feel stupid. But before I can respond, he grins and pulls off his shirt.

And there it is: black ink, bold on his bicep, the unmistakable mark of *The Deathly Hallows*. Then he turns a little more, revealing an intricate tattoo of *The Tale of the Three Brothers* running across his shoulder blades.

I exhale in exaggerated relief, playfully tossing my discarded shirt in his direction. "A man after my own heart."

He catches it easily, his grin widening.

And just like that, I know.

I'm going to have sex with this man.

The thought arrives unbidden, slipping into my mind as naturally as breathing. The way the water shimmers against his skin, the way his muscles flex beneath the weight of his tattoos. He is temptation incarnate.

No. Stop it.

"Wait," I say, forcing myself back to the conversation, "have you read the books? Or just seen the movies?"

He scoffs putting a hand to his chest, feigning offense. "Come on now. 'Dumbledore said calmly'."

I laugh, impressed by the reference. He's one of *those* fans.

I should walk away. End this here. But instead, I start moving toward the river, deliberately slow, my body humming with anticipation.

He follows.

Game on.

No.

Game off.

Dr. Jenson's words echo in my head. But Tim. Tim should be the one at the forefront of my thoughts, not my therapist. Not Brandon. And definitely not Leven.

*Leven.*

I shove the thought down before it has the chance to take root.

"You're choosing the 30-degree river over the 90-degree hot

springs?" Brandon's voice is teasing, but his curiosity is real.

I glance back, slowing so he can catch up. "I don't know... I've always liked pools over hot tubs. And besides, the hot springs will feel better after the cold plunge. But you don't have to come with me."

I turn away, stepping closer to the edge of the river. The scent of the water is sharp. The current moves fast, carving its way through the rocks like a creature with its own agenda.

Brandon hesitates only a moment before stepping beside me. "This is my first time hiking," he admits. "I want to experience everything."

*Everything?*

There's something about the way he says it that makes my stomach clench.

He means the river.

I am already thinking of other things.

I inhale deeply, letting the cool air settle in my lungs. I should tell him to go back to the hot springs. I should create space before this turns into something I can't stop.

Instead, I smirk, my eyes flicking up at him through my glasses. "Then let's jump in."

Brandon grins, and I already know he won't hesitate to follow me.

And that is exactly what I'm afraid of.

I climb onto the boulder, its surface warmed by the relentless desert sun, rough and ancient beneath my fingertips. From here, the world unfolds beneath me; the deep, winding river snaking through the canyon, the red and ochre boulders standing tall like silent sentinels, and the group of hikers watching from below, their faces expectant, amused.

"We have an audience," I murmur, tilting my head toward the others gathered at the riverbank or lounging in the steaming hot springs.

Brandon follows my gaze before flashing me that easy, effortless smile. The kind of smile that makes a woman feel like she is the only one in the world worth looking at.

"Can you swim?" He asks, his voice dripping with mock concern.

I give him a look. "Seriously?"

He shrugs, teasing. "I have to ask. You know *our* people usually can't. Gotta protect the hair." He gestures toward my braids wrapped on the top of my head.

I roll my eyes, bending my knees and taking the leap before he can say anything else.

The cold slaps against my skin like a thousand tiny knives, and I sink fast and deeper than expected. The shock steals my breath, and for a split second, the world is nothing but a silent, weightless abyss. Suspended in time. A perfect, fleeting moment where nothing exists but the water around me. My thoughts dissolve, my sins forgotten.

It feels like freedom.

I let my body float, waiting for the burn in my lungs to tell me which way is up. When I kick off the unseen riverbed and break the surface, the warmth of the desert sun kisses my skin in welcome.

Cheering erupts from the riverbank. I look up just in time to see Brandon launch himself off the boulder in a dive so smooth it cuts through the water without a splash. His body disappears beneath the surface, and I catch myself staring; admiring the way his limbs move with practiced ease, the strength in his frame.

Brandon resurfaces with a shake of his head, water streaming down his face. "Damn," he laughs. "I didn't plan on getting my hair wet today."

"Didn't have to follow me," I say, my tone light, but something else lingers beneath it. A dare.

He swims closer, his presence thick in the water, charged with something neither of us are acknowledging. He is in my space, the way a man knows exactly when a woman wants him there.

I could straddle him now, let my legs wrap around his waist and my hands find the muscles at his shoulders. It would be so easy to let our bodies fit together, to let my lips graze his. Not quite kissing, but close enough to taste the warmth of his breath. Tim would never know.

The thought sends a sharp thrill through me.

I take a step back, breaking the spell, inhaling deeply as if that alone could cleanse my thoughts.

What the hell am I doing?

Before I can spiral any further, a voice cuts through the tension.

"Can I jump in too?"

I turn, and Wendy is standing at the water's edge, toes digging into the warm, damp sand. Her blue one-piece clings to her curves, her expression hesitant but hopeful.

I welcome the distraction. "Of course. Want to go together?"

She nods eagerly. "Please."

"We'll go too." Two more women from the group step forward, their excitement contagious.

I glance at Brandon one last time before swimming toward

shore, as if distance will erase whatever just passed between us.

But I know better.

The universe intervened on this one.

One more moment in that water, and I probably would have...

No. I wouldn't have.

***

Later, I sink into the hot springs, my body warm, but my mind is far from settled. The contrast between the icy river and the bubbling, mineral-rich heat is jarring, yet comforting. Two extremes, just like the thoughts clashing inside me.

Around me, the group is talking, laughing, their voices echoing off the canyon walls. I am supposed to be making friends. That was the whole point.

Instead, my mind is somewhere else. On someone else.

Brandon.

Dr. Jenson.

Tim.

God, what is wrong with me?

I force myself to focus on the conversation, on the way the steam rises into the air in delicate tendrils, the scent of earth and sulfur thick around us. The heat soaks into my muscles, loosening the tension I didn't realize I was carrying.

I glance at Wendy, who is now fully relaxed, her earlier grief softened, at least for now. She deserves to enjoy this moment. I should too.

But then I catch Brandon watching me from the other side of the spring.

Not just watching—*studying*.

And I feel it again, that pull, that dangerous magnetism that has always led me down the wrong paths.

I drop my gaze, pretending I didn't notice, but the damage is already done.

I close my eyes, exhaling slowly. Think about Tim. Think about the man who loves you, who has stood by you.

Instead, my mind conjures a different image: Dr. Jenson. The way he leans forward when I talk, the way his voice steadies me, the way his hands look strong, capable. I wonder what they would feel like on my skin.

My stomach tightens.

I open my eyes, forcing myself to focus on the people around me, on the sound of laughter, on the warmth of the water.

I am here to be better.

I am here to break the cycle.

# Chapter 21

**Before**
**18 years old**

I never planned on being someone's first choice. I never wanted to be loved so recklessly. That kind of devotion had always felt like a weight, an anchor dragging me into the deep when all I wanted to do was float; free, untethered, untouched.

But Dorian? He loved me despite the rumors, despite the warnings.

And that made him easy prey.

When I first met him, I barely noticed him. He was dating a girl named Ally. She was sweet, kind, probably too good for him and I had my own distractions. I had Rob. I had whoever I wanted, when I wanted. Love wasn't something I chased; it was something I could make people beg for.

But when Dorian and Ally broke up, I saw something in him that caught my attention.

He hurt.

And that kind of devotion (the kind that left him hollow when it was taken away) I wanted that for myself.

So, I pursued him.

We sat in his car, the stale scent of old cologne and something faintly sweet filling the air between us. I could already feel him falling before I even opened my mouth.

"There are a few things you should know," I told him, leaning back against the seat, my tone light but firm. "Number one, don't take me seriously. I'm only going to cheat on you."

His brows furrowed, but he didn't speak.

"Two," I continued, holding up two fingers, "don't fall in love with me. I will hurt you."

His throat bobbed as he swallowed.

"And three?" he asked, his voice quiet, hesitant.

"Don't ask me for more than what I can offer."

"What can you offer me?"

I smiled, but it didn't reach my eyes. "Nothing. I can't give you the life you want, Dorian. I'm no good for you."

Silence. The words should have been enough to push him away, but instead, they only seemed to draw him in.

"Reya…" He inhaled sharply, shifting so he could look at me fully. "What if I already love you?"

And there it was. The inevitable fall.

I forced another smile, softer this time, more convincing. "You shouldn't."

But I knew how to play the game. I let my gaze drop, pretending to search for the right words when in reality, I was calculating, weighing my options.

I didn't love Dorian. I would never love Dorian.

But I wanted the attention. I wanted to be wanted.

"You shouldn't love me," I repeated, then added, "but I love you too."

A lie so smooth it rolled off my tongue like honey.

Even as I sat there, feeding Dorian the words he needed to hear, my mind drifted elsewhere.

To Rob.

Rob, who had nothing remarkable about him except for the fact that he belonged to someone else.

Rob, who barely spoke to me outside of hushed meetings in parked cars and stolen moments behind the bleachers.

Rob, who made me feel chosen, not because he loved me, but because he betrayed for me.

That was the thrill.

Not the sex.

Not the secrecy.

It was Tasha. The way she adored him. The way she *thought* she had him.

And yet, he would leave her waiting at restaurants, made excuses about practice, all so he could have me.

I was a nobody. Nothing special. But with him, I was something.

"Reya?"

Dorian's voice yanked me back to the present.

"I, umm, I have to go." I leaned back, away from him needing space, needing air.

"Okay," he said softly. "I love you, Reya."

I didn't say it back. Not this time.

Instead, I walked to my car, grabbed my phone, and dialed the number I knew by heart.

"Hey, you busy?"

"Never too busy for you," Rob replied, his voice dripping with anticipation.

"Meet in the usual spot?"

"Yeah," he answered, and I could hear the grin in his voice.

I smiled too, excitement curling in my stomach.

Even though I had seen him just the day before, seeing him always felt dangerous.

Fifteen minutes later, we met at the empty park, where only the distant hum of streetlights and the occasional rustle of wind in the trees bore witness to our sins.

I kept the car running but turned off the headlights as I climbed into the back seat.

Rob joined me, his movements familiar, practiced.

"Hey," he said as he pushed down his football shorts.

"Hey," I whispered back as I kicked off my jeans.

No pretense. No unnecessary words.

Just skin on skin.

Four minutes later, we were fully dressed again, standing outside the car as if nothing had happened.

And really, nothing had happened.

Because none of this meant anything. Not to me. Not to him.

I never asked why Rob cheated on Tasha. Never felt guilty for it. I didn't want him.

I just wanted to be wanted.

And in those fleeting moments, I was.

"I'm pregnant."

The words slipped before I could decide if I even cared about the consequences.

Rob blinked at me, unfazed. "So?" He shrugged.

"Soooo, it might be yours."

He scoffed, crossing his arms. "Reya, I'm going to college. This was fun, but that ain't my baby. I know I'm not the only one you're sleeping with."

The dismissal stung more than I wanted to admit.

"And if it is mine, I know a clinic."

I clenched my jaw. "I'm too far along for that."

Rob shrugged. "Then it's not my problem."

And just like that, he was gone.

***

The next day, I stood in Dorian's room, shifting my weight as he rummaged through his drawers. The room smelled like him: clean, warm, familiar.

"I'm pregnant," I told him, my voice shaking just enough to be believable. "And I'm too far along to do anything about it."

He turned, his face unreadable. Then, without hesitation, he pulled something from his drawer and walked toward me.

A small velvet box.

"I was saving this for after we graduated," he admitted, flipping it open to reveal a ring. "But... will you marry me, Reya?"

The pride in his voice. The love in his eyes.

I felt sick.

I never wanted to be a mother. Never wanted to be a wife. *You can't turn a hoe into a housewife.* The thought made me giggle, but I covered it with a choked sob.

Then I looked at Dorian, this crazy person who wanted me more than anything, who would never know the truth.

And I nodded. "Yes."

Maybe I could learn to love him.

Maybe I could learn to love this baby.

Or maybe I could just keep pretending.

# Chapter 22

## In the After

"Nothing happened."

I say it out loud as if speaking the words will make them real. As if repetition can scrub my conscience clean before I make it to my house.

The tires hum against the pavement, the rhythmic sound filling the silence in the car. I keep my grip steady on the wheel, but my fingers twitch, restless.

I pick up my phone and dial.

"Hey, Jory," I start, my voice bright, eager.

"Dr. Jenson," he corrects.

The formality in his tone is sharp, cold. Like a blade cutting through the warmth I had built up for this conversation.

My stomach twists. Why does this hurt?

"Sorry, Dr. Jenson. I just wanted to call and say I did the hike," I continue, ignoring the sting.

"That's great, Reya. Are you calling to schedule your next appointment?"

His words are professional, detached. What did I expect?

The rejection is subtle, but I feel it all the same.

"Actually, yes. Are you available tomorrow around three?"

"I can pencil you in. See you then."

And just like that, he hangs up. No lingering words. Just an end.

The car feels colder now, the silence pressing against my chest.

I should be thinking about Tim. About how I'm going home to him, excited to share my day, eager to see his face.

Instead, my mind drifts elsewhere.

To Leven.

Dr. Jenson told me to let him go, and I tried. Maybe I'm thinking about him now because Dr. Jenson was just so… dismissive. Maybe I want to stick it to him. Maybe I just want to hear a voice that isn't shutting me out.

My fingers hover over my phone, my heart already racing.

Before I can talk myself out of it, I press the call button.

"Hello?" His voice sends a jolt through me: familiar, frustrating, intoxicating.

"Hey, how are you?" I force the words out, steadying my breath.

"I'm good. I haven't heard from you in a while."

A flicker of resentment sparks inside me. *You ghosted me.*

I don't say it. I can't say it. I've learned my lesson. Leven is a flight risk, and if I push too hard, he'll disappear again.

"Yeah, I went through a depression and kinda isolated myself from everyone. I'm sorry." The lie slides off my tongue with practiced ease. I roll my eyes at myself, hating how much effort I have to put into keeping him.

"Naw, you're good," he says, his tone lazy, indifferent. He doesn't ask how I am. He doesn't ask what I've been going through. He doesn't care. Why did I ever think he'd be the one to help me when I told him my car had broken down?

And yet, here I am, caring too much.

"I'm probably going to go back to work soon," I offer, searching for something to hold onto.

"Oh. Okay. Yeah, let me know when."

"I will. Well, I'll talk to you soon."

The pause lingers.

"Don't be a stranger," he says, and there it is. The faintest hint of something. Interest? Affection? A smirk I can't see but know is there?

I don't know.

The call ends.

I don't feel happy. I don't feel disappointed either.

Leven has more walls than I do, and I have spent too much time trying to scale them. Trying to reach him. Trying to matter.

***

Home, Sweet Home.

The moment I pull into the driveway, a weight lifts off my chest.

This is home. The house Tim and I built together. The plants in the yard that I meticulously care for. The welcome mat at the front door, slightly frayed but still inviting.

I love our home.

I just wish I could love Tim the same way: effortlessly. Without complication. Without hesitation.

The front door opens before I can reach for my keys.

"Hey, babe," Tim greets me, arms open.

I step into them, inhaling the familiar scent of Old Spice and beard oil. The warmth of him wraps around me, grounding me, making everything feel easy.

"I can't wait to tell you about the hike."

"I can't wait to hear it." His eyes shine with excitement, genuine and untainted.

He takes my hand and leads me to the couch. A tea party is set up; strawberries, blueberries, cucumber sandwiches… and chicken wings.

I laugh softly. *He loves his chicken wings.*

This is what love should be. Easy. Comfortable. Real.

I settle beside him, the warmth of the tea in my hands mirroring the warmth in my chest.

"…And then I met this woman named Wendy," I tell him. "She's never hiked before, and when we got to the river, she jumped in with us without realizing how deep it was."

Tim's eyes widen.

"Babe, Brandon had to jump in and save her!" I exclaim, shaking my head. "She didn't realize how deep it was." I repeat, laughing.

"Brandon should've been asking *her* if she could swim instead of you," Tim jokes, a playful smirk on his lips.

My heart stutters.

The sound of his name on Tim's lips…it feels like being caught, like a thread unraveling too soon.

*Nothing happened,* I tell myself again.

Nothing happened.

And yet, something did.

I felt good about myself today.

I listened to Wendy's pain and didn't run from it. I helped

guide others through the hike. I connected, genuinely, without manipulation.

I was…likable.

Not because I was seducing.

Because I was *me.*

The realization sinks in, warm and unsettling all at once.

Is this what it feels like to be good?

Is this what it feels like to be enough without giving something first?

Tim looks at me with love in his eyes, completely unaware of the storm brewing inside me.

I smile back, pressing a kiss to his cheek.

"I think I learned something about myself today," I say.

"Yeah? What's that?"

I hesitate, choosing my words carefully.

"I think… I might actually be a good person."

It feels like both a revelation and a lie.

Because if I were truly good…why am I still thinking about Leven? About Dr. Jenson? About the things I want that I shouldn't.

Tim squeezes my hand. "Of course you are, Reya. You've always been."

I close my eyes, soaking in the comfort of his belief in me.

Even if I know it's misplaced.

I sit across from Tim, watching him, feeling his love wrap around me like a warm, steady force. He has done everything right: cleaning the house, setting up our tea party, waiting to listen, wanting to listen.

And yet, it isn't enough.

I am a terrible person.

What would younger Reya say?

The girl who cried herself to sleep because she had no one to love her. The one who was surrounded by people but felt completely alone.

I imagine her sitting on the couch beside me, staring up with hollow eyes, disappointed.

I let a single tear fall.

"What's wrong? What happened?" Tim asks gently, reaching over to wipe it away. His touch is light, careful, like I might break.

"Nothing," I lie.

I don't want to be vulnerable, but at the same time, I do. I want to let the sadness consume me, let the tears fall freely for the pity I feel for myself. But I blink them back, swallowing the grief before it can spill over.

Tim watches me carefully. "I thought you had a good day."

"I did…" My voice is quiet, unsure. Should I tell him? Should I let him in?

*Sometimes healing isn't about resolution. Growth can just be letting yourself be vulnerable.*

Dr. Jenson's words slip into my thoughts, settling like a weight in my chest.

Maybe I can't love Tim because I won't let myself love him. Maybe I've never let myself love anyone, not really. Even after nine years, Tim has never seen the real me.

Maybe today is the day I let him.

I exhale shakily. "Crying is normal for me," I whisper. "The reason I started seeing Dr. Jenson was to figure out why the tears are always there. Why they stay perched on my eyelids, never too far away. Why I can't allow myself to be happy." My voice cracks, and suddenly, I can't stop it. First one tear, then another, then a waterfall, cascading down my cheeks, unstoppable.

"And even now," I choke between sobs, "I don't know how to let myself feel happy about my day."

Tim shifts closer, his face strained with concern. "Why not?"

I squeeze my eyes shut, but the words still escape.

"Because I am a terrible mother."

The confession rips out of me, raw and bitter.

I can't seem to catch my breath, my inhales sharp and shallow, my chest rising and falling too quickly. I don't bother wiping the tears anymore. They slide down my face, over my lips, dripping into the hollow of my collarbone. It's uncomfortable and wet, but the tears are too steady to stop.

Tim shakes his head, his voice firm. "You are not a bad mom, Reya. Don't say that."

But how could he know that?

Because that's what I tell him? Because that's the image I keep up?

He doesn't know that I haven't called Delilah in weeks.

And she hasn't called me.

She is in Virginia, living her life without me, while I am in Las Vegas, living mine without her.

"I always struggle with this feeling," I confess. "Am I allowed to be happy without her? Or should I just accept a life of… mediocrity?" The words feel pathetic the moment they leave my mouth, but they are real. They are mine.

This is why I haven't called her.

How do I pick up the phone and tell my fourteen-year-old daughter, "Hey, I just got another tattoo, and I'm going on a cruise soon. Oh, and I went on this amazing hike and had the best time! I love you!"

My heart aches.

I wasn't there for her first tooth, or her first steps, or her first day of school.

I don't even know how to talk to her. If Dorian isn't there to be the buffer, our conversations are strained, awkward silences filled with surface-level pleasantries.

Dorian.

The name alone sends a pang of guilt through me.

I still remember the way his face lit up when he proposed. The pride in his eyes when he slid that ring onto my finger.

He looked at me like I was his world.

And I let him. Because it was easier. Because he loved me, and I needed to be loved

Tim watches me closely, waiting for me to continue.

I hesitate, then reach for his hand, lacing my fingers through his.

"I had a good day," I say softly, wiping the last of my tears. Repeating my revelation from earlier. "And I think... I might actually be a good person."

Tim tilts his head, studying me. "Reya. You've always been."

I wish I could believe him.

I let him pull me into an embrace, my head resting against his chest, his heartbeat steady beneath my ear. His warmth seeps into me, grounding me.

This should be enough.

Tim should be enough.

And yet, even as he holds me, I can't shake the feeling of something lingering in the air between us.

The weight of something unsaid.

The hint of something unfaithful.

# Chapter 23

**Before**
**18 years old**

As I laid in the hospital bed, the sterile smell of antiseptics clung to the air, mingling with the faint scent of sweat and something else, something raw. My fingers tapped against my phone screen, mindlessly scrolling as Dorian sat beside me, droning on about the baby. The baby he thought was ours. His voice was soft, gentle, expectant. I didn't want to hear it. I didn't want to have this conversation.

"Are you comfortable?" He asked, getting up, his chair scraping against the tile as he moved closer.

"I'm fine." I barely glanced at him. I wished he would just leave. I didn't need him here, yet something about his presence kept me from being entirely alone with my thoughts. "The nurse gave me an epidural, I don't feel anything."

"I wish you wouldn't have done that," he murmured, his fingers massaging my legs. I could tell he thought this was some tender moment between us, as if he had any right to be here, rubbing me, talking to me about experiencing childbirth as if that mattered. "You should feel it at least once…it's natural."

I wanted to laugh in his face. I didn't even want this baby, let alone the pain that came with it. There was nothing "natural" about bringing a child into a world where I didn't care for it. The only thing I had actually enjoyed about this entire pregnancy was the sex; undeniably the best I had ever had. My body had betrayed me, heightening every sensation, making me wet at the slightest touch. That was the only thing I would miss. That and my breasts, now gloriously full. Uneven, sure. Irregular, sure. But full.

"Cliff is coming," I said, finally tearing my gaze away from my phone long enough to see Dorian's reaction. It was inevitable, so I might as well prepare him.

Dorian stiffened. "Why is he coming?"

"Because we're friends." The lie slipped from my lips as smoothly as every other one I had told him over the years. Cliff wanted this baby to be his. And maybe it was. Or maybe it was Rob's. Or someone else's. The truth was, I didn't care enough to count.

Dorian exhaled slowly, gripping the armrest of the chair. "I don't want him at the birth of my child. He can wait in the waiting room."

"Delilah is my child too," I said, voice sharp, final. "And he's coming."

The steady beep of the heart monitor filled the silence that stretched between us. This was why I could never love Dorian, why I could never be satisfied with him. He let me win. Every time.

And if a man would let me walk all over him, why wouldn't I? He had no self-respect. And I had none for him either.

"Reya, I really don't want—"

"I feel pressure in my butt," I cut him off, uninterested in hearing whatever pathetic protest he had left in him. "I think it's time."

I picked up my phone, my fingers flying across the screen. I'm going into labor. This is it.

The nurse came in, her chipper voice grating against my ears. "It's time," she said, lifting the hospital gown to check my progress. "Time to poop your baby out."

I let out a hollow laugh, laying back, more relieved that this ordeal was almost over than anything else.

Dorian clutched my hand, his grip warm and steady, but I barely noticed. My attention flickered to the doctor between my legs, his hands ready, waiting.

"We have the head and one shoulder. Just one more push, Momma."

I pushed, feeling the pressure dissipate, and then it was over. The baby was out. The doctor lifted the wriggling thing and placed it on my stomach. It was crying, covered in a layer of slime and fluids that made my stomach turn.

I stared down at it, waiting, *waiting*, for that rush of emotion, that instant connection everyone always talked about. But all I felt was disgust.

I wanted it off me.

I turned my head, looking at Dorian, who was crying. His hands still gripped mine, but his eyes…his eyes were locked onto the child, filled with something I couldn't understand. Love? Awe? Irrational pride?

"Can I hold her?" He asked, voice thick with emotion.

"We'll let Momma hold her first," the doctor said.

"No, I'm okay," I cut in quickly. "Can you clean her off, please?" I didn't want this moment. I didn't want *her*. Let Dorian have his little moment, let him pretend this was the happiest day of his life. I just wanted to be done with it.

I had hoped, truly hoped, that when I saw my daughter, something inside me would change. That some part of me would wake up, like all those sentimental mothers said it would. Instead, I felt the opposite. The instinct didn't kick in. If anything, it shut off completely.

The door creaked open, and Cliff walked in. Perfect timing.

I smiled at him, not bothering to hide it.

The doctor handed Dorian a surgical tool. "Dad, would you like to cut the cord?"

Dorian looked at me, eyes wet, face glowing with joy. "Can I?"

"Of course you can."

And just like that, I was free.

# Chapter 24

## In the After

The dry Vegas air is already burning my skin before I even make it to the site entrance. The morning sun glares off the steel beams of the half-built casino, bouncing light in sharp angles, making the world feel jagged and unforgiving. The air smells of sawdust, hot metal, and sweat. These are the scents I used to take comfort in, but today, they churn my stomach.

I adjust my hard hat, plastering on my best *I belong here* expression as I step through the gates.

A few of the guys notice me immediately, some nod, others whisper. No one says what they're really thinking.

Reya's back.

I feel it in the way their eyes linger, the way the conversations shift the second I walk by. Foremen don't just disappear for months, and when they do, they don't usually come back. Yet here I am, stepping back onto the dirt like I never left.

I scan the site, noting the progress since I've been gone. The casino's skeleton has filled out, more steel, more concrete, more life. The electricians are wiring up the second floor, conduit running along the steel framework like veins. My crew is working, but the pace feels off. Slower. Less precise.

That's what happens when you take me out of the equation.

A figure emerges from the site trailer. Jason. My superintendent. My boss. The man who made me work double shifts, piled on extra responsibilities, and then acted surprised when I burned out.

He sees me and hesitates. *Good.*

I walk straight toward him. "Morning, boss."

Jason crosses his arms over his chest, eyes unreadable. He's a thick guy, barrel-chested with a beer gut that strains against his high-vis vest. A man who's used to barking orders and getting results.

"Didn't expect you this early," he says.

I smirk. "Didn't expect to be back this early."

"Listen, Reya," Jason sighs, rubbing the back of his neck. "Maybe we should ease you back in…"

"No." My voice is firm, cutting him off before he can finish. "I want my old responsibilities back."

He exhales sharply, like he's already exhausted by this conversation. "Look, I get it. You were a hell of a foreman, but things have changed. We had to adjust while you were out. The guys…"

"The guys have been doing sloppy work since I left," I say, shifting my weight, making sure my stance reads power, not desperation. "I can fix that. You know it. I know it."

Jason watches me carefully, measuring his next words. "You think you can just walk back in like nothing happened?"

I tilt my head, giving him the same knowing smirk I've used to get my way for years. "I think you know you need me."

The moment stretches between us. He doesn't want to admit it. Jason doesn't like being backed into a corner. But I've seen his site reports. The delays. The rework orders. The mistakes.

"You already gave my job to someone else, didn't you?" I ask, watching for the slightest flicker of guilt.

His nostrils flare. There it is.

I lean in slightly. "Who is it? Greg? Chris? One of those guys who barely knows how to run a crew?"

Jason shifts, uncomfortable.

"That's what I thought," I say smoothly. "You know they can't do what I do."

His jaw tightens. He doesn't want to give me ground. But Jason is predictable. He likes efficiency, likes things done right. And I'm his best shot at making sure this project doesn't fall further behind.

Finally, he exhales. "You get your old crew back. But don't expect special treatment."

I smile, victorious. "Wouldn't dream of it."

Control.

By midday, I'm walking the site like I never left. The crew is watching me, waiting to see how I'll assert myself.

"Hey, you guys got that conduit squared away?" I call out to a pair of apprentices.

They hesitate. "Uh, Greg told us to wait on it," one of them mumbles.

Of course he did. "Yeah, well, I'm telling you to get it done," I say, flashing them a smile that's just on the edge of challenging. "Unless you'd rather wait for another delay report."

They scramble to get moving.

The thing about a construction site is: respect is everything. You have to earn it, keep it, command it. And I refuse to let it slip through my fingers.

I make my way to Greg, my supposed replacement. He's standing near the gang box, checking his phone as if he doesn't have a job to do.

"Hey, Greg," I say, too sweetly.

He glances up. "Oh. You're back."

"I am," I say, stepping in close enough to make him shift his weight. "You have done great while I was gone. Honest. But Jason wants me to get back into the position"

His mouth tightens. He doesn't like it, but he doesn't argue. Smart man.

"Do you want to walk me through where we are?" I ask him, turning toward my guys.

The crew hears it. They exchange looks. The silent, unspoken agreement that things are back to the way they should be.

By the time I finish my rounds, something settles in my chest. Something familiar.

I was gone, but now I'm back.

And I'm making damn sure everyone remembers why they need me.

The moment I reclaim my position; I feel a shift. The site bends around me, adapting, readjusting. It's what I do best, I control the atmosphere, shift the power, and make people dance without them even realizing they're following my lead.

I scan the site, eyes darting through the sea of high-vis vests and hard hats, searching for one face in particular.

*Leven.*

The moment I spot him, something inside me tightens. Like a taut rope pulling me toward him, like gravity itself shifts whenever he's around. He doesn't look up, doesn't even acknowledge my presence at first, and somehow, that makes my pulse quicken.

Dr. Jenson once told me that I have a tendency to fixate on emotionally unavailable people. I had rolled my eyes at him. I didn't fixate; I conquered.

But Leven?

Leven is the one goddamn person I haven't been able to conquer.

And it drives me insane.

I approach, keeping my strides controlled, casual, like this is just another interaction and not the thing I've been anticipating all morning. *All month.*

"I'm back." I say it lightly, smiling, as if my heart isn't pounding against my ribs like a caged animal.

At first, nothing.

Disinterest.

The exact kind of reaction that would make any other woman turn away. But I know Leven. He's always strategic with his attention. It's a game to him, even if he doesn't realize he's playing it.

Then, there it is, a small smile, barely noticeable. But it's there. And he doesn't give those away easily.

"What's up? You're back?" His voice is unreadable, calm, distant.

I tilt my head, studying him. How do you make someone want you when they're completely uninterested in wanting anything at all?

"Yeah, so I guess you can't keep avoiding me now." I tease, but I know there's truth wrapped inside it.

Leven exhales, not quite a sigh but close. "I wasn't avoiding you, Reya. We just didn't have anything else to talk about."

Ouch.

I feel the rejection slice through me, but instead of flinching, I smirk. A defense mechanism, I guess. Leven might be a mystery, but I am a force. I win people over. That's what I do.

"Can we talk later?" I ask, knowing full well that I hate asking for anything.

Leven nods, nonchalant. "Sure. I have to get back to work, anyway."

Dismissed.

I turn and walk away before he can see the irritation flashing across my face. But before I even make it to the boss's office, my phone vibrates.

It was nice seeing you today. You look good.
—Leven

A slow smile spreads across my lips before I can stop it.

This is what I live for. The little crumbs of attention, the slivers of validation that keep me on the hook. I should ignore it. I should stop playing this game.

But I don't.

Because Leven is different.

And different is a challenge.

I make my way to Jason's office, my mood buoyed by Leven's text. But the moment I step inside, the air shifts again.

Jason doesn't look up right away. He's sitting at his desk, flipping through paperwork like I'm just another item on his to-do list. The audacity.

I cross my arms, leaning against the doorframe. "Gonna pretend I'm not standing here?"

He finally looks up, his expression is a mix of amusement and something else…something unspoken.

"Didn't realize I had to acknowledge everyone who walks into my office."

I arch a brow. "Funny, that's not how you felt the last time we were in here alone."

Jason's jaw tightens just slightly. He shifts in his chair, adjusting his posture like he's physically trying to put distance between us.

Oh, this is going to be fun. I love watching men squirm.

I step inside, closing the door behind me, not all the way, just enough to make him nervous.

"Relax," I murmur, voice laced with mock innocence. "I just came to talk shop."

Jason exhales through his nose, shaking his head. "You need something, Reya?"

*Yeah, I need you to remember the way you used to look at me.*

"Just making sure we're clear on my role here." I smile, slow and deliberate. "You did say I have my crew back, but I also want my authority back. Full control. No micromanaging."

Jason leans back in his chair, watching me. He's thinking. And thinking means I already have him exactly where I want him.

"Full control, huh?" He repeats, rolling his pen between his fingers. "You gonna stay long enough to follow through this time?"

I feign a pout. "I'm hurt, Jason. Truly."

He scoffs, rubbing a hand down his face. I watch his movements carefully, tracking every nervous tick, every glance. He's avoiding looking at me too long, which means one thing:

He's still affected.

And if he's affected, that means I still have power here.

Jason exhales, then nods. "Fine. You're in charge of your crew. Don't screw it up."

I flash him a satisfied smile. "I never do."

By the time I step back onto the site, I feel high off control. This is my world, my arena, and every move I make is deliberate.

I check my phone again. Leven's message still lingers there, unanswered.

I should let him wait. Make him feel the absence of my attention.

But my fingers betray me before my brain can stop them.

> You always say that. I'm starting to think you actually
> miss me.
> -Reya.

Delivered.

I lock my phone before I can second guess it.

I know how this goes. Leven will respond…eventually. Maybe hours later. Maybe not at all. But I'll be waiting.

That's the worst part.

I hate the waiting.

I hate the way Leven doesn't need me the way Jason did. The way Greg does. The way every other man I've encountered has.

Leven is the one who gets away with not wanting me.

And somehow, that makes me want him even more.

Dr. Jenson once told me that the chase is what excites me. That the moment I have someone, I lose interest. That it's not about love, or passion, or connection, it's about control.

I laughed at him. Told him he was wrong.

But as I stand there, staring at my unanswered text, heart pounding for a response from a man who refuses to be caught…

I wonder if he was right.

# Chapter 25

## In the After

Yesterday, I told Tim I thought I was a good person.

Today, I find myself in one of the empty rooms with Leven, listening for the muffled sounds of other workers moving around outside the door.

Am I a good person?

I'm seeking clarity. I'm seeking validation. Reassurance. Leven hardly gives me any of those, so any opportunity I can take, I hold onto it. I yearn for it.

Looking into his eyes, I see nothing but black solar spirals where his pupils should be. A black hole. Endless. Consuming.

And I wonder if this is a sign of who he truly is, a soulless creature.

I sit on the unfinished counter, boots knocking lightly against the edge of plywood still waiting for cabinet doors. The air in the room is thick and warm from our breath, from our proximity, from the weight of the things we aren't saying.

I take off my hard hat, setting it beside me as I rake a hand through my braids. My scalp itches beneath the weight of my own thoughts.

*I shouldn't be here.*

But I always find my way back to him, drawn by an irresistible magnetic pull between our hearts, yearning for each other's presence.

"Listen," I start, swallowing the lump forming in my throat. "I'm sorry. I'm a *very* impulsive person. But I didn't mean to hurt you."

My voice wavers just enough. Just enough to let him know I mean it. Just enough to let him know I'm vulnerable.

I search his face for understanding. For something that tells me he sees me. That he forgives me. That he wants me.

But Leven doesn't blink.

Doesn't move.

Like he didn't hear me. Like he doesn't care.

Instead, he reaches for my vest, fingers sliding beneath the zipper, tugging it down with a slow, deliberate ease.

"What are you doing?" My voice is soft, but there's tension in my breath, in the way my thighs clench instinctively around the edge of the counter.

Unintentionally, of course.

Or was it?

I tell myself it was unintentional. Because what he's doing now is unexpected. Because what he's doing now is unwanted.

But my body betrays me. My back arches. My lip's part. My breath catches the way it always does when he's near.

I knew what I was doing.

Leven doesn't speak. Doesn't acknowledge the way I'm studying him. The way I'm waiting for some kind of reaction. Instead, his fingers move lower, to the first button of my work shirt.

"Stop," I whisper. I don't pull away, though. My hands find his, holding them, but not removing them.

"Stop," I repeat, softer this time, lips grazing the edge of his ear as I exhale into his skin.

I want him to stop.

I want him to keep going.

I let my hands grip his shoulders lightly, let my mouth hover near his ear as I murmur, "We shouldn't."

It's an invitation. It's a warning. It's a test.

Leven finally pulls back and looks at me.

And for the first time, his eyes aren't empty.

They're burning.

Dark fire smolders behind them, a slow, consuming thing. Desire, maybe. Or something else. Something deeper. Something dangerous.

"Isn't this what you want?"

No.

Yes.

"No," I lie. "I want to talk, Leven." I push him back, barely moving him, but making my point. "Why did you ghost me like you did?"

His expression doesn't change. His shoulders don't shift. His stance doesn't break.

"Like I said earlier," he says, voice flat, detached, "we have nothing to talk about."

We have *everything* to talk about.

"That's crazy," I blurt out, eyes locked on him. "Seeing as how last time we saw each other face to face, you told me you loved me."

Leven exhales sharply, like he's bored of this conversation already. Like the words mean nothing now.

"Reya, are we going to fuck or not?"

The words punch the air from my lungs. Not because they're crude. Not because they shock me.

But because I already know my answer.

"Not until we figure this out."

Leven shakes his head, exasperated, already stepping back. "There's nothing to figure out. You have Tim." He says, his finger unconsciously in my face. "Tim proposed to you, you said 'yes' and I meant nothing."

His jaw clenches. The only real emotion I have ever seen from him.

"So if we're not fucking, then what are we doing?" His voice is cold, calculated, like he's done with this conversation. Like he's done with me.

I feel it then, that familiar panic. The one that claws at my chest whenever I feel him slipping away. "That's not fair, Leven. You knew I was in a relationship when you met me." The words fall from my tongue too easily. Too rehearsed. "And I told you not to fall in love."

*That was rule number one.*

Leven scoffs, shaking his head. "Yeah, I should've listened." He exhales, stepping back further, distancing himself from me. "I should've listened when you said you were no good for me, too."

And there it is.

A glimpse of pain behind his eyes. Just for a second. Just long enough for me to see it.

And it makes my chest tighten because Leven is the first person I have ever truly loved.

The kind of patient love I wish I had for Tim.

The kind of unconditional love I wish I had for my daughter.

The kind of love I'd received as a child.

The kind of unfailing love I wish I had for myself.

I blink back tears, but they betray me. They fall anyway.

Leven's face is unreadable. "Don't cry, Reya."

"I can't help it, I love you." I whisper, and I mean it. Every damn word.

Leven doesn't move, doesn't react, doesn't break. He just stares.

"Then why did you do it?" His voice is quiet. But I know what he's asking.

Why did I choose Tim? Why did I choose the easy thing instead of the real thing?

I inhale, the smell of dust and metal shavings filling my lungs. It steadies me. Just a little.

"I told you; it was impulsive. I was going to break up with him."

Tears are falling in full force now. I hate this. I hate him for making me feel this way. I hate myself for letting him.

Leven shakes his head, fists clenched at his sides. "That should've been us, Reya."

His words slice through me like steel.

Because he's right.

Because my heart has only opened for this one man. Because I never knew true happiness, true emotion…I never knew what it was like to only crave one man until I met Leven.

He reaches for my pants.

Unzipping.

Moving with purpose.

"Leven, stop." My voice is serious now.

But he doesn't stop.

He's relentless. Persistent.

I grab his hands, firmly, so he understands I mean it.

But he pushes them away.

The air changes. My body stiffens.

I realize I'm cornered.

He stands between my legs, his hard, muscular body unmovable against my weak pushes. His face is stone, emotionless, determined.

I look around.

No way out.

"I don't want to do this." I breathe. I struggle against him.

It's no use.

# Chapter 26

## In the After

"How are you doing today, Reya?"

A familiar question from a familiar voice.

Dr. Jenson studies me, his deep blue eyes scanning my face like he's searching for the truth beneath my carefully placed mask. He always knows. He reads me like an open book, as if my thoughts are scrawled across my forehead in ink only he can see.

I shift in my seat, still in my dusty work clothes, and glance at the clock. This session feels different. Dr. Jenson doesn't wait for me to answer before he moves on.

"You went back to work today?" His voice is light, but there's an edge to it. He knows this means I saw Leven. "How was that for you?"

I fidget with the sleeves of my long-sleeved work shirt, rolling the fabric between my fingers, stalling.

"Oh, it was as good as it could be expected," I mutter.

"If you don't mind," he says, leaning forward slightly, "I'd like to pick our starting point for this session."

That's new. He usually lets me dictate where we begin, where the conversation flows. He usually lets things unravel naturally. But today? Today he's pushing.

He smiles gently, patiently, but I know that look. It's a calculated patience. A look that says he already knows the answer before he asks the question.

"Did you see Leven today?"

I freeze.

The air in the room shifts, thickening between us.

I don't answer right away, but a nervous laugh escapes before I can swallow it back down. That's all the answer he needs.

"I take it you did, by the way you're fidgeting," he says. His tone is calm, even. But there's something beneath it. Something sharp.

Dr. Jenson is rarely this direct. He usually lets the silence do the work. But today? Today, it's pointed.

And I can't help but wonder if it's because he told me to stay away from Leven.

"Talk to me, Reya."

His voice is softer now, the concern in his tone unsettling. His hand rests lightly on my knee, the one place he can reach on my body, and I feel myself crack under his touch. Under the weight of his knowing eyes.

"There's nothing to talk about," I say, forcing a casual shrug. "*We* had nothing to talk about."

Lie.

It's becoming easier and easier.

Dr. Jenson leans back in his chair. "I don't believe that." He jots something down on his notepad, and I hate how it makes my stomach tighten.

I should tell him the truth. That's why I chose him in the first place, I felt I couldn't lie to him.

And I haven't lied to him.

Until now.

"I had sex with him."

The confession falls from my lips before I can stop it, spoken so softly I almost convince myself I didn't say it out loud.

Dr. Jenson doesn't react right away. He just looks at me; not with judgment, not with shame, but with something far worse.

*Compassion.*

"Okay."

That's all he says. He's letting me think.

"I didn't want to," I blurt out. "I put myself in that position. It's my fault."

His expression doesn't change. He waits.

"I went in the room with him to talk," I continue, my voice tight. "But he said we had nothing to talk about."

"Okay."

"I didn't want to have sex with him." I said again and swallow hard. "Well… I did at first. But really, I just wanted to see where we stood."

Tears slip down my cheeks. I don't even know why I'm crying.

"I sat on the counter. He started touching me, grabbing me. And I… I couldn't stop him. So, I gave in."

Dr. Jenson tilts his head slightly. "Why?" His voice is careful. "Why did you give in if you didn't want to?"

I take a deep breath, but it does nothing to steady me.

Because the truth? The truth hurts more than anything else.

"I gave in so I didn't feel like…" I stop talking. What am I saying? Why am I saying it? I don't have to. I can just keep my mouth shut. But instead, the words come out like vomit. "So I didn't feel like I was being raped."

The words gut me.

The moment they leave my mouth, my breath hitches. Tears fall harder now, breath uneven, hands clutching the tissue I hadn't even realized I grabbed.

Silence.

Thick. Heavy. Suffocating.

Then, finally...

"Did it work?"

I blink up at him, thrown off. "Did what work?"

"You said you gave in so it wouldn't feel like you were being raped." He holds my gaze. "Did it work? Did you *want* what happened to you?"

I refuse to answer.

Because this is Leven we're talking about. The only man who's ever made my heart jump. The only man who has ever had the ability to make me feel like I was on cloud-9. The only man who's ever made me feel *alive*.

I will not let Dr. Jenson take him away from me.

"Reya." His voice is softer now but weighted. He sets his notepad aside, wheels his chair closer to me. "This isn't love."

I tense.

"You think you love him because he gives you nothing," he continues. "He's the one man you can't tame, can't control. And it's tricking your brain into thinking it's love."

I flinch at his words.

"When he gives you the barest hint of attention, you cling to it. You live off it. But Reya…" He exhales, shaking his head. "That. Isn't. Love."

I stare at him, blank-faced, refusing to let his words sink in.

Because Dr. Jenson doesn't know.

He doesn't know the nights Leven opened up to me. The nights Leven told me things he'd never told anyone else. The nights he *let me in.* He doesn't know that I've confided in Leven, told him things I would never tell anyone else.

And Leven still loved me.

"I have clients who have told me similar stories," Dr. Jenson says gently. "That they 'gave in' so it wouldn't feel like they were being raped. But at the end of the day, they still didn't want what happened to them."

"I wanted it at first," I whisper. "I told him no, but I didn't resist. Maybe he thought I wanted it."

Dr. Jenson sighs. "You're making excuses for him."

I shake my head. "I love him."

His expression tightens. "That's not love, Reya. Tim loves you. Delilah loves you." He leans forward. "It doesn't feel like love because it feels easy. But real love isn't hard, Reya. It isn't supposed to feel like this. It isn't supposed to make you question yourself. It isn't supposed to force you into things you don't want to do."

I shift in my seat, uncomfortable under the weight of his words.

Dr. Jenson studies me carefully.

"You were doing so well, Reya," he murmurs, voice almost pained. "You were making tremendous progress. I was so proud of the woman you were becoming."

Something inside me twists.

Our history lingers between us, unsaid.

The way he's always seen something in me, something worth saving.

But right now?

Right now, I don't want to be saved.

I want Leven.

Even if it destroys me.

# Chapter 27

**Before**
**13 years old**

"I have never had only one girlfriend," Luther said, his voice thick with arrogance. He sat at the counter, cracking open a beer while my mother stood at the stove, the sizzling of pork chops filling the air. The smell was rich, familiar, but somehow, it felt tainted by his presence.

I looked at him, then at my mother, whose back was turned but whose shoulders stiffened at his words.

"Even now," he continued. "I have more than one girlfriend."

I was thirteen. Too young for this conversation. Too young to be dragged into his world of filth. Too young to be forced into understanding that love didn't mean the same thing to men as it did to women.

But I wasn't too young to recognize what my mother refused to see.

That Luther was a liar. A manipulator. A man who sat comfortably at our kitchen counter, drinking his beer, bragging about his conquests while my mother, his so-called "love," cooked his damn dinner.

I hated him.

I hated that I had to sit there, had to listen. I hated that my mother let him talk like that. That she never fought back.

"The problem with women," he continued, completely unbothered by my silence, by the way my mother refused to turn around, "is that they catch feelings. When men cheat, they just cheat to have sex. Women? They want to form relationships. They fall in love. That is their mistake."

I didn't want to hear this.

I wanted to go to my room. Do my homework. Pretend I lived in a normal house where men didn't talk about women like they were disposable.

But I couldn't leave.

Not because I was physically being forced to stay.

But because I didn't dare.

Luther liked to test boundaries. He liked to see how far he could push someone before they pushed back. But my mother never pushed. She just took it.

And that's when I learned that some women get walked on because they refuse to stand up.

I wasn't going to be like her.

I wasn't much of a talker back then. I had learned over the years that silence was easier than the confusion of knowing what I was supposed to lie about, what I wasn't supposed to ask about, and what I had to pretend I never saw.

So, I stopped talking.

Stopped asking.

Stopped caring.

And in this instance, it was no different.

What could I even say?

What should I say?

*I agree, Luther. Women should get cheated on.*

Was that what he wanted?

"You see, sex doesn't mean anything," he went on, taking a long sip of his beer. "I can have sex with a woman and not care about her at all. But your mom? I love your mom. That's why I come home to her."

Love?

I stared at him. This filthy, self-righteous man who spoke about my mother like she was some gold medal prize for enduring his cruelty.

Then I looked at her.

I looked at my mother.

Her body, small and frail, standing over the stove, shoulders hunched as she turned the pork chops.

She heard him. I knew she did.

She heard every word, and yet… she didn't react.

Didn't turn around. Didn't throw the pan at his head like she should have.

She just…existed.

Like a ghost of a woman who had long since faded into something tragic.

And yet he was thriving.

Luther sat there, beaming with pride, chest puffed out, radiating power, confidence, and victory because he had won.

He had broken her.

And that's when I realized something.

Men like Luther didn't want strong women. They wanted women like my mother: women who shrank. Women who withered under their words.

And women like my mother deserved what they got.

She deserved it.

Because she chose it.

She chose to stay.

She chose to be weak.

She chose to let a man like Luther turn her into nothing.

And I made a vow to myself in that moment, one that burned into me like a scar.

*I will never be my mother.*

I turned back to Luther, studying him now, not with hate, but with understanding.

I hated him, but I also admired him.

Not because of who he was, but because of what he represented.

Power. Control. A man who could break a woman down to dust and still sit at the table, unbothered, drinking his beer.

And my mother?

She represented what happens to women who loved too much, who gave too much, who trusted too much.

I. Would. Not. Be. Like. Her.

I would never let a man turn me into that.

No man would ever be able to break me the way Luther had broken my mother.

And if a man ever tried?

I would break him first.

# Chapter 28

## In the After

Driving home after therapy is somber.

Dr. Jenson's disappointment lingers in the air like a thick fog, suffocating and unshakable. His words churn inside my head, replaying themselves over and over like a taunting whisper.

*You think you love Leven because he gives you nothing.*

But he's wrong. He has to be wrong.

There are too many variables. Too many secrets. Too many lies I've had to keep. So many lies that sometimes I forget which ones belong to who.

Tim is the easy option. The safe option. The comfortable option. Tim is a great guy, he's just not *my* guy. I have tried, really tried, to love him. Nine years of forcing myself to feel something. I look at Tim and wish my body would react to him the way it does when I see Leven.

But it never does. And it never will.

I fell in love with Leven fast.

I met Leven eleven months ago, shortly after I found out about Tim's affair. And within two weeks of meeting Leven, I told him I loved him. And I meant it.

Within a month, we were talking about moving in together.

And now?

Now I'm clawing for scraps of his affection, desperate for the smallest bit of validation.

When I pull into the driveway, Tim's car is gone.

Perfect.

The house. The perfect house I bought with Tim two years ago, feels hollow. It's beautiful and meticulously designed, and yet, it's nothing more than a stage prop for a life I was never meant to have.

Sometimes, I imagine what it would have been like if Leven and I had bought a house together instead.

Would we have painted together? Would we have danced in the empty living room, barefoot, high on the thrill of accomplishing something together?

Or would it have been like everything else: me begging for a moment of his attention, holding my breath every time I spoke, afraid of saying something wrong and ruining the entire night? Me begging him to show me any feeling other than indifference?

I strip down the moment I make it upstairs, stepping into the shower and turning the water as hot as it will go.

I let the scalding heat burn my skin until the pain is the only thing I feel.

And then I cry.

I cry loud, unashamed, ugly sobs that I swore I wouldn't let out in front of another human being. But in the comfort of my solitude, I allow myself to feel the hurt.

I did not want to have sex with Leven today.

But I love Leven.

And I am so conflicted.

I sit in the shower until the steam becomes unbearable, until the water runs cold, until my sobs have been drained from my body along with everything else.

When I'm finally numb again, I wrap a towel around myself and walk into my office.

I reach for my journal because I need proof.

I need to relive the love I had for Leven before everything turned to rot.

I need to feel the warmth of sitting on his couch, his legs tucked underneath me, the soft hum of his old fan spinning above us, the faint scent of his cologne (cedar and something smoky) embedded into the cushions. I remember the way the couch creaked beneath us as we sat close, not touching at first, but somehow always drawn together like magnets denying physics. That was when things were still sweet. Still unspoiled.

Back then, I didn't question the way I felt when I was with him, I just knew. My chest would tighten when he looked at me, but not in fear...in anticipation. Like I was about to discover something I never knew I was missing. I'd never felt anything close to love before Leven. Not real love. Not this type. This was the kind of love that grabbed me by the throat and kissed me slow. It was heavy, addictive, and reckless. Like heat under the skin, it moved through me without permission.

He is the only man who has ever loved me without falling for my mask first.

He saw past my flirtation, my dramatics, the way I would storm out just to see if someone would chase me.

Leven never chased.

He would let me go, but when I came back, he would be

waiting…with a sigh, maybe, and a furrow in his brow, but always waiting for me to return. And man, do I love the way his eyebrows furrow.

He never let me manipulate him. He'd call me out with a smirk and a raised brow, that same damn smirk that made me feel small and known all at once. When I'd get pouty, he wouldn't coddle me. He'd just say, "Stop acting like a brat, Reya," with a calmness that disarmed me. And when I was irrational, spinning in circles over things I couldn't control, he wouldn't argue. He would offer me advice or a piece of chocolate from the stash he kept in his nightstand drawer. That's when I knew he studied me. Not just watched, but studied.

Understood.

He knew that I needed sweetness when I couldn't find it in myself.

No one had ever done that. Not Tim. Not anyone.

They gave in, tiptoed around me, or gave up completely. But Leven? He held his ground. And it made me crave him even more. He felt like control in a world where I had none, and that feeling—God, that feeling—is what I became addicted to.

More than him.

More than his body.

More than the sex.

I became addicted to the way he made me feel anchored when I felt like a hurricane.

Loving him was a high I've never come down from. Even now, when everything has turned sour and sharp, I still chase that first feeling. That version of him before the distance, before the silence, before the slammed doors and thrown words. Before *I* shattered us. I chase it like a drug, knowing I'll never get back to the purity of the first hit.

And still… I can't stop trying.

I flip through the pages until I find his name.

I need to know: Is Dr. Jenson right? Or am I?

*March 17, 2023*

*Four months ago, I found out about Tim and Nola.*

*So maybe I moved too fast with Leven. Maybe part of me was still raw and reacting, reaching for something that felt like comfort.*

*But this doesn't feel like a reaction.*

*Whatever this is, it's already more than anything I ever felt for Tim.*

*Leven has every part of me.*

*And I've only known him for two weeks.*

*When I first met him, he was perfect.*

*Forty-six years old. Dark skin, smooth as onyx. Smart, the kind of razor-sharp intelligence that reminds me of someone on the spectrum. His memory is impeccable. I revel in the way he can recall events from when he was six years old with details so vivid it feels like he's pulling me into the past with him.*

*And he was funny. Once you got past his hardened exterior, once you cracked through that unreadable mask…he actually smiled. And when he did?*

*It was rare. Precious. Addictive.*

*I was intrigued.*

*By the mystery of him.*

*By the challenge of him.*

*The first time I went to his house was for the Super Bowl. He had just brought groceries in, flustered and "razzled," for lack of a better word. It was cute. I wanted to fuck, and he wanted to put away groceries.*

*We had great, regular sex, then watched the game.*

*The second time? He made me breakfast.*

*He was nervous, and it was adorable.*

*We watched The Woman King that day—a movie that should have lasted two hours stretched to four because we kept pausing it to talk. Talk about nothing. Talk about everything. Talk about pain and history and how hard it is to be soft when life has spent so long trying to harden you.*

*Time didn't pass the way it normally does that day. It melted. It bent around us, stretched itself wide to make room for us. There were no clocks, no phones, no interruptions. Just his voice, his laugh, his shoulders shaking when I told him stories from my childhood that weren't even funny but somehow became funny in his presence. There was something about his energy that made the air feel lighter. Something about the way his eyes didn't judge me when I told him about my mom, about the dad I hated, about the way I always felt like I was fighting to be seen.*

*He didn't flinch. He didn't try to fix it.*

*He just… listened.*

*In those hours, in that cramped living room filled with old candles and the scent of bacon lingering on the walls, I felt it.*

*Love. Or the beginning of it.*

*Like our shattered pieces had been carved from the same jagged history. Like I had known him before. In another life. In another body. And maybe in that life, we hadn't gotten it right. But this time? This time we were going to try.*

*I wanted to climb into his soul.*

*It was like the universe carved a space in him just for me. And I knew, with terrifying clarity, that I had never felt anything like this before.*

*I fell in love with him.*

*It happened fast, and it happened hard.*

*Now? Three weeks later…*

*He's a stranger.*

*We don't laugh.*

*We don't kiss.*

*He doesn't even look at me the same way.*

*And yet, I am still here.*

*Still holding on to something that hasn't existed in a while.*

*What did I do?*


*April 6th, 2023*

*He reached out to me today, and I was completely disarmed.*

*The moment I saw him walking toward me, I melted. His beauty, his presence, the way he carries himself with that effortless confidence that makes me weak; it was all so overwhelming to my mental state.*

*I love him.*

*He ghosted me for weeks because I said I didn't like his spaghetti.*

*Spaghetti.*

*Out of everything we've been through, he disappeared for weeks because I made a comment about his food.*

*"I'll never cook for you again," he said.*

*But he came back. "If you were anyone else, I would have never talked to you again."*

*I should have walked away then.*

*I didn't.*

*May 4, 2023*

*I was supposed to tell Tim I was moving out.*

*And I did tell him I was leaving, but he decided to propose to me instead of packing his bags. He felt like a ring would fix our problems.*

*I agreed to marry him.*

*Not because marriage is something I want, but because the look in his eyes gave me the same feeling it did when Dorian proposed. He was beaming with pride at the thought of me being his wife, and I couldn't say no.*

*But how do I explain to Leven that I went to break up with my boyfriend and came back engaged instead?*

*I saw the heartache in Leven's eyes when I told him. We had planned our future together, and I shattered it.*

*But he knew.*

*He knew I was in a relationship.*

*He knew not to fall in love.*

*He knew I was no good for him.*
*So, was it really my fault?*

*May 10, 2023*
*He hit the wall next to my face.*
*Yelled inches away from my nose.*
*My heart raced.*
*And I became painfully aware that I hardly know this man at all.*
*In that moment?*
*I was afraid. We talked about domestic violence, I told him about Luther, and he said he would never be that in my life. He promised me he could control his temper. But thinking about it now, what man would openly admit to putting their hands on a woman? What man would openly brag about it?*
*I have no idea what Leven was capable of.*
*And so, I did the only thing I knew would calm him down.*
*I got on my knees.*
*And I stayed there until he finished, until he was satisfied.*
*Until he was calm enough for me to get the hell out of there.*

*June 23, 2023*
*Leven.*
*After all this time?*
*…Always.*

*What can I say? My heart aches for this man. My body—God, it craves him. Even now, when I know better, when everyone around me would scream run if they knew even half of the truth, I still find myself looking for his face in every crowd.*

*There's something about his voice that calms me, like a melody I've memorized, even if the lyrics never really make sense. Sometimes his stories contradict themselves, sometimes they feel... off. But I don't care. He's talking. And when Leven talks, it feels like God is giving me a second chance to feel whole.*

*If I need clarity, even when he's ignoring me, even when I haven't heard from him in days, I close my eyes and imagine his words. I hear him in my mind before I ever hear from him in real life.*

*Most of the time, the only emotion I can wring from him is irritation. But when he touches me? I lie to myself and call it intimacy.*

*So, I stay.*

*And I write.*

*And I call it devotion.*

*But in the quiet moments, even I know...*

*This isn't love.*

*It's just the most convincing lie I've ever told myself.*

I close my journal. I stop in June because I'm sure the rest of the entries just describe the emotional rollercoaster I have been riding since I met Leven.

Leven. The reason I quit my job and began seeing Dr. Jenson,

Leven. The reason I know real love.

Leven.

My hands are shaking.

And yet, I still love him.

Even now.

Even after everything.

Because love isn't supposed to make sense.

Right?

My phone vibrates loudly on my desk, interrupting me. It's a pleasant distraction from the uncomfortable truths in my journal. Truths I was desperately trying not to face. The screen lights up with Delilah's name, and I sigh as I answer.

"Hello?"

"Hi, mommy!" Delilah's cheerful voice pierces through the silence. My chest tightens instantly. She's fourteen years old and still calls me "mommy." The word never sits right with me. Maybe because I don't deserve it. Maybe because she hardly knows me, aside from the forced phone calls and a few awkward visits. Our entire relationship has been distilled down to brief conversations, photographs, and secondhand stories from Dorian.

"Hi, baby," I say, forcing warmth into my voice, even though the term feels foreign rolling off my tongue. She'll always be a little girl to me, not because I cherish those memories, but because that's the only way I've ever known her.

The last time I saw her was when she was six months old. Six months, and then Dorian took her far away, across the country. I don't blame him. He did what I never had the courage to do. He made a choice, for Delilah's sake.

She deserved a parent who wanted her.

I cringe, remembering those early months. Every diaper change, every midnight feeding, every cry...I resented all of it. The maternal instinct everyone promised would awaken in me never did. Even now, hearing the hopeful innocence in her voice fills me with irritation rather than warmth.

I glance back at my journal, the page still open to Leven's name, his rage-filled eyes haunting me from the scribbled words.

"Guess what, Mommy?" Delilah's voice is eager, pulling me reluctantly back to the present. "I made the track team! I'm going to be number one, just like you." Her excitement is tangible, and I know Dorian must have filled her head with exaggerated stories from my high school days. I've never shared those moments with her.

"You give me too much credit," I say lightly, brushing off her excitement. "I was never number one." I force a laugh, pretending to be humble. "You'll be better than me." God, I hope she is better. I hope she avoids every mistake I ever made. I pray she never feels the loneliness and self-hatred that defined my teenage years.

"Can you come to one of my track meets?" She asks quietly. Her voice is suddenly cautious; hopeful yet prepared for disappointment.

*Of course, I could.* But I won't.

"We'll see," I say easily, the familiar lie slipping off my tongue. It feels better than flat-out saying no, even though it's no less cruel.

As Delilah chatters on, sharing details about her practices, I only half-listen, nodding occasionally and humming acknowledgment at random intervals. My focus drifts back to the open journal, back to Leven, back to the night he nearly lost control because I questioned him about a book.

The book: another lie he'd told. The time I'd spent scouring Targets across the city, searching for proof, obsessively piecing together his story until I uncovered the truth: he was lying.

Again.

I can still feel the rush of fear, the racing of my heart when he looked at me with rage in his eyes, devoid of humanity.

"And guess what else, Mommy?" Delilah says, her laughter breaking through my anxiety-filled memories.

I gasp theatrically, pretending engagement. "What?"

"She fell down…like, all the way to the ground!" Delilah giggles, the innocent joy evident in her voice.

"No way!" I echo her laughter, though I've completely missed her story.

Guilt nudges me briefly, but I push it aside, returning my attention to the journal, to Leven, to the dangerous thrill he gives me despite all the warnings, despite all the red flags.

Delilah deserves better.

Tim deserves better.

But Leven? Leven gets all of me, even the parts that terrify me, even the parts I won't admit exist.

My mother withered away because she let a man consume her.

And I tell myself I am not like her.

But am I?

At least my mother stayed. At least she tried to be a present mom.

I didn't even do that.

I turn the page in the journal.

Leven's name stares back at me.

I want him.

I hate him.

*I will always choose him.*

Even if it destroys everyone else in the process.

The knock on my office door makes me flinch. *Shit.*

I scramble to shut my journal, sliding a few random papers over it as if that could erase the words I just read. The evidence of my own pathetic, desperate obsession. I click my laptop open for good measure, pretending to be busy. Pretending, like I always do.

"Come in," I call out, my voice smooth, unaffected.

Tim steps inside. "Hey, lady. Sorry to bother you."

"You're not bothering me." Lie.

I hold up a finger, signaling for him to wait. "Hey baby, I have to call you back," I say into the phone.

"You promise, Mommy?"

*No.* I never do.

"Yes, I promise." Another lie. But we both know better. That's why she makes me promise. She knows it doesn't mean anything.

Tim watches me as I hang up. "You didn't have to get off the phone. I know how important conversations with Delilah are to you."

I smile at him. Another lie I told long ago, another version of myself I carefully crafted to be more appealing.

The truth? I don't need an excuse not to talk to her. I was hardly listening anyway.

"It's okay," I say, shrugging it off. "We were done."

"How is she?" He asks.

"She's good," I say automatically. "She made the basketball team." Or volleyball? Or softball? Who the hell knows?

Tim frowns. "Isn't basketball season over?"

*Damn.*

"I don't know. I guess it's different in Virgina." I wave my hand dismissively. He doesn't press. He never does.

Then I deflect. "You didn't come home last night?" Not because I care, but because I don't want him to ask what I'm doing in here.

Tim shrugs. "Yeah, I was at my dad's. You should come over. He misses you."

"I would, but all you guys do is drink until you're drunk and then pass out." I take a sip of water, casually, like his drinking is just an inconvenience instead of something that makes my skin crawl. "That doesn't really sound like a good time."

Tim gestures to the empty chair as an invitation to talk. I nod toward it, and he sinks down with a sigh.

"If you come, I won't drink that much, I promise." He smiles, a little hopeful, a little pleading. And for some reason, I believe him.

I study him. Really study him.

Tim is perfect outside of his drinking (and the affair). And maybe if I approached it differently, he'd actually change it for me.

When he hurts me, he actively tries to do better. He is kind, and patient, and admires me.

I admire that about him.

"How was your first day back at work?" He asks, that genuine smile never faltering.

This is easy. Talking to Tim. Laughing with Tim. Playing the role of the good girlfriend with Tim.

"Work was crazy," I say, exaggerating the word with a playful eye-roll.

Tim perks up. "Wait…what type of crazy?" He stands abruptly. "Should I make us some tea crazy or pour a glass of wine crazy?"

I know he just wants a beer.

I could tell him the truth.

That I slept with my boss.

That a year ago, he made me foreman.

That eleven months ago, I started sleeping with Leven.

That eight months ago, all hell broke loose.

That Jason noticed how much time I was spending with Leven, so he started giving me shitty jobs, pushing me into a corner, forcing me to choose him (my boss) or Leven (the man that I love).

That I chose Leven. And Jason? Jason had no choice but to back off.

That Leven got mad when I got engaged, so he started treating me like garbage. And I took it, because I thought I deserved it.

That things at work got so overwhelming I had to take a hiatus and start therapy.

That today, my first day back, I saw Jason.

I saw Leven.

I saw my past colliding with my present, and I still couldn't make sense of it.

That Leven may or may not have forced himself on me today, but I won't call it that, because then I'll have to admit what it was.

That my daughter, the one I keep pretending to care about, made the volleyball team. And I lied to her again.

That I've been lying to you for nine years about who I really am.

That I think about Dr. Jensen in inappropriate ways.

That I've been thinking about Brandon all day.

I could tell him all of this, but instead, I take a slow breath, let the web of lies settle back into place, and say...

"Wine."

Tim's whole face lights up. His child-like glee makes me laugh, and for a moment, I almost believe this life is real.

As soon as he turns on his heels out the door, I scribble something in my journal.

*Dear Young Reya,*

*I don't know what I'm doing with our life.*

*I feel like such a disappointment to you. To myself.*

*We hated Luther. Hated the way he loomed over us like a storm cloud, the way his voice could crack the air like thunder. We hated the way Mom shrank under his words, how she curled in on herself, a woman dissolving into nothing, waiting for the next blow: physical, verbal, emotional. The way she cooked his meals with shaking hands, how she cleaned up after him like he was a goddamn king, how she tried so desperately to hold on to a love that was never really there.*

*I hate that. I hate me for that.*

*We swore we would never be like Luther. We swore we would never break someone the way he broke Mom.*

*And yet here I am treating Tim like garbage.*

*And Tim still loves me.*

*So now I wonder: was Luther right? Is this what love is supposed to be? Is love just one person bending, breaking, sacrificing while the other takes?*

*And then there's Leven.*

*Leven, who treats me like nothing. Who uses me, ignores me, hurts me. And I... I cling to him. Desperate to make him happy. <u>Obsessed</u> with making him happy. I lay awake at night, running through conversations in my head, analyzing every word I said, every move I made, wondering where I went wrong. I think of new ways to please him, to keep him, to make him love me, as if love is something that can be earned through suffering.*

*And I don't know why I'm telling you all this, little one.*

*Maybe because I picture your big, innocent eyes, looking up at me, scared and alone. And I remember what we wanted most at your age...*

*To be loved.*

*To be chosen.*

*To feel like we mattered.*

*And now? Now, at my big age, I don't even know what love is supposed to feel like.*

*Is it supposed to look like Tim: safe, predictable, forgiving?*

*Or is it supposed to look like Leven: volatile, consuming, passionate?*

*My heart and my head are at war.*

*And I know what you would say: You would choose Tim.*

*You would tell me that he is everything we ever dreamed of when we used to lay awake at night, imagining a world where love was gentle, kind, safe.*

*And maybe you're right.*

*But, little one…I don't know which one is worse: a love that is safe but makes me feel nothing, or a love that ruins me but makes me feel <u>alive</u>.*

*And if I tell anyone this (anyone at all) they will all say the same thing.*

*"Choose Tim."*

*"Tim is good for you."*

*"Tim loves you."*

*But I don't want to hear that.*

*I don't want to hear the right answer.*

*I want just one person to tell me to choose Leven.*

*Because either way, I choose Leven.*

*And I will ALWAYS choose Leven.*

*- Your Older Self*

# Chapter 29

## In the After

I walk up to the door that used to be so familiar, once a second home, now a monument to everything that has changed. The chipped navy-blue paint feels colder, more distant than before. I stare at it, hoping it'll feel like it used to, but it doesn't. Nothing does.

My hand trembles as I lift it to knock.

And then I freeze.

I let my arm fall to my side and take a shaky step backward. The world around me blurs. The apartment complex feels different, the faint hum of traffic behind me feels consuming, the relentless hum of the Vegas heat pressing against my skin feels like a punishment. I press both hands to the top of my head and inhale deeply, trying to steady the storm inside me. I bite down on my bottom lip, hard enough to taste blood, just to feel something I can control.

But I'm unraveling.

Drowning in my own mind.

Drowning in questions he'll never answer.

Drowning in this love that feels more like obsession dressed in romantic desperation.

I retreat to my car, pressing my forearm against the searing-hot roof like a grounding ritual. I unlock the door and slump into the seat without starting the engine. The door remains open, letting the heat spill in like retribution. It's suffocating, but I welcome it. Sometimes, I think if I can make my body as miserable as my heart, it'll balance out.

The tears come without warning, sliding down my cheeks silently at first, then with heaving sobs. I cry because I'm ashamed of myself. Because I know better. Because I'm still here.

After a few minutes, I wipe my face, check my reflection, and take another breath. I get out of the car and walk back to the door, legs heavy, heart heavier.

This time, I knock.

When the door swings open, the scent hits me first; sandalwood, and something sharper underneath. Tension. The air is thick with it. The hallway behind him is dim, the only light a sliver of blue from the TV flickering down the hall.

*Leven.*

He says nothing. His face unreadable, expression carved from stone. He turns without a word and walks back toward his room.

I follow. Of course I follow.

This script has played out before. Too many times.

I step inside and slip off my shoes at the door, one of the silent rules he never says aloud but always expects. The first time I forgot, he didn't yell. He didn't scold. He just looked at the spot where I left my shoes, and I swear the air in the room dropped ten degrees. That was enough. I never forgot again.

As I walk deeper into his house, a strange sense of familiarity washes over me. This place once made me feel safe, like maybe

I'd finally found someone who understood the quiet violence of loneliness. Now, it just feels haunted; by memories, by tension, by the echo of things he never says.

Still, I undress. Slowly, deliberately. Shirt. Pants. Socks. Each layer peels away like armor I no longer need, or maybe never had. The mattress welcomes me like a lover: soft, broken-in, and deceptive. I sink into it like it might cradle all my guilt.

He lies on his back, his head turned away. Silent. Still.

He won't turn toward me. He never does when I show up like this; seeking something he won't name. Still, I scoot closer. I place my arm around his chest, kiss the back of his smooth, shaved head.

No reaction.

He's a fortress, emotionally barricaded. But I cling to the walls like ivy, desperate to grow somewhere he'll see me.

I close my eyes, draw in his scent, and let my lips press to his skin like a prayer.

*Please see me.*

*Please love me.*

*Please let this mean something.*

I reach for his hand beneath the blanket, but he pulls it away. No words. No apology. Just a quiet rejection I've learned to endure.

But I tell myself it's okay. I tell myself that just being near him is enough.

I lie to myself like it's a religion.

Because the truth is unbearable.

He is a riddle with no answer.

A man who lives in his own world, and I keep knocking on

the outside like a child asking to be let in.

There's something tragic in how deeply I've convinced myself that he needs me. That I was chosen to heal him. That his coldness is just another language, and if I love him hard enough, I'll become fluent.

But what if I'm not the exception? What if I'm just another woman hoping to matter?

Still... I scoot closer, heart pressed against his ribs, as if proximity could translate into connection.

I love him.

And God help me...

That love might be the most irrational thing I've ever known.

After a few more moments of rejection, his body stiff, his silence loud...I give up. I turn away, curling into myself like a bruised petal in a storm. Sleep. That's the best I can hope for now.

This was our routine once; me coming over before work, slipping into his sheets like I belonged there, as if I hadn't spent the previous night in bed with Tim. Sometimes we made love. Mostly, we just existed beside one another, our bodies close, our minds galaxies apart.

Leven's love language was supposedly physical touch, but his version of it felt transactional, controlled. Whenever I reached for him, he flinched. Not physically, always. But emotionally? He'd recoil like affection was a flame and he'd already been burned by it too many times.

I lay on my side, facing the wall, letting my eyelids grow heavy. Two hours before I need to leave for work. Two hours to pretend I belong here. I close my eyes and do the one thing I know how to do well: fantasize.

Leven consumes me. Every crevice of my thoughts is shaped around him. His voice. His laugh. His frown. His distance. I've stopped trying to escape the obsession and started treating it like comfort. Like hunger.

Then, as if he hears my thoughts begging for him, he turns. A grunt, a shift in weight, and an arm wraps around me.

I still.

He pulls me close, slow, purposeful. His breath warms the back of my neck, and my body betrays me, melting into him like wax.

He cups my breast, firm and possessive. Like they've always been his. My body arches into his without hesitation, hungry for his approval. His touch.

I turn to face him, our noses nearly brushing. His eyes, those deep, unreadable voids, stare back at me with nothing in them. Still, I whisper to myself, *He's here. He's touching you. He wants you.*

But then Dr. Jenson's words echo: *You love him because he gives you nothing.*

I kiss him hard. Desperate. I cling to his head with both hands, like I can tether him to me.

He doesn't pull away. He kisses back. Deep. Urgent. He groans into my mouth and rolls on top of me, his body heavy with lust, or maybe just convenience.

As he enters me, he whispers, "Yes," like he's claiming something.

When he pulls out, I gasp, a quiet "No" slipping from my lips before I can catch it.

He returns, deeper, and another "Yes" rumbles from his chest.

I pull him in deeper hoping that his next stroke will touch my soul and erupt something in his.

This is us.

This is what we do.

A push and pull.

A dance of power and longing and denial. And I beg him with my body to stay. I search for a connection that might not even exist. Maybe it never did.

I run my hands over his shoulders, his neck, his bald head, the parts of him I've memorized. My legs wrap around him and I try to feel whole. Our skin tones blend like a painting I don't want to wash away.

Moans, gasps, apologies tumble out of me. "I'm sorry," I whisper. "I'm so fucking sorry."

He doesn't say much, he never does. But he whispers back, "It's okay," in broken breaths. His face is a storm; brows furrowed, mouth parted. But there's no softness.

This isn't making love. This is release.

He flips me over, tells me to get on top.

I obey.

I pleasure him like it's my purpose. I want to impress him, captivate him, win him. I suck him until I gag, until my eyes water, until he grips his head like he's overwhelmed before I get on top.

I ride him with intention, guiding myself onto him, rocking my hips like we're in sync. I moan into his ear, "Stop being so fucking mean…" hoping it'll soften him.

"Okay…" He breathes, but it sounds rehearsed. "Okay," he says again between breaths.

He cups my breasts like he's studied them, like he knows what I like. And maybe he does. Maybe that's what makes this harder: he *knows* what to do. He holds my breast like he is palming all my insecurities in his hands, and he holds the power of my pleasure.

I explode around him, my body giving him everything, hoping he'll meet me in that moment. He doesn't.

"Did you cum?" He asks.

"Yes," I answer, smiling weakly. Still trying to catch the breath that just left my body.

"Bend over."

I comply.

Always.

As he thrusts into me again, his grip on my waist is tight. Commanding. But when I glance over my shoulder, he's not looking at me. His eyes are fixed on the ceiling, expressionless.

Emotionally vacant.

He moans, sure, but it's mechanical. Like a sound effect, not a feeling. His hands move with precision, not passion. He's calculated.

Always calculated.

I could be anyone.

I *am* anyone.

And that's what devastates me.

Because while I am worshiping him with every fiber of my being... he is simply going through the motions.

Still, I let him.

Because even if I don't have his heart, at least, for now, I have his body.

And I pretend that's enough.

After Leven finishes, he gets up without a word. He doesn't look at me. He walks to the bathroom, turns on the sink faucet, then the shower. The sounds echo through the quiet house like a signal. I hear the rustle of a towel, the hollow clang of the rag he wrings out under running water. When he returns, he drops it next to me on the bed. He doesn't hand it to me. He doesn't speak.

Then he turns on his heel and disappears into the steam.

I know my place.

After him.

Always after him.

I once tried to shower with him, playfully. I thought it might be intimate, romantic. He stepped out. Told me the water was already hot enough. That was all he said. The message was clear.

So now, I wait. I take the rag and wipe myself clean, silently, methodically. I'm careful to leave no trace. Leven doesn't like messes.

But I linger in the bed, the sheets still warm from us. The ache between my legs is a soft echo of what just happened. A reminder. A reward. I close my eyes and let myself feel him again.

Every time with Leven is better than the last. He reads my body like a book he's memorized but never stops studying. I let the thought of him stretch out inside me, wrapping itself around my bones. This could be our life.

Morning sex. Morning coffee.

Routine.

If I could just spend more time with him, uninterrupted time, maybe I'd know for sure if this version of him is permanent, or just a wall he keeps up because I'm still wearing Tim's ring.

Leven wasn't always like this. He used to be warm. He used to kiss my forehead and tell me I made him feel good. We used to share secrets, not just bodies. He used to touch me without needing something in return. I've seen the softness in him; I've touched it. And I keep thinking, if I just try harder, I can bring it back.

Maybe that makes me a fool.

But I'm already in too deep to climb out now.

"Are you going to shower?" His voice cuts through my thoughts like a knife.

I jump slightly. "Yes, sorry." I gather my things and slip into the bathroom.

Even here, in the steamy silence, I feel like a visitor. Like a trespasser. His soap is aligned, labels facing forward. His towel hangs perfectly folded. There's no space for me here.

Not really.

I study him like an exam. I take mental notes on what pleases him, what ticks him off. Not because he asks me to... but because something in me wants to earn the right to stay.

I finish the shower, dry off, redress in my wrinkled work clothes and take one last glance over the bathroom to make sure everything is in its place before I find him on the couch, scrolling on his phone. I sit beside him, one cushion over, waiting for his next move. His presence always sets the pace.

He glances up briefly. "Are you going to stay here until you go to work?"

The question slices through the quiet like an insult disguised as a sentence.

I tilt my head. "What do you mean?" I always stay. Or...I used to. He knows this. These hours before work was ours once. Now it feels like I'm overstaying a welcome that was never offered.

He doesn't answer.

I swallow hard, my gaze flicking around the room as I try to read him. Is this a trap? Is he testing me? Did I do something wrong again?

"Do you want me to leave?" I ask softly, hoping he'll say no. That he wants me to stay. That he likes having me here.

He shrugs. "Do whatever you want."

And that hurts more than a yes or no ever could.

Because his indifference says what his mouth never does: I don't care.

And God help me, his not caring makes me want him more.

I turn away, pretending to check the time, but really, I'm holding back tears. This is the unraveling. I can feel it. The slow, deliberate withdrawal of someone I've built a world around.

I know I'm unreasonable. I know this doesn't make any sense.

I have Tim at home. I sleep beside him. I cook with him. I said yes to a ring I didn't want.

And yet, here I am, sitting in Leven's living room like I've earned the right to be heartbroken. Like I earned the right to question him about his emotions. Maybe I'm selfish. Maybe I'm cruel.

"I forgot how much I missed you," I say, my voice low, laced with longing. I study his profile, trying to catch a flicker of emotion. "I forgot how good you make me feel."

He smirks without looking up. A short laugh escapes him, and he finally meets my eyes.

"I missed you too," he says casually.

It's enough to make my heart stutter.

"Do you want me to make you breakfast?"

"No, babe, I'm okay." He turns his attention back to his phone.

"What do you plan on taking for lunch?"

His jaw tightens. His fingers flex and release, once. Twice.

He sucks in a loud, dramatic breath like he wants me to see his chest rise, like he's performing the act of being annoyed. "I don't know yet," he mutters, eyes back on his screen.

The silence is a third person in the room, thick with tension and things we never say. And I'm suddenly tired of the game. Tired of guessing, of dancing around his moods, of earning scraps of tenderness.

"You suck sometimes, you know that?" I say, standing to gather my things.

His eyes narrow, confusion etched across his face. "Why do you say that?"

"Because I'm trying, Leven! I'm here. I'm showing up. I'm trying to talk to you, and you're just...so fucking closed off all the time. You don't even try to meet me halfway."

His body stiffens, phone dropping to the couch.

"Why should I care?" His voice is sharp now, eyes dark. "When I did care, you walked through my door with that damn ring on your finger and a smile I'd never seen before. And you expect me to just... be okay with that?"

The sting in his words burns deep.

"Leven, I..."

"I was done with love, Reya. Done trying to fix people, carry people. I wanted to live my life, finally. Just be a grandpa and chill. But then *you*...you walked in *my* life. You pursued me. And I fucking let you."

He moves toward me, and there's something different in his eyes. Raw pain. Unfiltered emotion. What's usually unreadable is suddenly loud and screaming.

"I let you into my world. That meant something to me. But clearly it meant nothing to you."

I've never seen him like this. Exposed.

"I'm sorry," I whisper, reaching for his hand. "I'm impulsive. I was scared. I thought maybe if I said yes to Tim, maybe it would fix everything that was broken inside me."

"Why didn't you just say no?"

"Because I didn't want to hurt him."

"But you were okay hurting me?"

His voice is hoarse. My heart aches.

"I thought I could love him eventually. That's what I've always done. I pick the easy love. The one that won't break me. But you..."

"I do break you," he says. "I see it. I know I do. And it kills me, Reya. I don't know how to be anything else, but I was willing to try for you."

Something clicks in me. The fire that's always brewed between us ignites.

"Loving you is so damn hard," I blurt. "Never knowing what mood you'll be in. Never knowing if I can touch you, or if I'll say the wrong thing, or where I'm allowed to sit in your fucking house."

He runs his hands down his face and looks at me, finally, truly looks at me.

"You can handle me, Reya. That's why I love you. You don't

give up on me when I shut down. You see the man I want to be, not just who I am. You challenge me. You call me out on my bullshit. And I need that."

I blink back tears. He confuses the hell out of me.

"I need you too," I whisper.

He shakes his head like he doesn't believe me, but I see it: the softening in his eyes, the grief behind his silence.

And for the first time, we're both standing in the wreckage of our love, too stubborn to walk away, too scared to rebuild.

***

Later that day I sit in my car outside the therapy office, sweat beading along my hairline from the stale, unmoving air. I'm still in my work clothes smeared with drywall dust and regret. Leven still on my breath.

My phone rings,

Tim.

"Hey baby," his voice is soft.

"Hey," I whisper, already ashamed.

"I made dinner. I know you're heading to therapy, but it'll be waiting when you get back, okay?"

Tears sting my eyes.

"Okay."

"I love you, Reya."

I close my eyes. I wish I could say it back without feeling like a liar.

"I know," I say instead. I hang up the phone and walk toward the office of Dr. Jory Jenson. The thoughts in my head are taking over and consuming me.

"Come on in, Reya."

Dr. Jenson is standing at the door, his tie slightly loosened, sleeves rolled to the elbow. His presence is always composed, but lately, there's a tension between us.

He watches me as I enter. I feel his eyes trace over the tired lines in my face, the weight on my shoulders. The way I linger before sitting down.

"I'm glad you made it."

"Barely."

"Rough day?"

"Rough everything." I sink into the leather couch. "I saw Leven this morning."

He lets the silence settle. He's good at that.

"Do you want to talk about it?" He asks, voice low, even.

My eyes meet his and I dive in. "I don't know what's wrong with me. He barely speaks to me. He doesn't look at me. I know I don't matter to him, but I keep going back."

Dr. Jenson leans forward, his hands clasped. "What makes you say that?"

"He looks through me. Like I'm just… furniture. Convenient. Replaceable."

"And you stay?"

"Because when he does look at me, when he touches me… I feel like I exist."

He inhales sharply and removes his glasses. His blue eyes are soft, but something burns in them. Frustration? Compassion? Something he's not saying.

"Reya… you deserve more than breadcrumbs. You deserve to be seen when it's not convenient."

I nod, biting my lip. "But I think I love him."

His jaw clenches. Reya we've talked about this, "that's not love. That's trauma bonding."

His words cut, but they come from somewhere deep in him. A place that knows what I'm going through. Maybe even feels it for me.

"I know you think he's special. But you're building a life around a man who doesn't even open the door for you emotionally. You show up with your heart in your hands, and he closes the blinds."

I shift in my seat. "Why do you care so much about Leven?"

He pauses. His gaze lingers.

"I care because you remind me that people can be hurting and still show up. I care because I see your potential."

"And?" I press because I need to hear it. All of it.

"And… it's hard not to want better for someone who deserves so much more than she accepts."

The air thickens between us.

There's a beat. A pulse.

We both feel it.

But neither of us moves.

# Chapter 30

## Dr. Jenson

She said it during our first session. She said it so casual, so dismissive, I almost didn't register it.

*"I knew I wouldn't try to fuck you."*

She smiled when she said it. A sharp smile, daring me to react. I didn't. I was trained not to. But it's haunted me since.

No client has ever unraveled me. Not until Reya.

Tonight, she walks into my office carrying exhaustion on her shoulders and sadness in her eyes. Her clothes are dusty, construction dust, I assume. She sits without a word and curls into the worn leather like she belongs here.

And maybe, she does.

Reya is magnetic, and it's not just her looks, though they are undeniable. There's a slow, sensual, clumsy grace in the way she moves, even when she's exhausted. A confidence that masks her brokenness. Her smile is a smokescreen. Her laugh is always slightly delayed, like it's filtered through something sad first. She leans forward just a little too far when she's making a point. She bites the inside of her cheek when she's about to lie. Everything about her is intentional, and yet it all feels raw.

Honest, even when it's manipulation.

There's something so deeply human about her. Unfiltered. She doesn't hide her darkness, she bathes in it. And that, more than anything, draws people in.

*Draws me in.*

I sit across from her and pretend I'm fine. Pretend her scent, warm vanilla, and coconut, doesn't make my thoughts blur. Pretend I haven't thought about her more than I should. My wife and I have a good marriage. Quiet. Steady. Real. But Reya is... something else. Something loud. Something cracked and beautiful and infuriating. She's a fire I should never walk toward.

She stares at the floor.

"I saw Leven this morning," she says, her voice soft.

Of course she did.

"Do you want to talk about it?" I ask, already knowing she does. She always wants to talk about him.

"I don't know what's wrong with me," she says, rubbing her hands together. "He barely speaks to me. He doesn't look at me. But I keep going back."

I nod, resisting the urge to move closer. She needs space. I need distance.

"Because when he does look at me, when he touches me," she continues, "I feel like I exist."

That line. It crushes something in me. She's always using sex to find meaning, to search for love in places she'll never find it. She deserves so much more than what she takes.

"I just want him to see me," she says.

"I see you." The words slip out before I can stop them.

Her head snaps up. Her eyes widen.

I clear my throat. "I mean... I hear you. I understand you."

She watches me for a beat too long.

"Leven doesn't deserve you," I say, more harshly than I intended. "You give him everything and he gives you scraps."

She flinches and I immediately regret the sharpness.

"I'm sorry," I say. "That came out—"

"No," she cuts me off. "You're right."

Silence stretches. It's thick, humid. She's looking at me like she knows. Like she feels the shift happening between us.

I see the pain in her. The stubbornness. The deep yearning to be chosen by someone who will never choose her the way she wants. And I want to take it from her. I want to wipe every trace of Leven from her memory and show her what it's like to be loved without condition.

But I can't. Because she's my client. Because I'm married. Because this isn't a fantasy. Because this is unethical.

"I need you to see what you're doing," I say carefully. "You're using Leven to validate your pain. And you're using me to talk yourself out of healing."

Her lips tremble. I want to touch her.

Just enough to calm whatever is storming inside of her.

"You don't get it," she whispers. "You don't know what it's like to want someone who treats you like a burden."

"I do," I say before I can stop myself. My wife's distant voice on the other end of late-night phone calls. The dinners eaten in silence. The years of doing everything right and still feeling wrong. Our marriage is good, sure. But after 15 years of marriage, we've run out of excitement.

Reya leans back and studies me.

"Why haven't you ever asked me to stop talking about Leven?" She asks.

*Because I want to know everything about him. Because I want to know everything he's done to you so I can be the opposite.*

"I told you," I say, "you can talk about anything in here."

Another silence.

I watch her chest rise and fall, her fingers twisting the hem of her shirt. My gaze catches on the birthmark next to her eye, the scar near her elbow she thinks I don't see.

She is chaos.

She is a story I've read a thousand times and still don't understand. She is the slow burn of longing. She is every wrong choice you want to make just to feel something.

And I can't save her.

But God help me, I want to.

"Reya," I say, quieter now. "You can't fix Leven. You can't turn indifference into love. You can't bleed yourself out trying to make someone whole."

Her eyes shimmer.

"And what if I'm not fixable either?" She whispers.

I lean forward. Our knees almost touch. My voice catches.

"Then let me prove you wrong."

And the air shifts again.

She blinks. Slowly. Then looks away.

"Same time next week?" She asks.

"Yes," I breathe.

And when she leaves, her scent lingers in the room far too long. Just like her.

# Chapter 31

**Before**
**19 years old**

I stood quiet in the bathroom, staring at myself in the mirror like the reflection might blink and reveal someone worth loving.

Why was I made like this?

A tear slipped down the slope of my cheek. I didn't bother with wiping it. A birthmark bloomed from the corner of my eye to the edge of my ear, discolored smear that marked me from the moment I was born. Acne flared across my cheeks, red and angry. My hair, thick and coiled, refused to lay flat no matter how I pressed or braided it.

But it was my chest I hated the most.

My eyes dropped to my breasts. I tried to ignore them, pretend they didn't exist. But every bathing suit, every side glance in a changing room mirror reminded me. They weren't like other girls. The tips were too large, too puffy, too…wrong. So, I grabbed one in my hand, squeezed until the skin paled under pressure, and wrapped a rubber band around the nipple. Tight. As tight as I could get it. I bit down on my lip to stifle a cry.

Then I did the same to the other.

Pain burst behind my ribs, sharp and unforgiving. But beauty is pain, right? That's what they say.

Maybe if I could stop the blood flow, they'd just fall off. I could be left with something, anything, closer to normal.

My knees trembled. The rubber bands burned. My hands shook.

"Are you okay in there?"

Dorian.

His voice on the other side of the door was light, teasing, always infused with laughter. He didn't know I was spiraling.

"Umm, yes. Give me a minute."

I leaned over the sink, panting. My breasts throbbed, but I refused to remove the bands. Not yet. Not until I felt like I was in control.

Dorian was leaving for the Air Force in two weeks. My stomach twisted with every sunrise, every morning closer to his departure. He was the only person who saw light when everything around me felt dark. His humor, his relentless optimism, it was infuriating. And necessary.

I stared back at the mirror. *I will never be normal.*

A few moments later, Delilah woke up screaming. Her wails pierced through the apartment like tiny knives. I was supposed to make her a bottle, but I couldn't remember if it was two scoops of formula or three. She was already months old, and I knew nothing about her. Dorian's boots echoed against the hardwood before I even reached the kitchen.

"I got it," he said, already pulling the formula can from the cabinet.

"I was gonna…"

"You're tired," he said, smiling. "And flustered. Sit."

I sank into the couch, arms limp, eyes hollow.

He bounced Delilah on his shoulder, humming something under his breath as he fed her. He looked like a father. He looked like the parent she deserved.

"I don't want to be a mom," I whispered.

Dorian didn't flinch. He just kept rocking her.

"I know."

Tears stung my eyes. "It's not because I don't love her."

He looked at me then. "It's because you're afraid to fail."

I nodded, ashamed.

"Then fail forward," he said. "Fail with your whole heart in it. But don't lie to yourself and say you never wanted her."

I turned away.

Because I did want her. I wanted to be the kind of mother who braided her hair before school and kissed her on the forehead. But what if I couldn't? What if I gave her all my brokenness instead?

So I told myself I never wanted to be a mom.

Because if I failed, at least it wouldn't hurt as much.

Even though I loved her.

God help me, I loved her so much it scared me.

Dorian shifted Delilah to his other arm and sat next to me on the couch, his free hand resting gently on my knee.

"Do you remember how lonely you felt in high school?" He asked quietly. "How you used to say you had no one to talk to, that no one really got to know you?"

I nodded slowly, my throat tight.

"Do you want Delilah to feel like she has no one either?"

"No," I said immediately, barely a whisper.

He nodded. "Then you've got to try, Reya. You've got to show up. You can do this. Not because it'll be easy. Not because you feel ready. But because she needs someone, and I believe you can be that person."

His words wrapped around me like a blanket, soft and suffocating all at once. I wanted to believe him.

"I've messed up so much already," I said.

He chuckled gently. "You're not supposed to have it all figured out yet. That's the lie they tell you. What matters is that you keep going. That you love her enough to keep trying."

I stared at the baby in his arms; her tiny fingers wrapped around his thumb.

Maybe he was right. Maybe I still had time.

Maybe love didn't have to be perfect.

Just present.

# Chapter 32

## In the After

Apparently, rock bottom has a basement.

Everyone's rock bottom looks different. Mine looks messy.

Tim.

Leven.

Dr. Jenson.

Delilah.

I thrive on control, on staying five steps ahead. So how did my life end up here, unraveling in slow motion, slipping into everything I swore I would never allow?

No one is sabotaging me.

I do this.

I *always* do this.

When I hired Dr. Jenson, I thought I was buying clarity. A solution. Maybe even permission to feel better without having to change much.

But therapy doesn't hand you answers. It holds up a mirror.

And I don't always like what I see.

Even Dorian. Sweet, optimistic Dorian. He still thinks he knows me. Still believes he's the only one who's seen the real me, when the truth is: I just painted a version of myself that appealed to his hero complex. He fell in love with a mask.

My phone vibrates on the console as I sit in my car, engine off, the memory of Dorian's voice from years ago still echoing in my mind. It's him. Of course it's him.

I answer with a smile in my voice. "You must have felt me thinking about you." I tease.

He eats it up. I can hear the shift in his tone. Like I've given him something sacred.

"What a coincidence, I was thinking about you too."

I sigh, soft and calculated. "You always seem to check in when I need you. It's like you know me. Better than anyone."

He hums, pleased. "That's because I do. Always have."

And just like that, I've fed the ego. Just enough. Not too much.

"I miss you, sometimes" he says.

"I know," I reply. "I miss you too…sometimes."

"I don't know if Delilah told you, but she's on the track team."

"She did," I answer.

"But spring break is coming up, so she gets some time off of practice."

"Good for her, she gets some time to rest." The conversation flows effortlessly from years of history between us.

I hang up shortly after, make some vague promise to talk soon, and toss my phone onto the passenger seat. I sit there a moment longer, letting the silence wrap around me like a secret. My thighs still ache from Leven. My lips still taste like him. I haven't even brushed my teeth.

When I walk in, the air smells like butter and garlic. Tim's cooking. The soft clatter of dishes greets me before his smile does.

"Hey, babe," he calls over his shoulder. "You hungry?"

"Starving," I lie.

He puts on a movie, something light, something Tim. He sits close, his arm draped around my shoulders, his fingers tracing absentminded circles on my upper arm.

My mind travels to the warmth of Leven's body pressed against mine. The way he grunted in my ear. The weight of him still lingering in my core.

I curl into Tim and press my cheek against his chest.

Tim kisses the top of my head. He's sweet. Steady.

Leven is hell and hunger.

Tim is peace and promise.

Dr. Jenson is temptation and salvation.

And I am the storm in the middle.

I disappear into the bathroom. I look at myself in the mirror and stare hard. My eyes are tired. I am tired.

But still, I'm desirable.

I let my mind wander. I know what to do with a man like Dr. Jenson.

I know I'm going to break him.

Because married men are the safest. They can't demand too much. They're already tethered. It makes me feel powerful to be the exception to their rule.

And Dr. Jenson? He thinks he's different. He thinks he's safe.

But no one is safe.

When I get back to the couch, Tim wraps his arm around me, pulling me close. I let him.

Snuggling closer to Tim, I think about Leven.

And Dr. Jenson.

And the chaos I've built with my own two hands.

Because if I can control the mess, maybe it won't consume me.

Maybe.

The hum of the dishwasher is the only sound in the house, a low, soothing growl that fills the silence Tim and I have settled into. Tim is scrolling through his phone and occasionally muttering something about a client or a co-worker. I nod along, barely listening.

My phone buzzes in my lap.

Delilah.

My heart sinks.

I let it buzz once... twice... three times... before I finally answer. My voice comes out softer than I intend, like I was caught in a memory.

"Hey, baby."

"Hi, Mommy!" Her voice is bright, happy. Too bright, too happy. I hate how beautiful she sounds. Hate that she still calls me that.

"You sound happy," I say.

"I am! Did you see the video I sent you? From my meet?"

I lie without hesitation. "Yeah, you looked so fast, baby. I'm proud of you."

She giggles, satisfied. "Coach said I'm the fastest freshman on the team."

"Of course you are. You've got my legs."

There is a pause. Then, "Can I come visit for Spring Break?"

My stomach twists so fast I feel dizzy. I look over at Tim, still oblivious to the quiet chaos growing inside me.

"Spring break?" I repeat, buying time.

"Yeah, Daddy said it's okay. But he said I should ask you first."

*Daddy said it was okay?* I think to myself, *he did not okay that with me.*

"That…sounds great. Let me check with work, okay?"

"Okay," she says, her voice softening. "I just miss you."

My chest tightens. "I miss you too."

Another lie.

No, not a lie. I miss the idea of her. The innocence. The little girl who used to babble over video calls. But the real Delilah? The person she's becoming? I don't know her.

"Okay, love you!" She says cheerfully.

"Love you too."

I hang up.

That voice. That tiny voice. I sit back on the couch. The dishwasher still humming in the background.

Tim is still scrolling.

Another buzz.

Dr. Jenson.

> Looking forward to our session tomorrow. Let's pick up
> where we left off.

I stare at the message.

He has no idea how much space he takes up in my head.

I imagine leaning across that little table in his office, letting my fingers graze his knee. I imagine his breath hitching. I imagine slipping my blouse off, slow, calculated.

The thrill of it, wanting him, knowing I shouldn't, set my skin on fire.

I imagine him calling me by my first name in a voice that doesn't belong in a therapy room. A voice that belongs in my ear, in my mouth, inside of me.

"Dinner's done," Tim says, pulling me out of my fantasy. He sets a plate in front of me. Salmon, rice, steamed broccoli. The kind of meal that says *I care*.

I swallow a piece of salmon and taste Leven. Still on my breath. Still in my lungs. Still in my bones. Still in my heart.

The part I love most is the duality of it. The mess I hold inside me, hidden beneath this calm exterior.

After we eat, Tim cleans up, humming a song he knows I like. I stare at him. At the soft curve of his back. The man who loves me with every part of himself.

And all I could think is: He has no idea.

I use this time to scribble something in my journal:

> *Delilah still calls me Mommy.*
>
> *She is fourteen years old now and I don't know what kind of music makes her dance, or how she likes her eggs in the morning. I don't know what makes her cry...or worse, what she keeps to herself.*
>
> *But she still calls me Mommy.*
>
> *Like I earned that title. Like I actually held on to her.*
>
> *I have to love her from a distance, because that is the only way I know how to love without breaking something. Without breaking her.*
>
> *I tell myself it's better that way. That if I stay gone,*

*she might turn out okay. That she won't catch whatever sickness is in me that makes everything I touch turn to shit.*

*My Mom stayed. She stayed and I still became this.*

*So maybe absence is a kind of mercy.*

*I used to think love meant showing up. Being present.*

*Now I wonder if love, for me, means restraint. Staying away.*

*What if I get too close and I want to hold her?*

*And what if I hold her then never want to let go?*

*She might never learn to run from people like me.*

Tim walks up behind me and presses a kiss on my forehead. "I'm going to go visit my dad, want to come?" His voice is gentle, laced with that soft Tennessee drawl he can't quite shake, no matter how long he's been out west. There's a flicker of hope in his eyes, the kind of hope that always makes me feel like a terrible person for saying no.

I hesitate. Almost say yes.

"No, I have to call Dorian and clean up a bit. But next time, I promise." And, for once, I mean it.

He kisses me again, this time with a little more weight, a little more pause, before heading upstairs. I wait until I can't hear his footsteps anymore before grabbing my phone and dialing the number I've been putting off.

Dorian picks up on the second ring.

"Hey, Reya. You must've talked to Delilah." His voice is easy, lighthearted, the way it always is even when he knows he's about to piss me off.

"I did. She mentioned you told her she could come out here for spring break?" I ask, my tone sweet and deadly, letting him hang himself with his own rope.

"I did," he says without hesitation. "She wants to see you. She misses you. She needs her mom, Reya."

I close my eyes. He's not wrong. She does need *a* mom, she just doesn't need me as her mom.

"Dorian, I have a job."

"Oookay," he says, drawing it out in that same playful, nonchalant way that used to both irritate and charm me. "Delilah is fourteen. She can cook, clean, and hasn't burned the house down yet. I work too, and we're still in one piece."

He chuckles, but there's a warmth underneath. A quiet push, the kind only Dorian knows how to deliver. "And by the way, I already bought the ticket. No refunds." He laughs again like he just sent me a surprise gift basket.

"Fine." I exhale like being a mother is a favor I've just agreed to do for someone else. Guilt pricks the edges of my conscience. "Next time, just ask me first."

"If I had asked, you would have put up a bigger fight. And Reya…" His voice shifts, serious now. "She doesn't need another friend. She needs her mother."

I swallow. Hard. My tongue feels heavy. "What do I even say to her, Dorian?"

"You don't have to say anything." He softens. "Delilah will do all the talking. Just listen. You can do that." He pauses. "I know you can."

I want to argue, but I don't. Because hearing him say he believes in me is something I didn't know I needed.

"We'll see you Friday." Click.

I don't even get the chance to respond before the line goes dead.

I sit in the quiet for a moment, heart pounding, when I hear Tim's footsteps bounding down the stairs. He comes around the corner with a small duffel bag in hand and concern written all over his face.

"Hey lady, you okay?" He drops the bag and slides onto the couch next to me, that comforting smile spreading across his face.

"Yeah, umm. Dorian is bringing Delilah out here for spring break. She'll be here on Friday. I'm sorry, I just found out or I would have told you sooner."

He takes my hand and squeezes it gently. "You don't have to apologize for your daughter coming. She's family, Reya. She's always welcome here."

My heart flutters at that. Just once. But it's real.

"Thanks." My voice barely holds together.

"Are you going somewhere?" I gesture to the bag.

"Yeah. Since I know you hate when I drink and drive, I figured I'd just crash at my dad's tonight. He just got engaged, and we're gonna have a few beers and celebrate. That way I get to drink, and you don't have to deal with it. Win-win, right?" He grins, proud of himself like he just cured cancer.

I force a smile. "Have fun, babe."

I do love Tim. Not the way he loves me, but I love the way he tries. The way he adjusts. The way he listens. But there's something behind that smile...something he hides. A weight. A past. Secrets, maybe. I can't quite name it and I don't care enough to ask.

And he doesn't offer.

And that's just another part of the quiet agreement we've never spoken out loud.

Since I found out about Nola, he has been perfect. Beyond perfect, but I still can't help wondering if he's hiding something more...sinister.

Once the door closes behind him, the stillness settles like dust around me. And that's when the unraveling begins.

The minute I'm alone, the masks start to slip. One by one.

I stare down at my phone and consider calling Dr. Jenson, or Leven, or even Dorian again.

Instead, I lay back on the couch and let the darkness crawl over me like a warm, familiar blanket.

# Chapter 33

## In the After

I stare at my phone for a long time, thumb hovering over the name that I haven't called in weeks. The one name I only associate with disappointment, confusion, bitterness.

Mom.

And yet, tonight feels different. Tonight, I need to hear her voice.

The line rings twice before she picks up, and her soft, worn voice filters through the speaker like warm tea on a sore throat.

"Reya? Everything okay?"

I hesitate. The vulnerability it takes to even make this call is enough to make me want to hang up. But instead, I ask, "Did you feel ready to have kids?"

There's a long pause on the other end, one that stretches so wide I wonder if the call dropped.

"No," she says quietly. "I didn't feel ready at all."

"But you did it anyway?"

She lets out a sigh, so tender and long it feels like it's been trapped in her chest for years. "Yes. Because I thought I was supposed to. Because I wanted to be loved so badly that I was willing to give up everything just to feel needed by someone."

Something shifts inside of me.

"Did Grandma approve?" I ask, barely a whisper.

"Of Luther?" Her voice tightens. "No. Not at all. She told me he was trouble. She said if I stayed with him, I'd lose myself. But I told her she didn't understand me. I thought she was just being controlling. I thought... I thought love was supposed to hurt a little."

I bite the inside of my cheek.

"What was she like? Grandma? I barely remember her." I ask, grasping for more of the woman I hardly know.

"She was strong," Mom says, her voice thick now. "Strong in the way that made people uncomfortable. She didn't smile unless she meant it. She didn't love quietly. She was fire and steel. But she was tired by the time you came around. I think... I think she'd been worn down by trying to save me."

Silence passes between us like a ghost.

"Why are you asking me this, baby?" She finally asks.

"Because... I'm scared." My voice cracks at the admission. "Delilah's coming for Spring Break and I feel like... I don't know how to be a mom. I'm afraid I'll mess her up. I think I already have."

There's no judgment in her silence. Only breath.

"You won't," she says softly. "Because you care. Because you're asking the questions I never had the courage to ask."

"But what if it's too late?" My voice cracks again. I can barely get the words out. "What if I already did too much damage by not being there? By choosing men, and comfort, and silence over her?"

"Then you start now," she says. "You show up. You do better. Every day. That's all we can do, Reya."

Something in her voice, something soft and unwavering, cracks the shell around my chest. I feel myself crumbling. The ache in my throat finally finds sound.

"I hate myself sometimes, Mom. I look at her and I see everything she could've had if I were different. If I were better. And I want to be better. I just don't know how."

She says nothing, but I hear it. The quiet tremble. The sniffling breath. My mother is crying.

"You're better than you think," she says, her voice shaking. "How do you think I looked at you when you seen me beaten. I spent so long thinking I failed you. That I failed myself. I thought if I just stayed quiet, stayed soft, maybe Luther wouldn't break me completely. And I thought you hated me for that."

*I did.*

"But the truth is," she continues, "I stayed because I didn't know what else to do. And I hated myself every day I let him silence me. I hated myself for not protecting you girls better."

Her sobs are quiet but unfiltered. For the first time, I hear my mother. Not the woman I despised for her weakness. But the woman who survived, who endured. The woman who still showed me how to be soft, even when the world tried to harden her.

"I'm sorry," I whisper. "I never really saw you. I never... I never asked how you were doing. I just blamed you."

"I know you and Ava blamed me," she says. "But I'm still here. I've always been here."

I sit with her words. Let them wrap around the darkest parts of me like a balm.

We don't say much after that. We don't need to.

Maybe that's the beginning of healing. Maybe that's how I learn to be a mother.

By first learning how to be a daughter.

*Healing isn't always about finding a resolution. Sometimes it's just about talking, saying the things you never thought you'd share. Growth is letting yourself be vulnerable.* Dr. Jenson's words echo in my consciousness.

After the call with my mom, I sit in the silence of the house and let it wrap around me like a wool blanket: itchy, stifling, heavy. The walls don't whisper anymore. They just absorb me.

I think about her, the woman I spent years judging without ever actually seeing. I think about Delilah too, and how I have already done to her what my mother never meant to do to me.

I love Delilah. But I don't know how to show it in the way she deserves. And maybe I've convinced myself I never wanted to be a mom because the truth, that I wanted to and failed, would destroy me. If I don't try, I can't fail. That's how I've survived.

But it doesn't feel like survival anymore. It feels like erosion.

I glance at my phone. My fingers hover over a name I should have deleted. But I don't.

I won't.

*Leven.*

I press call.

The line rings once. Twice.

He picks up.

"Yeah."

His voice is low and tired and rattles through my chest like a match striking an old wound.

"Hey," I say softly.

Silence on the other end. I can almost hear him deciding whether to hang up or not.

"What's up, Reya?"

I don't know how to answer that. So I just speak the truth.

"I talked to my mom today. About being a mom. About Delilah."

He doesn't respond. Not right away.

"And?"

"And… I don't know what the hell I'm doing."

Silence again. Then, his breath.

He's still there.

# Chapter 34

## Leven

I'm sitting on my porch, the air thick with the scent of rain that never came. Vegas heat clings to my skin like a second layer, but the night is quiet, save for the hum of a distant freeway. I'm rolling a black and mild between my fingers, not lit yet, just something to do with my hands. The silence helps me think. Helps me stay grounded. Helps me not think about *her*.

Then my phone lights up.

*Reya.*

She's a hurricane in heels, and I've been standing in her storm for way too long.

When Reya's name pops up on my screen, I should ignore it. I should remind myself of every late night I waited for her to choose me and every morning I woke up knowing she never would.

I hesitate. My thumb hovers over the screen. I don't move. Not at first. It's too late for casual conversation, and too early for her to miss me the way I miss her. She only ever calls when she's spinning. When the world inside her is too loud to live in, she crawls into mine.

And I let her.

I always let her.

I press accept.

"Yeah." My voice is low and calm. Always calm. I have to be when it comes to her.

She doesn't say much, not at first. Just her voice soft and unsure asking about her daughter.

It throws me.

She never talks about Delilah like this. Hell, she rarely talks like this at all. This isn't the version of Reya I know: the woman with fire behind her smile, quick to cut a man down with three syllables or less.

This Reya? She's unsure.

Exposed.

"Leven, I don't know how to be a mom."

I don't answer right away. My jaw tightens, that familiar tick in my cheek pulsing; the muscle right below my temple. "So, what are you asking me for? You want me to tell you how to be a mom?"

She lets out a weak laugh. It isn't her usual laugh, the one she uses to flirt or deflect.

This one is hollow. Real. Sad.

"I'm asking if it's too late to try."

Silence again.

It's hard for me to trust words. People lie too easily, especially when they want something. But Reya isn't asking for anything tonight.

She's just…unraveling.

I know the sound of unraveling. I've done it before. I've seen my kids do it. I've seen it in mirrors and prison cells and barracks.

"Naw, you still got time," I say. "If you didn't, you wouldn't be askin'."

She goes quiet.

And that quiet? It does something to me, makes me remember why I ever let her in.

Reya is magnetic, yeah, but not in the way she thinks. It's not just the way she walks into a room like she owns it, or how her voice drips honey even when she's lying. It's the chaos inside her. That ache for love she can't name. She doesn't even realize how loud her pain screams.

It pulls people in.

*It pulled me in.*

And it scares the shit out of me.

A woman like Reya, she wants to climb inside a man's soul just to see if she can rearrange it. But I've spent too long building walls and ain't nobody rearranging shit.

"You still there?" She asks.

"Yeah," I answer.

"You ever feel like…you're too damaged to do the right thing?" Her voice cracks. She's not bullshitting. Not this time. I can tell the difference.

But I still don't speak. I don't trust myself. Not when it comes to Reya. She is a tornado.

Heavy.

Bright.

Chaotic.

Beautiful.

Her smile has the power to change the temperature of a space, and her pain carries like smoke. I can smell it even when she's laughing. She doesn't believe me when I say it, but I love her. I tried to fight it at first, but she clawed her way into the pit of my heart with her clumsiness.

"You there?" She asks again.

"Yeah. We all feel that," I say. "But damaged doesn't mean done. It just means you gotta work harder."

She breathes into the phone like she is trying to hold herself together.

"I don't know how." She says and my heart reaches for her.

"Figure it out," I say, not unkind. Just real. "Delilah's not gonna wait forever."

"You ever feel like you were meant to love someone, but you don't know how?" She whispers.

I exhale slowly. I stare into the night. The stars are hiding. Is she talking about me, or Delilah? "You ever feel like," I pause, thinking carefully, "the person who broke you also gave you the only peace you've ever known?" I shouldn't have interjected, but Reya, the woman that broke me is also the only person who gave me a peace I didn't think would come to a man like me. And something swelling inside of me had to tell her.

She doesn't say anything. I know she's crying. I can feel it through the line.

"Leven… I want to be a good mom. I do. But I don't know how. And if I admit I want to be a good mom, and I fail, then what does that make me?"

"A woman who's trying," I say. Listening to her breaks my heart.

She goes quiet again.

"I'm scared," she finally says.

"I know."

She sniffles. "Do you think I'm a bad person?"

I don't answer. Not because I don't know. But because I've seen her heart and her damage. She's not bad. She's beautiful.

"I think you're scared," I say, after a while. "And when people are scared, they either run or they ruin shit."

"I ruin shit."

"Yeah. You do." I say as I tilt my head back and forth.

She laughs, but it's not happy. Just recognition.

"Leven?"

"Hmm?"

"Why do you still answer when I call?"

I clench my jaw again. That same damn muscle twitching. I press the bridge of my nose between my fingers, try to calm the storm rising in my chest.

"Because you're the only woman who ever made me feel like I could be soft… without feeling weak."

Silence.

I hear her swallow.

"I wish I could love you better."

I close my eyes. "Yeah, me too."

We don't hang up. Not yet. We sit in silence again, but this time it's not painful. It's full. Full of everything we can't say. Everything we want to say but don't trust ourselves to mean tomorrow.

I don't tell her this, but I think about her every day. I know the exact shape of her sighs. The pitch of her moans. The way her body molds to mine like it's been waiting for me.

But I can't give her the version of love she wants. Because it'll kill me. Loving Reya is like staring at the sun; you can only do it for so long before it blinds you.

"Get some sleep," I finally say.

"You too."

She doesn't say goodbye.

She never does.

And I never ask her to.

I want to ask her what she wants from me. Why she calls when she does. Why, after everything, she still pulls me into her world when I've been clawing to get out of it.

But I don't ask.

Because the truth is, I'd always answer.

Even when I shouldn't.

Even when I know she'll never love me the way I want to be loved.

Because something about her still feels safe. Even if it burns.

I sit in the dark, wondering what kind of man keeps standing in a storm just to feel something real.

Guess I already know the answer.

Me.

I sit in the silence after Reya hangs up.

The phone screen goes black. That's how it feels, how it always feels, when she disappears. Like something in me powers down with her.

I lean back into the couch and stare at the ceiling, arms folded on my chest, jaw ticking again. That twitch started in jail. Right after that guard slammed my face into the concrete. Didn't break anything, but the muscles on the left side of my face never stopped reacting. Sometimes it twitches when I'm mad. Other times, like now, it twitches when I'm holding too much in.

The silence creeps in around me like smoke, familiar and thick. I used to crave it. Now it just reminds me that nobody ever really stays in my life.

I was sixteen the first time I got locked up. They told me it was for "possession with intent to distribute," but they didn't understand: it wasn't distribution, it was survival. It was either sell or starve, and I wasn't about to starve. My mom had her demons. My pops did what he had to do. And I had to do what I had to do.

Jail didn't scare me. Not like home did. Home was where the door slammed too hard, where you slept light in case someone needed to throw something at your head to make themselves feel alive.

Jail had rules. Structure. Predictability.

The military came after. A deal. "Do four years for your country or do ten for the state." I chose the sea. Learned discipline. Learned how to be invisible. Learned how to fold a corner of a blanket so sharp it could cut a man's throat if he stared too long.

But none of that taught me how to trust.

And definitely not how to love.

Reya stirs something in me I thought was long dead. Not love, not exactly. It's not that easy, not that clean.

But something dangerous.

Something soft.

Something I have no business wanting.

She talks to me like I'm a man worth knowing. Looks at me like I'm worth something more than what I've done. And that's the part that makes me mad. Because she doesn't really know me. Not the way I know myself.

But fuck, I want her to. More than I want to breathe sometimes.

I think about her laugh. That cocky-ass smile when she knows she's said something too bold. Or when she pops off at the mouth. If she thinks it, she will say it, and it will be the death of her.

I crave the way she puts her hands on me, not like she owns me, but like she sees me.

She is a beautiful kind of wreckage. Every step she takes leaves dust and smoke behind, and I've been doing everything in my power to not get caught in her storm.

But it's too late.

I'm already choking on her name.

I don't bring women around my kids. I don't let women touch my toothbrush. I don't let women leave shit in my house.

And Reya?

She did all of that. Didn't ask. Didn't even pretend to ask.

And I let her.

I think that's the part that scares me the most.

She got past every wall without even trying. And now she thinks I'm cold when I don't give her what she wants. She doesn't know how many versions of myself I've had to kill just to survive. How much of myself I had to kill just to let her in my world.

Loving her feels like going back to war.

Only this time, I don't know if I'll come out alive.

Reya doesn't know this. No one does.

That's why I keep her at arm's length. That's why I pretend

not to care when she shows up late or leaves early or cries in my bed and thinks I don't notice.

I always notice.

But if I give her the softness she wants, the softness she deserves, she'll leave.

They always leave when the storm dies down.

So, I give her silence.

Not because I don't love her.

But because love has never saved me.

The only thing that has ever saved me, is distance.

People think I'm quiet because I don't have anything to say. Nah.

I just don't have anything left to give away.

I've had women lay on my chest and ask me what I'm thinking.

I lie. Every time.

Reya's different.

And that's the fucking problem.

She's trouble wrapped in warmth. A contradiction that calls to every broken part of me. And I don't want to need her, but I do.

But she doesn't get all of me. Not anymore. When I opened up, she hurt me to my core. A pain I can't recover from.

She gets my body. She gets my time.

But she'll never get the softest parts of me. Not again. Not while she's wearing Tim's ring.

# Chapter 35

## In the After

As I hang up the phone, my heart aches for Leven. That conversation was like pulling teeth. His indifference is becoming too much for me to bear.

I sit in the quiet of the living room for a few seconds, phone still in hand, as if waiting for something, anything, to follow. A message. A call back. A crumb.

But there's nothing. Just the echo of his voice still rattling in my bones.

Dry.

Cold.

Void of warmth. The way he ends every conversation like I'm asking for too much by simply wanting him.

I drop the phone onto the bed beside me and stand slowly, heavy with a loneliness that clings to my limbs like wet clothes. I stand there, staring into the darkness of my room.

Tim is gone. Dorian is three thousand miles away. Delilah is... well, she's a stranger I gave life to.

I should call my mom again.

But I don't. Because I already used up my "I need you" card once today, and somehow, I still feel just as empty.

And Ava? Our relationship is one I have yet to examine and I'm far from ready.

Why am I like this?

My heart wants what it wants, but my logic is throwing up red flags like a Fourth of July parade. Why am I so connected to Leven? Why do I feel as though I would suffocate if I ever walked away from him?

I wipe at my face, my cheeks sticky with dried tears.

God, I'm tired.

I crawl into bed, curling myself into the smallest version of me. The version that's too exhausted to pretend she's strong. The version that only exists when no one is watching. The one that is weak and confused. The one that is losing control every minute of the day.

I close my eyes and try to silence my thoughts, but all I can see is Leven's face when he used to laugh at my dumb jokes. The way he would look at me sideways like I had magic in my mouth. The face that would light up when he looked at me.

I haven't seen that face in a long time.

And it's killing me.

I let that final, shattering thought wash over me like icy water and press my face into the pillow, stifling the sob that rips from my chest.

I don't know what's worse.

Feeling unloved.

Or feeling loved by everyone except the one I want the most.

The darkness of the room is complete. The only sound is the whisper of the ceiling fan rotating lazily above me, and the faint thump of my own heartbeat in my ears. Sleep takes me slowly like a hand wrapping around my wrist and leading me somewhere familiar, but dangerous.

And just like that, I'm not in my bed anymore.

I'm in a hallway.

Narrow.

Endless.

The walls are the color of wet concrete, slick with something that glistens under the flickering overhead light. My bare feet press against cold tile, and every step echoes behind me, like someone (or something) is following close behind.

I walk.

The uneasiness begins to consume me as the hall stretches, bends, warps. Pictures line the walls but every time I try to look at them, the faces blur, twist, disappear. I know the people in the frames, but their identities slip through my fingers like smoke. They feel like my past, but I can't make out who they are. I strain and squint and stand in one spot until I force the images to reveal themselves.

My mother. My daughter. Me.

But younger.

More innocent.

Before I learned to tuck every wound into a grin and make it sexy. Before I knew pain, before I knew disappointment.

Suddenly, I hear laughter. Light and melodic.

It's Delilah.

I turn the corner, and she's sitting cross-legged on the floor, cradling a doll with broken eyes and a missing arm. She looks up at me, not fourteen, but five. Her cheeks are full, her eyes wide and glistening. Moist from something unspoken.

"Mommy," she whispers.

I freeze.

I can't move.

Because I know what's coming. I know this version of her. I remember her like this...right before I left, for the *second time.*

"Why didn't you love me?" She asks. Her voice is soft, but the words land like bricks on my chest. "Why can't you love me, mommy?" The look in her eyes shatters me to my core. Her innocence. Her pain. Her need.

*I did*, I want to say. *I do.* But the words are stuck in my throat. I watch her, helpless, as she holds the broken doll to her chest. What can I say to a child that will never understand I just wanted to protect her from *me.* From becoming the monster that brews inside of me.

"She's all I had," she whispers as she looks down at the doll. Her gaze lingers like she is letting out years of loneliness, and then she vanishes; her small body disappearing in a blink, leaving behind only the mess of the doll on the floor. I walk over and pick up the doll and it...looks like me. Caramel skin and a perfectly imperfect birthmark next to her her eye lighter than the rest of her skin.

I fall to my knees.

I can't breathe.

The doll she was clinging to looks like *me.* How can I...

Suddenly, the hallway shudders and the walls begin pulsing like a heartbeat, closing in. The pictures start to bleed: red smearing across the glass, the faces begin to melt.

And then I'm not alone.

He's here.

*Leven.*

Leaning against the far wall, arms folded, his face cast in shadow. That unreadable expression I know too well.

"I needed you to love me different," I whisper, standing slowly, my feet slipping in something warm beneath me.

Blood?

He tilts his head. "You want too much," he says, his voice harsh.

"No. I just... I just want you."

I step forward, and I try to reach for him, but the closer I get, the farther he feels. Like he's behind a pane of glass, watching me drown on the other side.

I take another step forward, and his presence rescinds another step backward.

"I let you into my world," he says, backing into the darkness. "And you threw it away for a ring."

And just like that, he's gone too.

Now I'm alone again.

But not really.

Because now I hear her voice.

My mother's.

"I did the best I could with what I had." This voice is small, almost fragile. "I'm sorry you feel I could have done more. I'm sorry I failed you."

"You didn't fail me," I say into the void. Spinning around to find where the voice is coming from. "You didn't fail me, Mom." I say desperately trying to convince her.

"She loved you," another voice echoes. "You were just too angry to see it."

I spin, searching for the source. A mirror appears in front of me: tall, cracked, leaning precariously against the hallway wall.

I walk up to it.

And I see myself.

But not the me I know.

This Reya is tired. Not the sexy kind of tired, not the sultry exhaustion I fake to get attention, but soul-tired. Worn. Eroded from the inside. Her makeup smudged, her eyes hollow. Her reflection breathes heavily, then steps forward, placing a hand on the glass.

"You're going to destroy every good thing in your life if you don't stop."

My throat tightens.

"I don't know how to stop."

"You do. But you like the pain. You like the control. And deep down, you don't think you deserve love unless you earn it by bleeding first."

The mirror shatters and the glass burst toward me. I put my arms up to protect my face and the glass cuts my skin, and I welcome the pain of every slice.

\*\*\*

I wake up with a scream caught in my throat.

My pillow is soaked.

My heart is racing.

The room is quiet again, but I can't get Delilah's voice out of my head. Or Leven's distance. Or my mom's pain. Or the version of me I saw in that mirror.

I sit up slowly, pressing my palm against my chest, like that might quiet whatever's breaking underneath.

I need help.

Real help. The kind Dr. Jenson is offering. The kind I asked for.

I don't know how to just receive help, though. I reshape it. Sweeten my voice, soften my eyes, say just enough to make him lean closer.

Dr. Jenson doesn't even realize he is stepping into this game of trying to make *him* need *me*.

He is steady. Patient. He's doing what he is supposed to: holding space, offering truth, trying to guide me out of this ache. But I keep wondering how far I can pull him in, instead.

Right now, wrapped in the residue of that dream, I don't even know who I am when I'm not breaking on purpose.

# Chapter 36

## In the After

As I clock in, the buzz of fluorescent lights overhead hums louder than usual, like a warning I can't quite decode. My steel-toed boots feel heavier today. Or maybe it's just the weight of pretending.

I'm surrounded by the sounds of grinders, the bark of supervisors, the beep-beep of lifts backing up. My crew moves around me like ants rebuilding a hill, efficient and unaware that their queen is crumbling.

They ask questions: Jason about the install on the mezzanine, Greg about conduit spacing. But the words fly past me, meaningless in my fog. I nod, answer mechanically, offer a smirk or two. But I'm coming undone beneath my hardhat, my safety glasses hiding a weariness that can't be measured in voltage.

"Yo, Reya," Jason says, raising his voice over the whir of a drill. "You good? You've answered the same thing three times and none of them matched."

I blink at him, caught.

Greg chuckles, wiping sweat off his forehead with his sleeve. "She's on auto-pilot today."

"Shut up," I mumble, forcing a smile. I take a sip of my Red Bull.

"Damn, you alright for real?" Jason leans in a little. "You look like you seen a ghost or quit nicotine. One of the two."

That gets a laugh from Marcus, who's wiring a junction box nearby. "Or both. She looks like she tried to fight sleep and lost."

I shake my head. "Just tired."

"Yeah? You workin' nights as a superhero now?" Greg says, grinning.

"Something like that." I want to walk away.

"Man, all I know is, don't drop anything today," Marcus warns, tapping his hardhat. "I'm standing under your pipe rack later."

The laughter fades quickly, the moment passing. They move on. I don't.

I'm not here.

I'm in Leven's silence.

I'm in my mom's voice, cracking for the first time in years, confessing she doesn't even like herself.

I'm in Delilah's name lighting up my phone screen and the guilt I pretend I don't feel every time I let it go to voicemail.

I am surrounded by people and still... so alone.

By lunch, I've lost count of the tasks I've half-assed and the warnings I've ignored. My phone buzzes with a reminder:

Therapy with Dr. Jenson 3:30 PM.

I don't want to go.

And yet, it's the only place I can breathe.

\*\*\*

The room is dim, as always, lit just enough for comfort, just low enough for confession. Dr. Jenson greets me with that same careful warmth. His chair is angled slightly today, open toward me more than usual. A subconscious shift, maybe.

"Rough day?" He asks, notepad in hand.

"I don't know how to stop choosing things that hurt me," I whisper, not bothering to fake a smile today.

"Why do you feel that way?"

"Because I am surrounded by people who love me, and I feel… nothing. Not gratitude, not connection. Just…distance. I feel like I'm watching my life through glass." I confess and I'm starting to sound like a broken record. How many times have I said I felt broken. I felt unloved. *I am not okay,* and I'm tired of people telling me that I am.

He sets his notepad down.

"I try so hard to be everything. For Tim. For my daughter. For my mom. I'm trying to fix everything that I've already fucked up, and I just keep… failing."

My hands are shaking. I don't even try to hide it. Dr. Jenson leans forward, his brows drawn tight, his mouth a thin line.

"You're not failing, Reya. You're surviving. You've learned how to cope in a world that never gave you the tools to thrive." His eyes are different.

"Then why does it still hurt?" My voice cracks. "Why does Leven get to have all of me, and still not want me? Why do I feel like I'm too much for him and not enough at the same time?"

Dr. Jenson's eyes glisten. Not just with sympathy, but something else. Something I've seen before in others, but never in him.

He stands up and paces for a beat, as if trying to shake something off. Then he comes back and crouches in front of me.

"You are not too much," he says, voice low, reverent. "You are complex. Beautifully so. And I know what it's like to be exhausted by your own mind." He reaches for my hand but stops short, hesitating.

I close the distance.

He lets me.

His fingers brush mine, just once, and it feels like static. Like finally admitting something we've both buried beneath our roles and restraint.

"I can't stop thinking about what you said that first day," he murmurs. "'I knew I wouldn't try to fuck you.'"

The heat in the room shifts. I blink, stunned by the memory. By the look in his eyes now. I think about all the times we crossed the invisible line, but pretended it meant nothing.

"You said it like a challenge," he adds. "But Reya... every week you walk in here and I feel like I'm losing my grip."

The moment stretches, dangerous and electric.

"I'm not safe for you," I whisper. "I ruin everything."

His hand finally wraps around mine, firm. Intentional.

"I know," he says. "But I still want to help you. Even if it means falling, too."

And there it is. The kiss.

The start of something we both know could end everything.

But right now, it feels like the only thing keeping me afloat.

But right now, for the first time, I don't *want* to conquer a man. I *need* my therapist. I need help.

# Chapter 37

## Dr. Jenson

She's crying again.

Not the small, quiet kind. This is the kind that crumbles a person from the inside out; the kind that softens even the coldest rooms, even the most disciplined men.

Her hands are trembling in her lap, eyes distant, drowning in things she can't quite say aloud.

She's breaking.

And God help me, I want to be the one who puts her back together.

I move without thinking.

Closer.

Close enough to smell the warmth of her skin, that faint cocoa butter scent she always wears like armor. My thumb hovers over her knuckles, unsure, until she laces her fingers through mine like she's been waiting for it all along.

I shouldn't touch her again.

I know better.

I've built a career on knowing better.

I shouldn't want this.

But I do.

Not as a therapist. Not as a guide. But as a man.

And that…that's the part I don't know how to justify.

"I feel like I'm never enough," she whispers. "Not for Tim. Not for Leven. Not even for my own daughter."

"You're more than enough," I breathe.

The words come out before I can swallow them back.

She looks up at me, and there's something in her eyes I've never seen before. Surrender. The kind of surrender that only comes from someone who's been fighting their whole life.

I kiss her.

I kiss her slowly, carefully, like I'm afraid she'll vanish beneath me. And for a moment, just one breathless, soul-bending moment, she melts. Every wall, every mask, every bitter laugh designed to keep people out… collapses.

Her body leans into mine, hungry for something more than lust. Hungry for something human. Something real.

I guide her gently onto the couch. Her breath catches, her hands clutch the collar of my shirt like she's holding on to the edge of a cliff. I want to be the ledge that holds her. I want to be the warmth that thaws her out.

Every touch is a vow I can't make out loud.

Every kiss to her shoulder, her neck, her chest is soft but deliberate. It is my apology for every man who's ever made her feel small.

When she lets out a sound halfway between a sob and a gasp, I pause.

"Are you okay?" I whisper against her jaw.

She nods, and her eyes beg me not to stop.

So I don't.

Not until I've worshipped every inch of the woman they've broken. Not until she's falls to pieces beneath me, not from fear, but from trust. From finally being held like something sacred.

When it's over, we don't speak. We lie there in the silence, her heartbeat echoing against my chest, her breath uneven in the dark.

I want to tell her this was a mistake.

But all I can think about is how much pain she carries.

And how much I want to carry it with her.

# Chapter 38

**Before**
**16 years old**

Running.

It was the only thing that ever steadied me. The only thing that drowned out the noise in my head. That filled the hollow space in my chest. It hurt in all the right places. The tightness in my lungs, the burn in my thighs, the pounding in my feet as they hit the track over and over and over again, it reminded me I was still alive.

When I joined the track team, I wasn't chasing medals or college scouts. I was chasing peace. And for a while, it worked.

Being on the team was the first time I remember feeling both powerful and powerless. Like my body mattered but my voice didn't. Like I was visible and invisible in the same breath.

Coach Marcus saw me.

Or I thought he did.

He was always there. Whistle around his neck. Stopwatch in hand. "Kiddo," he called me. He never said my name. Just "Kiddo."

Said I had drive.

Said I had something special in me.

He was thirty-two. Married. A father. A man everyone liked.

A man I admired.

I wasn't the fastest runner, not by a long shot. But I gave everything to every lap and Coach noticed. He always noticed.

"The 400 is gonna hurt no matter how you run it," he told me after I practically collapsed across the finish line my first race. "If you hold back, it burns. If you go all out, it burns. You just have to decide if you want that pain to mean something." He clenched his fist in front of his chest.

That stuck with me.

*No matter what, it hurts. So make it count.*

After one late track meet, the field was emptying out. I lingered. Tying and untying my shoes like I had nowhere better to be…because I didn't.

Home was a war zone of silence and slammed doors. My mother floated around like a ghost, while Luther dominated the couch, the house, the air we breathed.

Coach Marcus called my name from the bleachers. He held out a towel and a water bottle, like always. "You've been pushing hard lately, kiddo." He said, wiping sweat from his own brow like he'd just run with me. "Something going on?"

I shrugged, taking the towel. "Just wanna win."

He smiled at me. But it wasn't his usual smile. It held… something else. "You've got it in you. I see it."

He always said that: *I see it in you.* I used to think he meant potential. Now, I wasn't so sure.

We talked for a few minutes. Nothing heavy. But I felt warm inside. Like someone cared if I existed.

And I wanted to keep that feeling.

I wanted him to be proud of me. To see me and not look away.

Then, he reached out.

His hand on my shoulder was familiar. But the way his thumb moved slowly, circling near my collarbone, was not. My body tensed.

"I know you don't get what you need at home," he said. His voice was softer than usual. "But you've got me."

The world slowed down.

I looked at him and, for the first time, I didn't see a mentor. I didn't see a coach. I saw a man. A man looking at me like I was something he could take. A man looking at me like I wasn't sixteen.

He leaned in, slow and steady, like this had been building for months.

And I let him.

Not because I wanted to.

But because I didn't know what else to do.

His lips met mine, gentle, calculated. The kind of kiss that would sound sweet in someone else's story. And I remember thinking: *Is this what it feels like to be wanted? Is this love?*

But it wasn't.

It was possession. It was power. *His*, not mine.

And when it was over, I said nothing.

I never told a soul.

Not Dorian. Not anyone.

I told myself it wasn't a big deal. That I could've stopped it. That he didn't really do anything. That maybe I imagined the tension.

But deep down, I knew better.

Because I was sixteen.

And he was supposed to protect me.

And instead, he proved something I've never unlearned: Men will always disappoint you.

They'll make you feel seen just to take what they want. They'll make you feel safe just so you will let your guard down. They'll give you love wrapped in manipulation, and if you're not careful, you'll call it a gift.

That was the day I became the villain in my own story. Because I stopped trusting heroes.

I stopped believing they even existed.

# Chapter 39

## In the After

I snap out of the thought with a jolt.

My heart is beating against my chest like it's trying to outrun something, like it remembers what my brain tried so hard to bury. My skin is slick with sweat, my jaw tight, and my throat is dry.

Coach Marcus.

I haven't thought about him in years.

But his kiss… that moment… it felt like yesterday. His thumb circling my collarbone, his voice soft like silk wrapping around a bruise.

I sit up in my car, pressing the heels of my palms into my eyes until stars flicker behind my eyelids. I try to will the memory away. But I can still feel it: his lips, the confusion, the disappointment. The lesson.

Don't trust men with gentle voices and strong hands.

They only hold you until you become something to conquer.

I run a hand through my hair, stare out the window, and let the silence wrap around me like an old coat.

And then it hits me.

*Dr. Jenson kissed me.*

Not in that way, not like Coach Marcus…but still. A kiss that I invited. That I welcomed. A kiss that shook me in ways I haven't fully understood yet. But now, in the shadow of this memory, I wonder…

*What the hell am I doing?*

I press my fingers to my lips like I can still feel him there. It wasn't just a kiss, it was soft and slow and full of things he's never said out loud. It was full of pain he wanted to take from me. Like he saw the wound I was hiding and wanted to kiss it clean.

But it's never clean.

I start the engine and blink away the memories.

I think about Leven.

I think about Tim.

I think about my mom. About Delilah.

And I don't feel like I'm with anyone.

I feel… alone.

Like no matter how many bodies I share myself with, I am still this sixteen-year-old girl sitting in silence after a line was crossed, telling herself it wasn't a big deal. Still trying to convince herself it wasn't real so she could keep waking up the next day.

Today, of all days, I needed my therapist. I want to call him and scream and cry and crawl into the safety of his voice, but then I remember: I've done this before. I've trusted the wrong people before. And even though Dr. Jenson is nothing like Coach Marcus, men change. They all do.

I stare at Dr. Jenson's messages until the screen dims, until the silence in the room feels like it's echoing off the walls.

His last message:

How are you feeling today?

Everyone always wants to know how I'm feeling.

They want to pull it out of me gently like if they're soft enough, careful enough, I'll bloom into something worth saving. They all want to play therapist. Healer. Hero.

But none of them ever ask the real question.

What do you need, Reya?

Because if they did… I don't know if I could answer.

And if I did answer, I don't think they'd be ready for the truth.

I don't need another man who sees me as a broken thing to fix. I'm not a puzzle piece for someone else's self-worth. I'm not an experiment in patience or a project for someone's good intentions.

I'm exhausted.

Leven thinks he knows me. Thinks he's the only one strong enough to handle my chaos, but he doesn't want to understand it. He just wants to survive it without drowning.

Tim wants to love me out of my pain. Wants to soothe me into being the version of myself he can live with. But loving me isn't soothing, it's wild and messy and clawing and loud.

And Dr. Jenson?

He wants to take the pain from me so badly it consumes him. But it's not his to carry. And I never asked him to.

I don't need someone to save me.

I need someone to stand in the fire with me.

Someone who doesn't hand me a blanket when I'm cold, but pulls me into the storm and says, "We're going to scream together, run together, get struck by lightning together. And you're not allowed to crumble."

Someone who doesn't just accept me but forces me to evolve.

To grow the fuck up.

To stop using pain as an excuse for everything I ruin.

I don't want a man who kisses my scars and says, "It's okay."

I want a man who looks at those scars and says, "So what? Everyone's got them. Now, let's go."

No more tiptoeing around me like I'm glass.

I'm not glass.

I'm steel under pressure.

And I want someone who knows how to forge something with me. Someone who sees the fire in my bones and adds their own oxygen.

I close my eyes and let the tears run hot down my cheeks.

I pull away from Dr. Jenson's office, my mind racing.

I'm so tired of being cradled.

So tired of soft hands and whispered apologies. Of forehead kisses and empty words.

I want a man who can feel with me.

Not just hold me when I cry but shake with me when the pain rips through my chest. Not just tell me I'm beautiful, but grab me by the jaw and say, "You're out of your fucking mind— but I'm still here."

Someone who will crash into my soul and leave dents.

I think Leven can be that person, but he is just so hard to read.

\*\*\*

It's dark by the time I pull into the Thai spot near downtown. I sit in the parking lot for a moment, the engine still running, asking myself if this is a bad idea. Reaching out to Brandon wasn't part of the plan. But I needed… something.

I texted: Dinner?

> Only if I get to pick the appetizer.
> -Brandon

Now I'm here, staring at the neon-lit sign buzzing against the night sky, wondering what the hell I'm doing.

I don't want Brandon.

At least, not the way I want Leven.

But that might be exactly why I'm here.

I walk in and there he is, already at the table, glasses fogged from the heat outside. He looks up and grins that goofy, crooked smile. He is wearing a black tee with some obscure anime on it stretching across his chest, and his locs are tied up like a crown of no-nonsense chill.

I remember the way the sun kissed his skin while we were in the river, the way laughing with him was easy and straddling him seemed like it would be even easier.

"Hey," he says, standing to pull my chair out like we're in a 1950s movie.

I raise an eyebrow. "You're not about to call me 'M'lady,' are you?"

He laughs, and the sound hits something soft in me. "Only if you wear a cloak and call me Ser Brandon."

I shake my head as I sit, hiding my smirk behind the menu. "You're such a nerd."

"And yet, here you are," he quips.

Touché.

Dinner is easy. Too easy. We talk about everything but emotions. Which is exactly what I need. He tells me about a theory he's been reading on quantum entanglement and somehow connects it to Naruto. I make fun of him. He calls me a muggle. I throw a spring roll at him.

And for the first time in weeks, months maybe, I laugh.

Really laugh.

Not the flirtatious, controlled kind I use to manipulate or entertain. But the stupid, gut-punch, snort-through-your-nose kind that bubbles out before I can stop it.

It feels foreign. But good.

Somewhere between bites of pad Thai and a debate about who the best Hogwarts professor is (it's obviously McGonagall), I realize something: I haven't thought about sex once.

Not in the usual way. Not like a trade for intimacy. Not like a weapon. Not like something I could offer Brandon to keep him close.

I'm just… here.

Being me.

And that? That's terrifying.

When we step outside into the warm night air, I'm buzzing from the comfort. From the lack of tension. From the safety of being myself without needing to seduce or perform.

He walks me to my car and leans against the door casually. "You good?" He asks, eyes soft behind his lenses.

I nod. "Yeah. Actually, I am."

He studies me for a second. "You looked like you needed a

laugh. I'm glad I could deliver."

I smile, but it fades quickly. Because the urge is still there. The madness, simmering low in my belly. The need to feel something sharp. Something real. Something dangerous.

"Brandon?" I say, my voice dropping into that familiar tone, the one I use when I want to flip the script.

He doesn't move.

"I could get us a room tonight," I say. "We could hang out a little longer."

His eyes don't even flinch. "Nah," he says easily, almost gently. "I know what you're doing."

I blink. "What?"

"You're not into me like that. And that's okay. I'm not mad. But I'm not going to be someone you use to escape." He shrugs like it's no big deal. "We're good. You needed a friend tonight. Let's just keep it there."

Damn.

It doesn't sting. Not exactly.

But it settles in me like a stone.

He hugs me goodbye, arms strong and brief, and says, "Text me when you get home."

*Text me when you get home.*

Then he's gone.

And for the first time in a long time, I don't feel desired.

He didn't reach for me. He listened to me. And somehow, that feels louder.

I sit in my car for a moment longer than usual, the buzz of the streetlights humming around me, the remnants of laughter from nearby tables floating in the air. My reflection in the windshield isn't perfected or curated, it's just… me. Hair a little frizzy from the warm breeze. Lip gloss mostly faded. No effort left to give.

And still, Brandon made me feel enough. Not because he wanted anything from me. Not because he was trying to fix me. But because he let me just be.

Dinner was… easy. I didn't care if he was looking at my lips or my hips. I made dumb jokes. He made cornier ones. We talked about anime, and I didn't feel the need to pretend I knew more than I did. We debated *The Prisoner of Azkaban* versus *Order of the Phoenix* like it actually mattered. And maybe it did.

Because something about tonight made me feel like myself. My real self. My nerdy, goofy, slightly messy, not put-together self.

And that self doesn't need sex.

That self doesn't need manipulation.

That self doesn't need validation.

It just needs air. Room. Laughter. Safe company. A seat at the table that doesn't come with conditions.

As I drive home, the lights blur a little, and I smile softly to myself.

Being authentic is surprisingly… refreshing.

For tonight, that's enough.

I text Brandon when I get home.

He replies almost instantly: Glad you made it safe. Let's do it again sometime.

No heart emoji. No kissy face. No pressure.

Just… sincerity.

I pull out my journal and write:

*Tonight felt… different. Not heavy, not dark—just still. Like I exhaled for the first time in years and didn't even realize I'd been holding my breath.*

*Dinner with Brandon didn't exhaust me. It didn't undo my seams or set my skin on fire. It just made me feel human. Not wanted. Not pursued. Just…human.*

*And maybe that's why I came home and cried.*

*Because I don't know how to exist in relationships that aren't built on performance.*

*I think about the girl who used to press her ear against her bedroom door to make sure Luther hadn't started yelling yet.*

*The girl who held her breath in the hall so she wouldn't be noticed.*

*The girl who could hear her mother crying through thin walls every night, and never once ran to her. Not because I didn't care. But because I wasn't sure if my presence would fix it or make it worse.*

*Every single night, I heard my mother break in pieces. And every morning, she acted like she hadn't.*

*I used to think she was weak.*

*But now… now I wonder if she was just surviving the best way she knew how.*

*I've been pretending for so long (like I'm just built different) incapable of real connection, destined to orbit every man I touch and leave a storm in my wake.*

*But what if that isn't true?*

*What if I've just been protecting something… soft?*

*What if I'm terrified that the moment I stop*

*performing, stop seducing, stop controlling; no one will stay?*

*I think everyone I've ever met has wanted something from me.*

*Or maybe I just thought they did.*

*Maybe I've internalized that every look, every compliment, every gesture comes with strings attached. And maybe that's why I can't tell the difference between love and possession.*

*Maybe tonight was the first step.*

*Maybe I don't need to fix everything.*

*Maybe I just need to feel it.*

*To sit in the stillness.*

*To stop running.*

*Even if I have no idea who I'll be when I finally stop.*

*—Reya*

The journal sits open in my lap, the pen still warm in my hand. I haven't moved since the last word. I haven't needed to. The stillness in the room feels sacred, like if I shift too soon, I'll lose the clarity I found tonight.

I let my head rest on the headboard and close my eyes.

This is what peace must feel like. Not loud or celebratory. Not explosive. Just... quiet. Gentle. Uneventful in the most profound way.

The hike.

*That damn hike.*

The dust on my shoes, the heat biting at my skin, the breathlessness from the climb, God. It was everything I didn't want to do. But I did it. And somewhere between slipping on loose rocks and laughing with strangers in the frigid river, I felt something crack open in me.

Brandon reinforced that tonight. I didn't care about how my lips looked when I smiled. I didn't care if he noticed the scar on my chin or the faint stretch marks on my arms when I reached across the table. I didn't perform.

And still, he stayed.

He listened.

He made me laugh.

And when the night ended, he hugged me like a friend.

I didn't even know I missed that kind of touch until I had it.

Yes, I was attracted to him, physically, sexually, and intellectually, but I didn't have to spread my legs to make a connection with him.

God, I think, maybe therapy is working.

*Dr. Jenson.*

The thought of his name shifts something in my chest, a tension I've been trying to ignore. It burns quietly.

He wanted to help me and I took that, I twisted it, and I made it something else. Something intimate. Something physical.

Something it was never meant to be.

I wanted to be held in that moment. I wanted to be touched like I mattered. But now I wonder if I sabotaged the one connection that could have saved me from myself. I wanted to feel desired but instead, I ruined the safest space I've ever had.

I miss the boundaries.

I miss the trust.

I miss the way he used to look at me like I was worth helping: not fixing, not claiming.

*Helping.*

And now… I don't know if I can ever get that back.

I pull the blanket over my shoulders and curl into the bed, the pen still in my hand, the journal still open.

Tonight, I feel something different than desire.

I feel the weight of change.

And for once, I'm not running from it.

# Chapter 40

## In the After

It's slow getting my bearings back at work. Everything feels like it's moved on without me, like the building has exhaled and is learning to breathe again without my presence. The halls hum differently. The crew is more efficient. Even the walls feel taller. Or maybe that's just me, smaller somehow.

I walk through the site with my head high, chin set like a sculpture, but inside, I'm screaming. Drowning in a silence only I can hear.

I wish I could tell Jason that I'm overwhelmed. That I took on too much, too fast. That I shoved my way back into a life I wasn't ready for because I thought coming back would fix the hole inside me. But I can't. I can't backtrack now. I demanded my crew. I demanded control. If I take it back, I'll fall apart. And worse, they'll see it.

Delilah is flying in tomorrow.

Dr. Jenson and I are circling a disaster we can't name.

Tim is being too good. Too present. Too kind.

And Leven…God, Leven.

I *need* him.

I scan the jobsite like a woman hunting oxygen. The incessant clatter of drills and steel hitting concrete rattles my ribs. I feel like I'm being buried alive in noise.

I pull out my phone, hands trembling.

"Hey," I say when he answers. "Can you meet me on 35? I kinda need you."

There's a pause. A long one. Then: "Yeah. I'm on my way."

I hang up without saying goodbye. I never say goodbye. Maybe it's a habit I picked up from my mother, or maybe it's because goodbyes have never felt real to me. People leave anyway. Saying it doesn't stop them.

Leven appears ten minutes later, walking like he's been summoned to war. His brows are pulled together in that way that makes my stomach twist. His fists flex and release at his sides, his jaw ticking like a bomb, and I swear, for a moment, I feel safe.

His anger is protective. It always has been.

"You okay?" He asks, not even fully to me yet. His voice is low, steady, but edged like a blade.

"I just wanted to talk."

"You've been wanting to talk a lot lately," he says, and his words cut through me like glass.

I flinch, but I don't let him see it.

I could turn this into a fight. I could poke at him, say something sharp, get him riled up. It's easier to be hated than pitied. It's easier to feel something, anything, than be left with his silence.

But I don't. I breathe. And then I walk away. One step, two steps, three, and then I pivot back around.

"I never wanted to love you, Leven," I say, my voice flat but shaking at the edges. "I told you from the start, I don't do love.

But you made me believe I could. You made me believe I could trust someone."

He doesn't move, doesn't blink.

"How is this on me?" He asks, stepping toward me. His hand wraps around my arm gentle and steady. "How is it my fault that you walked into my apartment with that damn engagement ring and a smile like nothing was wrong?"

"I'm sorry…"

"Sorry doesn't unbreak a heart, Reya. You can't drop a bomb on my life and then expect an apology to sweep the ashes under a rug."

"What do you want from me, Leven?" I ask, voice cracked open like a raw nerve.

"I don't know. But sorry isn't enough."

He's trembling beneath the surface, like a man gripping too tight onto composure that's about to splinter. "What did you think would happen?" He asks.

"I don't know," I admit, barely a whisper.

"Did you think I'd just be your second choice?" His voice rises. "You thought I'd be your hidden lover while you played house with Tim?"

I look at him and realize how much damage I've done. I let myself believe my love would be enough to override all the ways I've hurt him.

"I thought…" I walk to him, slower now. "I thought if I loved you hard enough, if I gave you the parts of me I'd never given anyone else… I thought that would mean something."

His face doesn't soften. If anything, it hardens.

"It doesn't mean shit," he says. "Reya, you lay in my bed, you eat my food, and then you go home to Tim."

"I know," I whisper. "I love you. I know that doesn't fix anything. But it's the only truth I have left. You are the only man I've ever genuinely loved."

He steps back. "Then why did you treat me like nothing but an option?"

I don't have an answer.

He pulls his hand away from mine. The emptiness left in its wake is immediate.

"You thought I'd wait for scraps? You thought you could give Tim the title and me the feeling? You thought I'd be okay with that?"

"No, I…"

"You thought wrong, Reya."

He turns. Walks away.

I follow. Desperate. Breaking.

"Don't do this," I cry. "Please." I don't try to hide the ugliness I feel. I don't try to stifle the agony I feel with him walking away from me.

He doesn't look back. Doesn't flinch.

"And lose my number," he says over his shoulder, like it's nothing. Like *I'm* nothing.

"Please," I say again softer this time. "Don't do this."

And just like that, he's gone.

Gone.

I stand in the hallway long after Leven walks away.

"Please. Please, please." I cry into the empty hallway. Begging the stillness of the air to bring him back to me.

His words echo like steel through my chest: *You thought wrong.*

I don't move. I don't breathe. I just... exist, in this stillness that feels louder than any argument we've ever had. This can't be the end. My heart doesn't know how to comprehend what I'm feeling. "But...I love you." I say one last time into the shadow of what was once Leven.

By the time I make it back to my car, my throat is dry, my palms are slick, and there's a pressure sitting just behind my eyes that won't let me cry. Not again.

I sit in the driver's seat, fingers wrapped around the steering wheel like I'm holding onto something that might save me from myself.

Why won't I leave Tim?

The question punches through my chest, raw and demanding.

Why won't I just pack my shit, throw it in the backseat, and show up on Leven's doorstep like I want to fight for us? Like I believe in us?

If I love Leven the way I say I do, if he's really the man who lives in the deepest corners of my heart, then what the hell is stopping me?

Fear?

Comfort?

Control?

Do I love Leven... or do I love the way he won't let me manipulate him?

Do I love him... or do I love chasing a version of love that feels just out of reach, so I never have to sit still and feel unworthy?

I pull my phone from the center console and scroll down the contact list until I see his name.

*Dr. Jenson.*

I don't want to wait until our next session. I need...
something now.

I text him:

> Are you busy? I know it's late. But I don't know what to
> do.

His reply is almost instant:

> I'm here. You can call if you need to talk.

Unconsciously, I pull my fingers to my lips.

The kiss. The lines that were crossed. It all still lingers on me
like all the other bad decisions. But I need my therapist. I hit
"Call" before I can change my mind. His voice is steady when he
answers.

"Reya?"

"I can't stop messing everything up," I say without a hello.
My voice is shaky, quiet. "I push people away. I sabotage good
things. And I don't know why I won't just leave Tim if Leven is
the one I want."

He's quiet on the other end. But it's not an empty silence. It's
the kind that waits and makes room for the mess.

"I don't know what I'm afraid of," I whisper. "Maybe it's
easier to say I'm confused than to admit I don't think I deserve
something real."

Still silence.

"I think part of me likes chasing love that won't stay. At least
I don't have to sit in one place and wonder if I'm enough to keep
it."

"Reya," he says finally, his voice low. Measured. Gentle. "Have you ever been in a relationship where someone asked you to stay? Not because they needed you. Not because you filled a void. But because they genuinely saw you, and loved what they saw?"

I close my eyes. "No."

"Then it makes sense," he continues. His words sit heavy. They don't hurt. Not in a sharp way. But in the way only truth can. "Do you love Leven?" He asks.

"Yes."

"Do you trust him?"

I hesitate. "I don't know."

And that's the part that breaks me. The part I never say out loud.

I love a man I don't trust. Because trusting someone means handing them the pieces of me I've spent a lifetime gluing back together. And I'm not sure he'd know what to do with them.

"Then maybe it's not about leaving Tim," Dr. Jenson says. "Maybe the question is: Can you live with your choice to stay with Tim?"

I say nothing. I just sit there in the silence he leaves for me. The kind that holds me accountable without punishing me.

He's not trying to fix me.

He's making me face myself.

And somehow, that's worse, and better, all at once.

# Chapter 41

## Dr. Jenson

The phone call came late last night. I had just finished grading papers and was finally heading upstairs to my wife when the screen lit up with Reya's name. I should've let it ring. Should've silenced it and walked away.

But I didn't.

Instead, I answered and all I heard was her voice, breathless, shaky, asking if she could talk.

*About Leven.*

Of course it was about Leven.

And God help me, I almost let the jealousy slip. The sharp, unwelcome burn of knowing she turns to him for comfort, while I—her therapist, her confidant—am bound by everything ethical and sacred not to want more.

But I do.

I don't think she can comprehend how badly I want more.

Now I sit at my desk, staring at the grain in the wood, willing my breath to steady. The office is too quiet. The coffee's gone cold. I keep checking the clock like it'll offer some clarity.

She'll be here in five minutes.

And I've made my decision.

I will reestablish the boundary. I will be the man she needs, not the man I want to be.

The door opens softly before she even knocks.

"Hey," she says. Her voice is subdued, almost careful.

Her scent hits me first, vanilla and something floral. Always the same, always devastating. She takes a seat on the couch, and I catch a flicker of something in her expression: restlessness, exhaustion, maybe even guilt.

She doesn't look at me right away.

"How are you?" I ask, keeping my tone neutral.

She shrugs. "I don't know. I'm not sleeping much."

I nod and flip open my notepad, not because I need to write anything yet, but because it gives my hands something to do. Her presence undoes me more than I care to admit.

"Leven told me to lose his number," she blurts, eyes locked on her hands in her lap. "I thought... I thought we were going to figure it out."

I inhale through my nose, slow and careful. "And why do you think he said that?"

"Because I'm a mess. Because I ruin everything."

"No," I say, a little too quickly. "You don't ruin everything, Reya."

She looks up at me now. Her eyes are wet, but she doesn't let the tears fall.

"I love him," she whispers. "So why can't I leave Tim? Why can't I pack a bag and show up on Leven's doorstep like in the movies? Why am I such a coward?"

I set the notepad down.

"Because running doesn't fix the ache," I say gently. "And

maybe… deep down, you know that."

Her mouth opens to argue, but nothing comes out.

"Reya," I say, leaning forward, my voice low, deliberate, "the way you crave love, it's not about the men. It's about you. It's about a little girl who learned that attention meant survival. That if someone wanted her, she was safe. And now you're an adult, still fighting that war, still trying to feel enough."

Her lip trembles. Her shoulders fold in.

"You've spent your whole life performing. Shifting. Calculating what version of yourself people will love best. And now you're exhausted because you've never been allowed to just… be."

Silence thickens between us. I want to reach for her. God, I do.

But I don't.

She's quiet, too quiet. And I know what that silence holds: hope, confusion, maybe hurt. I have no right to ask her to stay, but I speak anyway.

"Which is why I need to say this," I begin, forcing myself to meet her eyes. "We can't cross that line again. What happened between us…" I pause. Swallow. "Whatever it was, It can't happen again. Not because I don't want it. But because you deserve to heal without having to wonder if the person helping you is just another man trying to take something from you."

She doesn't look away. Doesn't flinch.

And for a moment, I wonder if I have already lost her, for good this time.

But I keep going. I owe her the whole truth.

"I'm sorry," I say, my voice quieter now. "If I made you feel like it was transactional, like you had to give me something to get something in return. That was never my intention. But intention doesn't erase harm. I've beaten myself up over it every day since."

I shift in my seat, suddenly aware of just how much I've blurred the lines I was supposed to hold. "If you want to report me, I will understand." The words land heavy. "But if there is any part of you still willing to try, I would like to keep working. As your therapist."

I don't add how badly I still want her. I don't tell her how difficult it's been keeping my distance while knowing the taste of her mouth. *The taste of her.*

Because right now, none of that matters.

She deserves clarity. Even if it means I don't get to be the one to help her find it.

"I wasn't innocent in all this," she says, twisting a tissue between her fingers. Her voice is soft but certain. "I think we can both admit we were playing fast and loose."

She laughs. *God, that laugh.* And for a second, I forget to breathe. It's dangerous, the way I respond to her.

But I hold the line.

Because she needs more than infatuation. She needs belief.

So I shift. Gently. Grounding us back in what matters.

"Delilah is coming to town," I say softly. A pivot, but not a dismissal. A bridge. "And I know you're scared. But Reya..." I pause. Letting the weight of her name settle between us. "You are capable of being her mother. Maybe not the way you were taught. Maybe not the way you imagined. But in your own way. Because she doesn't need perfect."

"What does she need?" She asks, voice cracking.

"She needs *you*."

Tears spill down her cheeks now. She doesn't wipe them away.

And I don't look away.

"Thank you," she whispers.

I nod.

We sit in silence, but this time, it's not heavy. It's full. Full of pain, and growth, and everything we cannot say.

And for the first time, I feel like I've actually helped her.

# Chapter 42

## In the After

It was sometime in August when me and Leven took our first vacation together. I can't remember the exact date; I just remember the feeling.

It was hot, the kind of thick, sticky heat that clings to your neck and seeps into your clothes. Memphis heat. The sun spilled over the cracked pavement like syrup, and the cicadas cried from the trees in waves, a constant hum that never let up.

Leven was different there.

He moved slower, talked softer. His eyes stayed wide open, scanning the familiar. He drove me through streets that shaped him, pointed out stop signs and liquor stores like they were landmarks of significance. And to him, they were.

"That's where I learned how to ride a bike," he said with a soft chuckle, motioning toward the pavement. "Tore my whole damn face up on that speed hump."

I laughed because the image was funny, but also because I was nervous. Nervous at how vulnerable this man was being with me. There was a warmth in his voice I hadn't heard before. Like his chest opened just enough for me to peek inside.

He showed me his elementary school with boarded-up

windows, graffiti scrawled along the side, but he spoke about it like it was still standing tall.

"That place taught me more than the Navy ever did," he said, smiling to himself. "Ms. Townsend couldn't handle how smart I was. A little black boy that actually excelled in school. She did everything she could to keep me down."

Sadness consumed my heart, but he just stared at the building like it still had a heartbeat. Like somewhere behind the broken bricks, his childhood was waiting for him.

Then, he took me to the house he grew up in.

It was small, paint peeling from the sides, the screen door hanging crooked. But he stood in front of it like it was a cathedral.

"We used to all sleep in that back room," he said, voice low. "My brother, my sister, my cousins all in the summer. We didn't have much. But my Granny made it feel like we had everything."

*Granny.*

He said it like her name was stitched into the air.

"She's the reason I am who I am," he continued. "She never let us forget where we came from." We stood there for a while. We stood in silence. We stood in his memories. I looked at him and tried to feel the love he felt.

We got back in the car, and he drove in silence, like he needed time to recalibrate. I didn't say anything. I let the quiet be.

When we pulled into the museum, I assumed he had planned this all along. But the nervous glance he gave me before we walked inside told me otherwise.

"This isn't part of the tour?" I teased.

"This is…" He paused, exhaled. "This is sacred to me."

I followed him inside, through the corridors filled with Black Excellence, portraits and plaques and relics of resilience. And then we turned the corner, and I saw her.

A statue. Bronze. Regal. Beautiful.

*Lilly.*

"Leven, is that…?"

He nodded. His eyes already glistening. "She helped organize the Sanitation Strike March. Worked alongside women who cooked for protestors, hid injured men in her basement, taught Black kids to read before the state said they could go to school."

I was speechless.

I walked closer to the statue and touched the edge of her dress (cold, solid bronze) and I swear, I felt something pulse through me.

A strength.

A stillness.

"She was a warrior," he said. "She didn't take any mess. But she had this gentleness to her. She knew when to be steel, and when to be silk."

I turned to him. His face was soft, brows pulled together like he was holding in too much. His hands were at his sides, clenched, like he was trying to stop the past from flooding him.

"You look like her," I whispered, and he laughed through his nose.

We sat down on a bench in front of the statue. He told me stories. About how she prayed over the door every morning. How she made sweet tea so strong it could give you a cavity. How she once threw a cast iron skillet at a white man who spat on her son.

We laughed. We cried.

And in that moment, I saw every piece of him.

Not the man who clenched his jaw when he was frustrated. Not the man who shut down when things got too close. But the boy who wanted to be held. The boy who was raised in fire and came out whole.

"I don't bring people here," he said finally, his voice barely a whisper. "This is my safe space. My sacred space. I hold it near to my heart."

I reached for his hand.

My heart fluttered so hard, I felt dizzy. Because I believed him. Every word.

And in that moment, I knew.

I was in love with him.

Not because he had the gift of gab. Not because he was charming. But because he had depth. Because he had more darkness than light and never tried to hide it.

He gave me a piece of his world.

And I took it like it was holy.

*** 

That memory always calms my weary heart.

I think about the softness in Leven eyes.

The peace we felt sitting on that bench, talking about a life I never knew but somehow felt like I belonged to.

Leven calms me.

And I needed the strongest sense of calm I could get, because in just a few moments, Delilah would be walking through the door, so I cling to that memory and hold it near. I bring a hand to my chest, as if to push the memory into my heart.

Tim stands next to me, his hand gentle around my waist, thumb drawing small circles like he's grounding me. "You seem calm," he says to me.

"I'm calm because of you. Thank you," I say.

I lie.

The air inside the house is still. I can smell the cinnamon candle Tim lit earlier and the faint trace of bleach from my panicked cleaning spree this morning. Everything looks perfect. The living room is staged, the kitchen spotless. The hallway mirror gleams.

But *I'm* not ready.

I've rehearsed a thousand different versions of this moment in my mind. What I'd say. How I'd stand. If I'd cry. But now that it's here, this moment I've pushed away for fourteen years, I'm frozen.

The sound of a car pulling up feels like thunder in my ears.

Tim opens the front door for me.

I step forward.

There she is.

*Delilah.*

A whirlwind of pink sneakers, messy curls, and nervous excitement. She stands beside Dorian, taller than I remember, more grown than I want to admit. She's scanning the house with wide, curious eyes, clutching the strap of her backpack like a lifeline.

And then her eyes find mine.

Time stops.

I don't know who moves first, maybe it's both of us, but suddenly we're crashing into each other. Arms tight, bodies trembling.

And the hug…

God, the hug.

It stops everything. The self-loathing. The fear. The need to be in control.

Her arms wrap around me like she's trying to piece something broken back together, and I feel it: this warmth blooming in my chest that I've denied for so long.

A piece of me exhales.

The little girl inside of me who never felt hugged like this cries in relief.

I bury my face into her shoulder, trying to hide the tears that are falling faster than I can catch them. She smells like sweet conditioner and bubble gum. And she's real. She's here.

"Hi, Mommy," she says quietly.

My knees buckle at the sound of it.

I pull back and look at her. Really look at her.

Her face is mine. My same almond-shaped eyes. My same mouth. The same crooked little eyebrow when she's curious.

*She is mine.*

"I missed you," I whisper.

"I missed you, too," she says, her voice light but firm. "I love your house. It smells like cinnamon."

Tim steps forward and offers a warm smile, the kind he saves for special moments.

"You must be Delilah," he says.

She nods. "You must be Tim."

He laughs and scratches the back of his neck. "I've heard a lot about you."

She tilts her head. "Me too."

It's awkward. It's perfect. It's happening.

Dorian gives me a knowing glance, then turns to his daughter. "Alright, Peanut. I'll call you in a few days, okay?"

She hugs him tightly. He walks past me slowly, and for a moment, our eyes meet. There's no judgment. No lecture. Just a shared understanding.

"You've got this," he mouths, and then he's gone.

Back inside, Delilah plops her bag on the floor and starts asking about her room and the snacks she can have and the Wi-Fi password.

I nod, answer what I can. But my mind is still back at the front door, in that hug, in that brief second when I felt like I wasn't just a mother in name.

I was her mom.

And that terrifies me because now, I have something I don't want to lose.

Later that night, once the house settles and Delilah is tucked in, I sit on the floor of my bedroom and pull my journal into my lap.

I write fast. Sloppy. Emotional.

*March 12th*

*I don't know what I'm doing. But for the first time in forever, I want to do it right.*

*I felt her heartbeat against mine and I swear, I've never felt anything that real before.*

*She deserves more than what I've given her.*

*And I don't know how to be a good mom. I don't know how to show up for her like she deserves.*

*But I want to.*

*I don't want to run this time.*

*I want to stay.*

*I want to fight for something that isn't wrapped in desire or chaos or pain.*

*I want to be someone she can lean on…*

*And maybe that starts now.*


I close the journal.

I feel beginning in this moment.

Delilah's asleep. Curled up on the air mattress we laid out in the spare room, her playlist of lo-fi music still humming softly through the Bluetooth speaker. The lights are low, the dishes are done, and the day has settled into itself.

I'm sitting on the couch with my knees tucked under me, wearing one of Tim's oversized hoodies. It smells like laundry detergent and him. I don't know if I'm cold or just looking for comfort.

He walks in from the kitchen, two mugs of tea in hand, and passes me one without a word. Chamomile. No honey, just how I like it. He remembers.

"Thanks," I say, curling my fingers around the warm ceramic. The silence stretches between us again, not heavy, but waiting.

He finally breaks it.

"You were good with her tonight," Tim says quietly. "I know you don't think so, but I saw you."

I don't respond. Compliments make me nervous. Love makes me defensive.

"I mean it," he continues. "You didn't try too hard. You

didn't shut down. You were just… you."

I stare down into my tea, the ripples moving gently with my breath. "She's easy to love," I murmur. "From a distance."

Tim leans back onto the couch, one arm resting behind my shoulders. "Reya," he says, his voice different now. Firmer. "Can I say something without you biting my head off?"

I smirk despite myself. "Since when do you ask for permission?"

He chuckles. "Fair."

A pause. Then, "You punish yourself more than anyone else ever could. More than anyone else I know. You carry this guilt like it's part of your identity. But you're allowed to be different now. You're allowed to grow."

I look at him then. His face is so open, so certain. And suddenly, I see it, the man beyond the patience. Beyond the six-pack of IPA and the safe hands. He's got calluses on his soul too. He's fought his own battles.

"I didn't know I could be," I whisper.

"You can," he says. "But not if you keep trying to be everything for everyone and nothing for yourself."

His words slice through me, clean and careful.

"I don't know who I am without the lies," I admit, my voice cracking.

"You're someone who knows how to survive," he says. "But surviving and living are two different things."

The tears come before I can stop them. I bite the inside of my cheek hard, trying to will them away, but he sees them anyway. And he doesn't flinch. Doesn't try to fix it. He just puts his tea down and pulls me closer.

I let him.

The hoodie sleeves bunch up around my wrists as I curl into him, and right now, I don't feel like I have to perform for him.

He just... holds me.

"Sometimes I wonder if you really understand me," I whisper.

"I do," he says. "I see all of it. And I choose *you* anyway."

I don't know what to say to that. It's too much. It's not enough. It's everything.

He presses a kiss to my temple and rests his chin against my hair. "And Reya?"

"Yeah?"

"You don't have to love me back for this to be real."

Something breaks open in my chest.

Tim doesn't expect anything from me. Not sex. Not submission. Not silence. Not even love.

Just... me.

# Chapter 43

## In the After

Delilah talks fast. One thought tumbles into the next with no room to breathe in between, like if she pauses, she might forget something important. Her arms flail dramatically when she gets to the part about someone tripping over a backpack in the hallway, and she breaks into loud, unfiltered laughter that makes her cheeks glow.

I can't stop watching her.

I sip my coffee, barely tasting it, and nod in rhythm to her excitement. She's talking about high school drama, about some boy named Aidan, about her AP classes, and a teacher who plays lo-fi beats while they work. It's nothing like the phone calls I wait impatiently to be over.

It's a flood of life pouring out of her.

And all I can do is sit here, absorbing it.

Dorian's words echo in my mind: *Delilah will do all the talking.*

Boy, was he right.

She hasn't stopped since she walked through the door. It's as if all this time apart didn't matter. As if she just needed me to sit still long enough for her to fill the space between us with her world.

And maybe I needed that too.

She's funny. She's sharp. She's awkward in this charming, innocent way that makes e happy. She chews on her straw when she's thinking, and she trips over her own shoelaces when she stands too fast, laughing at herself like the world is always good, even when it's embarrassing.

And I see it: *me.*

Not who I am now, but the version of me before the damage.

The way her lips curl when she's trying not to laugh.

The way she sits with one leg under her, despite me reminding her not to.

The way her eyes flick to mine when she wants to make sure I'm still listening.

She is mine.

Not in the way a child is a parent's obligation.

She is mine like a soul twin born fourteen years too late. Like nature got impatient waiting for nurture to do its job.

We laugh the same.

Joke the same.

We're clumsy in the same exact way: her elbow knocks the spoon off the table, and I pick it up without a word because I've done the same thing too many times to count.

How?

How can she be so much like me... when I wasn't there?

Tears press hot behind my eyes before I can stop them.

She doesn't notice. She's too caught up in the rhythm of her story. Thank God.

I look at her and I swear I see a thousand versions of her in an instant.

Delilah at sixteen, crying in a bathroom stall because she feels invisible.

Delilah, comparing herself to filtered girls online, wondering if she's enough.

Delilah, trying to find her voice in a world that only listens when you scream or sell yourself short.

I can't breathe.

My throat closes.

What if she feels what I felt?

What if she breaks like I broke?

What if she looks in the mirror one day and hates what she sees?

What if she tears her body apart, piece by piece, and no one's there to stop her?

I push back from the table, knocking my chair just slightly, and excuse myself with a shaky smile.

"I'll be right back," I whisper, but my voice cracks and betrays me.

I make it to the bathroom before the sobs take me under.

Not soft tears. Not silent grief.

But the kind of cry that lives in your bones.

The kind that scrapes its way out of your throat like it's clawing to be free.

I sink to the floor, the cold tile against my skin grounding me just enough not to pass out.

*I should have been there.*

Not just the phone calls.

Not just the birthday cards.

But through her goddamn bad days at school.

Instead, I told myself I didn't want to be a mother.

I told myself it was better that way.

That it would be worse to try and fail.

That loving her from afar would hurt less if I just never loved her too much at all.

I bury my face in my hands, breath hitching, snot mixing with tears, the pain raw and unforgiving.

This is not guilt.

It's grief.

Grieving the version of me who didn't know how to love right.

Grieving the moments I can't get back.

And under all of it, blooming painfully in my chest, is the smallest spark of resolve.

Maybe I don't know how to be a good mom.

But I'll figure it out.

Because she is mine.

And I will not let her become a mirror of all the pain I couldn't escape.

Not if I can help it.

A soft knock raps on the door. "Mommy?"

I inhale, wiping my face on the sleeve of my shirt. The word mommy hits different when it's said like that: soft, uncertain, a question wrapped in love.

"Mommy, did I do something wrong?"

I shake my head even though she can't see me, then crawl toward the door on unsteady knees and press my back to it.

"No, baby. You didn't do anything wrong." My voice is still raspy. Still thick with emotion.

A pause.

I hear her take a breath on the other side. "Can I come in?"

I hesitate for half a second before turning the knob.

Delilah steps in slowly, cautious like she's afraid I might shatter all over again. Her eyes—my eyes—scan my face, and I can see the worry in them. She shuts the door gently behind her and kneels in front of me.

"I'm sorry," I whisper. "For everything."

She looks confused. "Sorry for what?"

"For not being there for you. For not showing up when you asked me to. For leaving you with questions and silence and stories instead of hugs. I…I don't even know what I'm doing, Delilah. I've been gone so long, I don't know where to start."

Her brow furrows as she processes my words.

Then, like she's been rehearsing it in her heart, she says: "Mommy…" She takes my hand and forces me to look at her. "Daddy told me about everything. He had a different story every time I asked about you. He told me you had to get your life together, and we decided we would wait to fly down here until we felt you were ready."

The tears fall again.

I cry differently this time, it's quiet, stunned by grace. The kind of grace that only children can offer because they haven't yet learned how to build walls like adults do.

Delilah rubs her thumbs on my knuckles like it's the most natural thing in the world. "I'm proud of you, Mommy."

I flinch.

*What?*

"I know you don't believe it yet," she says, "but I *am proud of you.* You're getting your life together. You're strong. And you don't have to be perfect…"

I cover my face, sobs creeping back through me like waves.

This child, my child, is offering me the kind of forgiveness I haven't even figured out how to give myself.

"I want to be better for you," I whisper.

"You already are, that's why I'm here," she says without flinching. "We're gonna be okay. I know it."

She wraps her arms around me. And I let myself hug her back like it's the first time I'm deeply holding her.

Not like a stranger.

Not like someone afraid of messing up.

But like a mother.

And for the first time in forever, I start to believe I can do this.

*Tonight,* my daughter *looked me in the eyes and said she was proud of me.*

*And I broke.*

*Because she has every reason not to be.*

*She waited for me. Chose to love me.*

*I don't know how to carry that kind of grace…but I want to learn.*

*For her.*

*For me.*

*God, please don't let me fuck this up.*

*—R.*

# Chapter 44

**Before**
**19 years old**

The adrenaline coursing through my veins was enough to drown out the sound of the men's voices in the backseat, but not quite enough to stop me from trembling. My hands were slick with sweat on the steering wheel as I tried to steady the car, but every bump in the road sent a fresh wave of fear through me.

"I'm taking you guys' home. I did not sign up for this," I snapped, my voice trembling despite my attempt to sound firm. The words felt hollow, meaningless. What had I even signed up for? Gas money and a reckless, selfish thrill? Leaving my sick daughter at home to do… this?

The men didn't seem to hear me or care. Their laughter filled the car, the kind of laughter that only comes from adrenaline and the high of doing something terrible.

"Did you see the look on her face?" One of them bragged, his voice deep and menacing. "She was so terrified. How much did we get?"

I bit the inside of my cheek, tasting blood as I fought to stay composed. My heart was racing, and I couldn't tell if it was fear, anger, or some twisted sense of regret. Not regret for my daughter or the mess I'd landed in, but regret for not getting what I really wanted: the party, the sex, the escape. What kind of mother was I?

The sound of sirens shattered the air like glass. My eyes darted to the rearview mirror, and there it was: a police car closing in fast, its lights an ominous red-and-blue pulse. My stomach dropped.

It's over. It was all over. My breath hitched as my heart pounded so hard it felt like it was trying to escape my chest. The reality was crashing down, but not fast enough to drown out the selfish thought that slithered through my mind: I'm not going to jail. I didn't do anything. I just wanted to have a little fun.

The siren wailed louder, the universal demand to pull over. My relief was immediate, almost grotesque. I slowed the car and pulled to the side of the road, eager to be rid of the men in my backseat. They were the criminals. Let them take the fall. I'll explain everything, and I'll be home tonight. Maybe I'll even laugh about this later.

But as I stopped, the chaos began. Lights flooded the car, and the world seemed to tilt on its axis. I caught movement in every direction with police vehicles blocking us in, officers were shouting commands, guns drawn. The air around me vibrated with the thrum of helicopters above.

"Driver, turn off the ignition and throw the keys out the window!"

The voice boomed, leaving no room for argument. My hands were shaking so badly it took two tries to grab the keys. I fumbled and nearly dropped them before finally tossing them out the window. This wasn't a misunderstanding. This was my life turning into a nightmare.

"Driver, put your left hand out the window and open the door from the outside!"

I followed the instructions, my movements robotic. The warm air hit me as I opened the door, and the sweat dripping down my back made it feel like a furnace. Every second stretched into eternity, and I was painfully aware of the guns pointed at me.

I didn't want to die. I just wanted to live a little. That's all. How did it come to this?

"Driver, with your hands in the air, slowly get out of the car!"

I reached for my seatbelt, and the tension in the air shifted. The faint clicks of weapons being readied froze me in place.

Chh-Chk.

Chh-Chk.

Chh-Chk.

The sound of every gun being cocked all at once was a sound I would never forget.

"DRIVER, SHOW US YOUR HANDS, NOW!"

"I'm… I'm just unbuckling my seatbelt," I stammered, my voice breaking. Panic rose to my throat, threatening to choke me. I moved slowly, doing exactly as they said, but the fear was suffocating.

When I finally stepped out of the car, my knees wobbled, and I struggled to keep my hands steady. The world around me was a blur of shouts, lights, and cold, unrelenting authority.

"Get on your knees!"

I dropped to the ground without hesitation, the asphalt scraping against my skin as I fell forward. My hands instinctively caught me, but the heat of the pavement burned my palms. The weight of everything crushed me: my mistakes, my selfishness, my stupidity.

An officer's knee pressed into my back, pinning me to the ground. The cuffs bit into my wrists, and the heat from the pavement seared my cheek. It hurt, but not as much as the truth that finally sank in: I deserved this.

I felt myself being hoisted up, the officer's grip firm but not unkind. As I stood, my mind shifted to the men in the backseat. For a brief moment, I felt nothing for them. No pity, no concern.

They were not my problem. They made their choices.

The officer grabbed me by my forearm, his grip rough and unyielding, and hauled me to my feet. The sudden movement made the world tilt. Red and blue lights blurred together, painting the morning in violent streaks of color. Sirens howled in the distance. The sharp barking of K9 units filled the air, their handlers shouting commands I couldn't process.

None of it felt real.

It was like watching a movie from the outside, like I was hovering above myself, a spectator in my own downfall.

My sneakers dragged against the pavement as I was marched toward the waiting police car. I was numb in a way I couldn't explain.

And then, I saw them.

The other men.

Laid out on the ground, faces pressed into the street, handcuffs biting into their wrists. They were still, waiting, their bodies tensed with the kind of fear that made a man's jaw lock, his breathing go shallow. But all I could focus on was how goddamn attractive they looked like that.

Pinned down. Restrained. Powerless.

I let my eyes roam over them, drinking them in. The curve of their muscles, the sharp lines of their shoulders, the way their arms flexed even as they lay motionless.

I swallowed hard, heat pooling deep in my belly.

The thought came so naturally, so instinctively, that I didn't even question it: *What would it feel like to have them on top of me?*

My legs moved without my mind's consent, my body still locked in that dreamlike trance, my thoughts slipping into the only space that had ever made me feel safe: lust. Sex. Distraction.

I barely even noticed the officer guiding me forward, my gaze still locked on the men, imagining their weight pressing me into the ground.

God. I would never get the chance to feel them.

The regret hit me harder than my own arrest.

Not the fact that my life had unraveled to this moment. Not the fact that I was being dragged toward the first police car I would ride in that day.

Not the unknown of what was coming next.

Just the deep, aching loss of something that was never mine to begin with.

The officer's hand pressed against my head, pushing me down as he guided me into the back of the squad car. I let him. I barely felt it.

The moment I was inside, the stench of vomit, sweat, and the sharp, artificial tang of disinfectant that failed to cover the filth, hit me.

The seat was rigid plastic, uncomfortable and intentionally unforgiving.

This space was designed to make people rethink their choices. To force reflection, regret, self-loathing.

But none of those emotions surfaced.

I had no regrets.

None.

The only thing that ached within me, the only thought that stuck like a splinter in my mind, was the missed opportunity. The fact that I would never know what it felt like to have one of those men on top of me, inside of me, pressing me down, making me forget.

And that?

That hurt more than whatever was waiting for me at the end of this ride.

As the police car drove through the streets of Las Vegas, nothing looked familiar. Nothing felt familiar. I was numb to the scenery, numb to reality.

I'm not sure how we made it to the detective's office, or into the interrogation room. I didn't even feel alive until the voice I heard outside the door was deep, authoritative, and unyielding. "All right, we are placing you under arrest and taking you to the Clark County Detention Center for booking and processing. Place your hands behind your back."

The words slammed into me, reverberating through the stale, damp air of the tiny room. My heart lurched, a heavy, painful thud, as my mind raced. It's him. I could feel it. Detective Harold was right outside. The thought twisted my gut, but not entirely with fear. I glanced around at the stark, suffocating walls. No two-way mirror like on TV, just a camera pointed directly at me. The room reeked of sweat and despair, or maybe that was just me.

The door opened, and in strode the detective with a presence that made the air heavier. Tall, muscular, and immaculately put together, he carried himself with a discipline that screamed military. His piercing gaze locked on me, cutting through my thoughts like a blade.

"Who were the men you were with?" His voice was like gravel and steel.

I froze, my mind flickering between reality and the absurd. Was this really happening? How had I ended up here? My fingers trembled as I clenched them together under the table. I could hear the faint rattle of the cuffs around my wrists.

"I… I'm not sure of their names. I just met them this morning," I stammered, my voice small. My own words felt foreign, detached, like they were coming from someone else. "The only one I know is Slim."

"What's his real name?"

"I don't know." The truth hung in the air, useless and unhelpful. "This was only my second time meeting him."

I thought back to earlier that day, the memory unfurling in vivid, chaotic flashes. Slim, his grin, the way his friends carried themselves. Tall, dark-skinned, and tattooed, they had a confidence that was almost intoxicating. They weren't just handsome, they were dangerous in a way that made me forget to think straight. My husband was training for the Air Force, and I couldn't wait to get these new men home. The thought embarrassed me now, sitting in front of the detective, but it had been real. Stupid, reckless, but real.

"Listen, Ms. Carter." The detective's voice broke through my foggy thoughts. "We can't help you unless you're straight with us. If you cooperate, we'll tell the judge."

*The judge*? A bolt of panic surged through me. Why would there be a judge? This wasn't my fault. I wasn't involved. I just wanted to have fun and let loose while Delilah was at daycare. My mind flipped to my daughter, my sweet, sick girl. Guilt knotted my stomach. I need to stop by the store and get her some Tylenol. Maybe Pedialyte too. When I get out of here, I'll…

The detective's stare burned through me, pulling me back to the present. He was waiting. Watching.

"I just met them this morning," I repeated weakly. "We were all supposed to go back to my house. I had no idea they had other plans."

The detective leaned forward, his pen poised. "What do you mean by plans? What were you going to do at your house?"

I hesitated. Every nerve screamed for me to stop, to think, but my dysfunctional mind couldn't resist spiraling into inappropriate fantasies. What would it be like to sleep with a detective? Would he take control? Would he let me? Would we laugh about this later? The thought almost made me smile, but I quickly shook it away. Focus, Reya. Get through this.

"We… we have these parties," I muttered, my gaze dropping to the floor. "You know, adults… just adults having fun together." My voice was barely audible by the end. I couldn't bring myself to say the word, but I knew he understood. His expression didn't change, but there was a flicker of something: disgust? Pity? *Lust?* I was nineteen, was I even an adult?

"So, I went to pick them up," I continued, filling the tense silence. I spoke fast, desperate to get it all out. "I barely made it because I didn't have gas. They gave me fifty bucks when they got in the car, and I filled up my tank. They said they were hungry, so we went to McDonalds."

"Uh-huh." He scribbled something in his notebook.

"I wasn't hungry, so I waited in the car." My heart began to race as the memory bubbled up. I could feel the heat rising under my sweatshirt, my skin prickling with sweat. Is my story making sense? Does he believe me?

"They came running back to my car, wearing masks and carrying guns," I blurted out. "I didn't know what to do. They told me to drive, so I did. I didn't know…"

"And you had no idea they were going to rob the place?" The detective interrupted, his tone sharp, his eyes narrowing.

"No! I swear. I just met them. I didn't know…" My voice cracked, and I swallowed hard. "I just needed the gas money…"

I trailed off, remembering the fear in the car, the sound of their voices, the weight of the silence afterward. My heartbeat thundered in my ears. My lies were unraveling, and deep down, I knew I wasn't fooling him. But somewhere, twisted in the fear and desperation, another thought lingered. Would this detective come to one of my parties? What would that be like?

I blinked, ashamed of my own thoughts, but they wouldn't stop. *Get out of here first, Reya. Worry about everything else later.*

I blinked, my vision blurry. The detective's office swam into focus, the sterile walls and fluorescent lights too sharp against the haze in my mind. I focused on the detective and the way his pen scratched notes into his notebook. He looked calm, focused, almost bored. The silence stretched too long, and I realized he was waiting for me to say something.

"Is that all you have to say on the matter?" His voice was

steady, but I thought I caught a flicker of judgment in his eyes.

"Yes," I replied, trying to match his calm tone. I took a breath, one that felt like the first all day. My thoughts wandered to Delilah.

The detective stood abruptly, and the scrape of his chair against the floor jolted me back to the room.

"Well, Ms. Carter, you are under arrest, and you are being transported to the Clark County Detention Center for booking."

I froze. My breath caught in my throat, and my heart hammered so hard I thought it might break free from my chest. I couldn't process his words.

"No…" The word escaped before I could stop it.

The detective didn't look at me as he came around the desk, reaching for my arm. His grip was firm but not rough, guiding my hands behind my back as if he'd done this a thousand times before.

"This can't be happening," I whispered, my voice trembling. "But… I didn't do anything."

"There's nothing more I can do for you, Ms. Carter. It's up to the judge now," he said, his tone clipped but not unkind. "I'll let them know you cooperated."

*Cooperated?* That word felt like a bad joke. I wasn't a criminal. I'd just given some strangers a ride, picked up a little gas money, and maybe made a poor decision about what I wanted out of the night. But none of that was illegal. Not really.

As he led me outside, the brightness of the sun stung my eyes. A metro officer stood waiting by a police car. His face blurred into the sameness of every other officer I'd seen. They all seemed like parts of a machine, something impersonal and unstoppable.

The officer took my arm, his grip practiced, and guided me toward the car. He ducked my head as he pushed me inside, the door slamming shut behind me. The sound reverberated through my skull.

The car started, but I felt disconnected, like I was floating just outside my body. The world through the window looked unreal, too bright and too fast. My chest ached with the weight of something I couldn't name. I didn't cry. I thought I should, but I didn't. It was as if my body had decided crying would be a waste of energy.

"Have you ever been to jail before?" The officer asked from the front seat, his voice breaking through the thick fog in my head.

"No," I replied automatically. My voice sounded far away.

"My advice to you," he said, glancing at me in the rearview mirror, "Keep your head down and your mouth shut."

I stared at the back of his head, trying to make sense of the words.

*Jail.*

He was talking about *jail*. I couldn't be going to jail. I didn't belong there. This wasn't my fault.

My thoughts spiraled, each one more frantic and disconnected than the last. Delilah was waiting for me. Who was going to check on her? Who was going to get her medicine? She needed me. But even as the thought crossed my mind, a darker one followed: This wasn't about Delilah. This was about me. I *wanted* this. The fun, the thrill, the men.

The officer's words repeated in my head: *Keep your head down. Keep your mouth shut.* I wasn't sure if I should feel grateful for the advice or offended. Did he think I was the kind of person who wouldn't survive jail?

# Chapter 45

## In the After

The shrill, incessant ringing of my phone jerks me awake, its sound tearing through the silence of the early morning. My heart races as I fumble in the dark, wiping the blur from my eyes. My hand brushes the nightstand as I search for my glasses, the cool metal frame finally meeting my fingertips. Everything feels off. Too quiet, too empty.

I cling onto that dream of my final days in the *before*. Before my life came to a screeching halt.

Instinctively, I reach to the other side of the bed, expecting to feel Tim's familiar warmth. My hand lands on cold, undisturbed sheets, the faint dent of his body barely visible in the muted light. A hollow ache spreads through my chest. Was he even home last night? I don't remember hearing the front door or feeling him climb into bed beside me.

The phone continues its relentless ring, cutting through my disoriented thoughts. The number flashing on the screen isn't one I recognize.

"Hello?" I answer, my voice hoarse and thick with sleep. A knot tightens in my stomach, the dread of a call from a stranger at an odd hour.

"Is this Reya?" The voice on the other end is female, unfamiliar, and sharp enough to cut through my foggy state.

"Yes," I reply, hesitation creeping into my tone.

"I'm sorry to bother you," she begins, her voice tight, almost trembling. A pause stretches on the line, thick with tension, and my grip on the phone tightens. "But I think you're sleeping with my husband."

Her words hang in the air, detonating like a bomb.

A cold, icy dread slithers down my spine. My breath catches, and my mind races, trying to process what she's just said. "What?" I croak out, my voice barely above a whisper.

"You heard me." Her tone hardens, and I can practically feel the weight of her accusation pressing through the line. "You've been seeing my husband."

I stare at the wall, my heartbeat pounding in my ears. "I don't know who you are or what you're talking about," I manage, but even to my own ears, my voice sounds unconvincing.

The woman lets out a bitter laugh. "You don't? I have texts, Reya. Pictures. Everything. So, let's not play dumb, alright?"

The room feels like it's closing in around me. My head spins as questions swirl in my mind. Who is she? And most importantly, could this all be some terrible mistake?

"Who is your husband?" I finally ask, my voice is steadier now, but my hands are trembling.

"Oh, you know him well enough," she snaps, her voice laced with venom. "You've been sneaking around with him, so I'm sure you can figure it out."

I open my mouth to protest, but the words catch in my throat. A part of me wants to scream at her, to demand proof, to deny everything. But doubt creeps in like a shadow and for the first time the lie doesn't come easily.

The woman exhales sharply, as though she's losing patience. "I don't know how you live with yourself, Reya. Destroying someone else's marriage." Her voice softens into something almost pitying. "I thought maybe you'd have the decency to own up to it, but I guess I was wrong."

Before I can respond, the line goes dead, leaving me alone in the suffocating silence.

I sit there, my phone clutched in my hand, the words replaying over and over in my head. My breath comes in shallow gasps as I try to make sense of what just happened.

I glance at the empty space beside me in bed, my mind spinning with suspicion. Where is Tim? Why didn't he come home last night?

But then, an even darker thought creeps into my mind, one I can't push away. The woman didn't name her husband.

Could she mean Tim?

Or... could she mean someone else?

I shake my head, trying to dispel the thought, but it's no use. The seed has been planted, and it's spreading its roots. A part of me knows this moment has been coming for a long time, like the slow build of a storm on the horizon.

I sit in the dark, the silence pressing in on me, and wonder:

Am I the betrayed?

Or the betrayer?

*I used to think love would save me.*
*Now I know it was never about being saved.*

*It was about surviving.*
*And I did survive.*
*Until the phone rang…*
*Living in the after has teeth.*

Zero points, Reya. One point, Karma.

# Chapter 46

**In the After**

Fuck.

# Acknowledgments

I want to thank my mom, first and foremost, because no matter how wild the idea, she always let me be wild. Her belief in me has never required explanations, outlines, or proof of concept. Just love.

Next, Deon. For standing beside me in all my chaotic creativity and never flinching. You let me be exactly who I am, even when that meant riding shotgun on the emotional rollercoaster that is my brain.

To all the people who told me not to publish this book, thank you. You fueled a fire you didn't mean to.

And to the three people who told me to publish it anyway, thank you. You reminded me I wasn't alone in my ache.

To my daughter: thank you for being your authentic, beautiful self. You are the most honest reflection of the parts I'm still learning to love in myself.

To my editor, Laurie, thank you for giving me the kind of honest, constructive feedback I didn't even know I needed. You challenged me to go deeper, to go braver, and to tell the truth.

I wrote this book to save myself. If it saves anyone else, that's just a bonus.

# About the Author

Rozia Bell is a Las Vegas native, an electrician by trade, and a writer by necessity. She has always believed that stories (especially the hard, uncomfortable ones) can create space for healing, connection, and radical self-honesty.

By day, she works with her hands. By night, she wrestles with words. *The Ache Within Me* is her first novel, but it's more than just a book; it's a reckoning. Writing it healed something within her that she didn't even know was broken. It gave language to the ache she had carried quietly for years.

Rozia didn't set out to write a story with perfect characters or clean resolutions. She wanted to write something real. Something that could sit with people from every walk of life and whisper, "You're not alone."

She is the founder of Banks & Bell Legacy, a storytelling-centered brand that blends literature, mentorship, and creative healing. When she's not writing, she's dreaming up the next project that will remind people how deeply human they are allowed to be.

This is her beginning. And she's just getting started.

Coming Spring 2026

# The Truth Within Me

*A novel of manipulation, control, and a woman's quiet rebellion by Rozia Bell*

You thought you knew him.
You thought she was losing herself.
But the truth was never that simple.

The second installment in the Within Me Universe doesn't begin where The Ache Within Me left off.
It begins after everything's already been ruined.

Told in haunting reverse, *The Truth Within Me* opens inside the mind of a man you've already met…but this time, it's from his point of view.
Cold. Calculated. Addicted to control.
He doesn't scream. He doesn't hit. He doesn't have to.
He gives just enough to keep her wanting more. Then he disappears (again and again) until her grip on herself begins to unravel.

But what if Reya wasn't unraveling?
What if she was planning her escape?

As both timelines move backward toward the moment everything cracked wide open, a darker truth is revealed: the truth about the cost of craving attention, the performance of submission, and the silent war women fight when no one is listening.

You didn't miss the signs.
You just believed the wrong version of the story.